THE TARNÓW GATE

Also by Saul Isler:

Novels

Babe Ruth Is Missing

Shakespeare Is Missing

Jesus Is Missing (due 2020)

The Cave at Devils Elbow (Young Adult)

Short Stories

The Man in the Parking Lot

The Blue Shoes

Acrostic Puzzles

The Majestic Acrostic (with Charles A. Duerr)

The Majestic Acrostic 2 (with Charles A. Duerr)

THE TARNÓW GATE

STORIES

BY

SAUL ISLER

POCAMUG PRESS

The stories in this book are products of the author's imagination, and places, people and things are used fictitiously. Any resemblance to actual people or occurrences is purely coincidental.

Pocamug Press^{TM}
May's Lick, Kentucky
Pocamug.com

The Tarnów Gate
Version 7/25/2019

Cover photo of the Tarnów Cemetery gate taken
at the Holocaust Memorial Museum, Washington, DC.
Photo © 2018 Alejandro Ortiz III. Used with permission.

The Interrogation first appeared in "The Blue Shoes."

Library of Congress Control Number: 2019938185

ISBN: 978-1-7333656-0-4

for

Susan J. Sullivan

a most remarkable woman

CONTENTS

The Tarnów Gate

D.C.'s Holocaust Museum had opened just the year before, in 1993, but I was not ready to visit it. I needed no reminders of the war I fought alongside my Jakob as Resistance fighters in Tarnów, Poland. But our son, Jake, whom only I call Jake, insisted that I accept the visit as my birthday present. He convinced me that such a visit might provide closure on the loss of the man I loved, the man Jake never knew.

Jakob, I was certain, had died at the hands of the Nazis while saving me, pregnant just a month at the time with Jake. Jakob and I had known each other for just three months and hadn't the time to become married. Still, certain as I was of his death, I felt married to him and chose never to marry another after he was gone.

Jake is very convincing, so I gave in. A week later, there I was, Hanna Topolsky Danzler at age 67, traipsing with him through the museum's exhibits, one more painfully observed than the other. I thought I'd buried these memories forever, so each was a stab in the heart: musty old Nazi uniforms, weapons and swastika flags, the heartrending Hall of Shoes that made you think of every victim who wore them, a boxcar that carried Jews to their death in the concentration camps. History for most visitors, harsh reality to me. I asked Jake if we could leave.

Walking toward the exit, I noticed an out-of-the-way alcove. It housed an exhibit with a steel gate. I gazed at it and stood frozen. I knew this gate. It was the original gate that once led to the Jewish cemetery in

Tarnów. It instantly pulled me back to the last time I saw it; and to the last time I saw my beloved Jakob.

Jakob Danzler was only 17 when I met him in October of 1943. I was a few months older. He was black-haired, handsome, short but powerfully built. He'd been an apprentice longshoreman when he lost his parents in the Warsaw Ghetto uprising. He escaped by joining the battle and, near its end, ripping the yellow Star of David from his sleeve and walking straight out of the ghetto to the dock on the banks of the Vistula where he'd once worked, slinging eighty-pound sacks of cement. There, that day, he shouldered two sacks of groats from a pile being loaded onto a southbound barge. He boarded the barge with them like he was a member of the crew and later jumped off in the countryside not far from Tarnów. In Tarnów he found my pod of the Resistance and joined. We quickly became the only family Jakob had left.

We fell in love the moment out eyes first met. Those were fast-moving days. We lived together in a one-room garret above the secret quarters of the Resistance, never apart after our first meeting. We had little money and little food, but we had each other. One evening we exchanged halves of a crude mizpah, a pendant worn by lovers to signify remembrance. Jakob had made it from a thin disc sawed off a broom handle. He inked his name into one half, mine into the other, each followed by the word "forever." Then he cut it in two, crookedly, as was the custom. We each wore our half on a silk cord strung around our neck.

Three months passed. I knew I was pregnant with little Jake but didn't want to inform Jakob till I could be certain the pregnancy would hold through the violent maneuvers we underwent daily.

On a moonless night, we attacked and overcame a truckload of Nazis. After dispatching them, we donned their uniforms and drove their truck to a rendezvous with another underground group at a strategically important, wood-supported bridge outside the city. Pulling onto the bridge, we cruised slowly toward the Nazi infantrymen guarding its eastern end while our compatriots were affixing RDX plastic explosives to the supports under the western end where we'd entered.

As we neared the Nazis we started firing and they fired back. We both took casualties. In seconds we were close enough for hand-to-hand skirmishing. I was knocked down by one of them and about to be bayoneted when Jakob jumped between us. He grappled with the Nazi, shouting to me to get back on the truck. When I refused, wanting to fight by his side, he shot the man, grabbed me and literally flung me onto the truck before going after more of the enemy.

With German backups fast coming upon us, we had to pull out. Jakob had stayed behind to hold off the Germans. I screamed for us to wait for him but he furiously waved us on. We had no choice but to retreat past the west

end before the bridge blew, collapsing it as planned, dumping two truckloads of the enemy pursuing us.

That was the last I ever saw of my Jakob. He was listed as Missing In Action. Just missing? I wanted to believe it but was certain he'd died on the bridge saving us. I had nightmares of the Nazis dragging him, dead, as they did with all their Tarnów victims, into its Jewish cemetery where they were thrown into open trenches dug by other Jews, often women and old men and children, who'd then be shot and thrown in with the dead. This was the way of Tarnów's infamous Kommandant Horst Gruber, who swore, "No filthy Jew blood shall ever contaminate the streets of the Third Reich."

* * *

"What is it, Mom? What's the matter?" Jake pulled me into his arms. I was sobbing. I buried my head in his chest. Others looked away as I pulled my eyes from the Tarnów gate. Was Jakob murdered and flung into a pit in the cemetery once guarded by that gate? Jake walked me to a secluded bench and held me until my tears subsided.

I'd told him his father had simply "died in the war." I didn't want him to bear any false hopes. Now, in this special place, I told him everything. It came pouring out of me through my renewed tears. When I finished, he sat a while absorbing what he'd heard. He too was crying. "Mom," he said, "What if my father were still alive? What if he somehow survived the bombing of that bridge? If there's any possibility of that, this is where to find out."

How could I argue with that?

Jake asked a docent to direct us to an information officer. The name plate on the officer's desk read "Mrs. Miriam Workman." She was about my age and I noticed, peeking from under her rolled-up sleeves, a concentration camp number. I wanted to ask her about it but she looked all business. After I finished my story, she led us to a room full of microfiche files containing information regarding known names, and photo, if available, of the concentration camp inmates. The records were separated into those who'd died and those who'd survived. The death list was, of course, by far the larger. Fortunately, Danzler was not a very common name. There were three Jakob Danzlers among the myriad of names on file. Unexpectedly, only one was among the victims, meaning two had survived. But now I knew my Jakob was among the survivors!

He was in one of the hazy photos of the seven thousand rescued on January 27, 1945 at Auschwitz, a hundred miles east of Tarnów. I spotted his face among a row of skeletal, stripe-suited prisoners standing in the snow, peering out from behind barbed wire. My heart skipped several beats. No doubt, it was Jakob, my Jakob! He was wearing a "coat" that appeared to have a former life as a potato sack. Bearded and emaciated, his head was swathed in filthy bandages. A vacant stare hung on his empty face but . . . he was alive when the war ended!

My heart would not stop pounding. I found myself sobbing again, this time with tears of unbelieving joy. But was Jakob still alive? If so, what had become of him? Where did he live? Had he married and had a family? Had he searched for me first? "Is there any way of knowing if those two Jakob Danzlers are still alive?" I asked Mrs. Workman.

"Research is working to learn that," she said. "We're still very new and our computers aren't quite up to speed. The Internet will help but it's not much older than us. I believe the information you seek may be available within no more than a month. That's what we've been promised. The moment it comes in I'll call you, Mrs. Danzler." I've used Jakob's surname ever since I could feel little Jake growing inside me.

We thanked Mrs. Workman and left, returning the next day to Buffalo. In less than two weeks, Mrs. Workman's call came in.

"I've found what you're looking for Mrs. Danzler." There was an upbeat quality to Mrs. Workman's voice. "The two Jakob Danzlers are still alive," she said. "I have contact information for both."

"Can you tell me their ages?" I asked. I'd been pacing back and forth, but had to sit down to receive her answer.

"One is 73, the other, 67."

I was too stunned to reply and felt very faint. Why couldn't Jake be here to take over?

"Are you there, Mrs. Danzler. Are you OK?"

Recovering, I said, "Yes, yes, please tell me about the one who is 67. That's how old my Jakob would be. I believe he's the one who's my husband."

"There's nothing to tell except that he was alive as late as the beginning of this year. But I do have his address and phone number, both of which may be old."

My pen was ready. "Go ahead," I said.

"Your Jakob Danzler resides in Wellington, New Zealand."

I nearly fell off my chair. Wellington, New Zealand? The other side of the world. But he was alive. I made Mrs. Workman repeat the information so I'd make no mistake. Thanking her, I hung up and immediately phoned Jake that his father was still alive and, through the auspices of the good Mrs. Workman, I had found him . . . in Wellington, New Zealand.

As he blurted "Dad? . . . Alive? . . . New Zealand?" I could hear Jake's wife Sunny and his 16-year-old twins, Ted and Terry, screaming in the background

They were at my place ten minutes later, a bottle of champagne in hand, pulled from their wine cooler on the run. After a ceremonial glass, we did some strategizing. How would we approach this unsuspecting Jakob Danzler? How would he react? We knew nothing of his physical or mental condition. Was he, in the first place, really my Jakob? Obviously, we'd have to phone him to find out. Too nervous to do the phoning, I asked Jake to do it. "No, Mom," he said, "He knows you but he doesn't even know I exist."

Jake was right. I had to make the call. It was 3:30, Friday afternoon, Buffalo time which made it—we figured out—7:30 am Saturday, Wellington time. So as not to awaken the man, we waited two hours; the most anxious two I've ever spent. Playing Uno with my grandsons helped. All nerves, this was the first time I lost to both of them.

Exactly at 9:30 we made the call. I held the phone as Jake punched in the 13 digits required. A woman answered. An older voice. His wife? "If this is the residence of Jakob Danzler, I'd like to speak to him, please," I said, my voice cracking, unable to hide my nervousness. What would I say when he came on the line? Why hadn't I rehearsed something? My usually steady hand was shaking. Jake was hanging over my shoulder. The others were hovering behind him.

"He's back in the garden where he usually is. Who's calling, please?"

"Uh, my name is Hanna. No H on the end." Now why did I say that? "Are you . . . are you his wife?"

"Me, his wife? Mercy, no, I'm his housekeeper. Wait, I'll have him to come in. What's your last name, miss?"

"Just say Hanna, please. He may know it. It's very important. I'm calling from America."

"America! I'll get him right away."

What will I say? I'll just let the conversation go where it goes. If he's my Jakob, will he remember me? If he's . . ."

"Hello, Hanna, no H on the end. This is Jakob Danzler. You're calling from America, is that right? Must be something important. What can I do for you?" There was no recognition in his voice but it was rich and warm, the way I remembered it. It was the hearty voice of a younger man, accented with a mix of Yiddish and Down Under, but I recognized it instantly. It was the voice of a healthy, living Jakob Danzler.

I went straight ahead, doing my best to hold my own still slightly Yiddishized voice steady. "Jakob Danzler, this is Hanna Topolsky, but I call myself Hanna Danzler. Do you recognize that name? Do you remember me?"

Several seconds passed that seemed to me like several minutes. "Hanna Topolsky? There's something familiar about that name. I don't know. Something . . . familiar. Maybe the first name. I just don't know, you'll have to excuse me. It would help if you explained your call."

He didn't remember me. I spent the next ten minutes telling him of my harrowed moments at the Museum. The moment I mentioned

Tarnów he said "Wait! Tarnów. I've been told I that I once did indeed fight there with the Polish Resistance, the NSZ, during the war. They said I was wounded in a gun battle, captured and sent to Auschwitz for the remainder of the war."

What a strange way for him to put it. "You indicate that you do not know this, Jakob, only that you were told it," I said.

"That's true," said Jakob. "They told me a piece of shrapnel from an explosion entered my brain. It took away my memory. Well, most of it. An operation after the war removed the shrapnel but unfortunately did not return all of my memory. But you said your last name is Danzler. Are we related? Please say more." I could feel his deep interest in my answer.

Without hesitation I said, "Jakob, I was a fighter with the same NSZ, the Resistance, like you. And I was your . . . your lover. You saved my life and the lives of many others of us by holding off the Germans at the mid-town Tarnów Bridge in early October of 1943. You insisted on remaining so the rest of us could escape. You were apparently injured when we exploded the bridge. But we were certain you were killed, if not by the explosion then by the Germans. I could not believe it when I learned, a few weeks ago, that you were still alive. Now please tell me what has become of you since the war."

His hesitation suggested that, like me, he didn't care to talk about it. But talk he did. "After the war, while recuperating from the operation, I realized I had virtually no recollection of my past. Only vaguely did I recall that I had even fought during the war. I became friends with my paraplegic roommate, a Zealander from Wellington. He urged me to resettle myself in his wonderful country. Without knowing of family or friends, or if any had survived the war, I had little to lose by heeding his suggestion. So I did exactly that. I accompanied him to Wellington and soon met a wonderful Maori woman, Nyree. We married and I studied to become an architect, which is what I am, though recently retired." Jakob stopped.

"Is something wrong?" I said.

"Nyree contracted ovarian cancer and died three years ago, Hanna. We never had any children—couldn't have them—but we did have a wonderful life together for forty-six years."

It was my turn to hesitate. "Jakob, I'm terribly sorry to hear about your Nyree."

"Thank you. But please tell me more of our connection, yours and mine."

"It was a brief one. We knew each other for only three months. But . . ." Should I tell him? Should I tell him?

"Go on," he said.

Jake, right at my side, could overhear enough of our conversation to move his head slowly, up and down. He could always read my mind. OK, I mouthed to him. "Jakob, I must tell you something. You have a child, you do have a child, a son. Our son. I named him Jakob after you but I call him Jake. He was born on May 5th, 1944, exactly eight months after I last saw you at the Tarnów Bridge. He is sitting beside me. Would you like to say hello to him?"

I could hear only heavy breathing on the other end. Then muffled crying. I waited. I was crying too. As, now, was Jake. At last, from Jakob: "Please put him on."

"Jakob?" said Jake, through his tears. Then: "Dad?"

No more words were said by either. No more could be said. Not for the next full minute. Jakob, me, Jake, Sunny and the boys too, we all were sobbing. Finally, from Jakob: "Jake? Your name is Jake Danzler? You are my son?" All Jake could say was yes. "And your mother's name is Hanna?"

"Yes, of course, she mentioned that, didn't she?"

"Yes, she did," said Jakob, his voice sounding far away. "Please put your mother back on the phone . . . but ask her to wait. She must wait a few minutes, she's not to hang up. Will you do that, Jake?" Now there was excitement in Jakob's voice.

"Yes, I will, of course I will." Jake handed the phone to me with Jakob's demand to wait till he got back on the phone. I took the phone, looked at it, then said, "Jakob?" But there was no reply. I waited five full minutes before I heard an answer, all the while looking at Jake and wondering what was going on.

Then Jakob's unmistakable voice: "Hanna, are you there?"

"Yes, I'm here. What kept you so long?"

He ignored my question. He talked fast. "Do you own a mizpah? Made of wood? You know what a mizpah is?"

"What? Yes." My free hand was locked vise-like on Jake's arm. "A wooden mizpah. A handmade wooden mizpah cut from a broom handle, right? Yes, Jakob, I do. I'm wearing it right now. It says . . ."

Jakob slowed down to finish my sentence. "'Jakob forever.' And I am now holding one that says 'Hanna forever.' I told you there was something familiar about your name. Then, when you spoke about the Tarnów Bridge, I began to remember. And I remembered that Hanna was the name on the mizpah found with my belongings when I left the hospital after my operation. I had no idea of its meaning, its significance. I'd put it away in an old jewelry box and pretty much forgotten about it until you called. Now a little bit of those days leading up to the battle at the bridge is coming back to me. I remember you, Hanna. Vaguely, but I do remember you. Even the garret is coming back to me."

Our conversation went on for over an hour. He told me a bit of his life with Nyree. And of his life as an architect. But he quickly returned to recalling the moments at the bridge and the wonderful moments before that in the garret that he was now recalling for the first time since his memory loss.

Everything was coming back to him in a rush. He wanted to meet with me as soon as humanly possible. He would come to America as quickly as he could catch a flight and "We will take it from there."

His choked sobs punctuated every other sentence.

I had found my Jakob. Jakob had found me. And Jake had found his father.

The Tarnów Gate

Bullwhip

Phil drifted into the back room at the Unurban Coffee House ten minutes late, as usual. Blithely greeting TJ, he took a minute to arrange himself at a rickety table in the rear of the nearly empty space.

Phil Adelman, late-twenties, and TJ Coe, mid-forties, had become friends through their mutual passion for writing. For months they'd met there every Wednesday at noon when they weren't working, to talk about writing and to critique each other's work.

No return greeting from TJ. "You know something, Phil? If you'd been writing, I wouldn't mind your always being late. But you haven't been doing much lately. And what you're doing lately is nothing to shout about. Ever been given lessons?"

"In writing?" Phil, lanky and nearly a head taller than TJ, leaned back and folded his arms while looking over his glasses at his friend. "You're kidding, aren't you? You about to suggest a teacher?"

"I am, Phil. Me. With your magnanimous permission."

"I don't get it."

"Didn't think you would, Phillip. You know something? In spite of your lazy persona and your lousy writing habits, you are one damn good writer. That's why I want to do this. Been thinking about it awhile. You write cleanly and you don't waste words. If Willie Nelson were a writer, he might want to be you."

"Yeah, and if I could wail and strum a guitar, I'd want to be him. Your point?"

"My point, my young friend, is not about the mess you are, which you are, it's about what you write, which, like I said, is damn good. But the way you are gets in the way of what you do. Look, I'm not here to analyze you, even if that's what I've been doing. I just want to teach you a few things you maybe don't already know. About what you write, but about who you are too. You up for it?"

"I'm sorry, TJ, but . . ."

"But? Wrong word. Get off your 'but,' Philly. And another thing, stop making excuses for not writing. That's Lesson Number One. And Two."

"But . . .

"Phil, look at me. Are you some kind of slow learner?"

"Listen, Teej, I appreciate what you're saying, but—excuse me—I don't especially like, well, the tone of your voice. And, forgive me, I'm really not too comfortable with this entire conversation."

"No shit, Phillip. Don't blame you. Wouldn't like anyone laying this kind of truth on me either. You too pissed to accept my offer? I mean, I'm not doing this for me, y'know?"

"What? No. Yes. I'm not sure. You've got to stop jumping all over me like you do. You're supposed to be my friend, not my father." By now, the two were standing face-to-face.

"OK, I'll stop jumping," said TJ, looking up at his friend. "I'll tread a little lighter. What say you?"

"Yeah, I guess so. Where do we begin?"

"Right there with what's in your hand. Your manuscript of Bullwhip. You've been dithering with that damn thing all year. So I'm going to shred it. Give it to me." TJ's hand was out.

"What?!"

"Not literally. But maybe I should. Look, Phil, your otherwise brilliant novel does have flaws. Teeny-tiny to merely huge. It's all bricks and no cement. Crying for a total re-write."

"You mean that? Why didn't you say so before?"

"I've been saying so for a dozen Wednesdays, you long stick, you haven't been hearing me. Now sit down and go to page seventeen."

Phil, his shaggy head wagging in denial, sat as ordered and went to page seventeen. TJ moved his chair beside him, reversed it and folded his arms over its back so he could look over Phil's permanently hunched shoulders.

The "lessons" began.

"You're good enough with narrative, Adelman, and maybe great with dialogue. But you've got to get a little smarter with plot. Or at least a little less lazy about building it. You can get away with a middling plot if you write well, if your story is well told and has interesting characters; real people. Plotting is hard, the rest is fun. But why not concentrate on narrative and characters and plot? Together in an entire whole, complete and totally killer way. Narrative and dialogue are downslope roads for you, man. But plot is the mountain you gotta climb."

Phil's wide, full-lipped mouth hung open. "I hate plot."

"Stop hating. Try making an outline for once like a normal writer. That way you won't paint yourself into a corner like you seem to have done with Bullwhip. An outline is the best way to see the plot; to get to the end. You don't have a plot till you can state the plot."

Phil mimed his feelings by sticking a finger down his throat.

"Outline," Phillip," said TJ, rubbing it in. O-U-T-L—"

"Yeah, yeah, I got it," said Phil.

"Then do it," replied TJ.

Within a week, accepting TJ's gospel, Phil had a full outline and had begun deleting old words and tapping out new ones. Slowly but steadily. With TJ practically sitting in his lap.

In eight more days of non-stop re-writing, buying most, but not all, of TJ's suggestions, and another few days of editing—only part of it proofreading—by TJ, the manuscript was reborn. Phil, with TJ hovering over him, had never worked so hard, so steadily. Phil called it "Final." TJ called it "Final, Number One." To celebrate its "finality," Phil bought a bucketful of Kentucky Fried, a Two-Buck Chuck red and a tub of Breyer's Butter Pecan. All he could afford. It would take four more re-writes, working together, before he could call the book truly finished, complete, done.

He began submitting it to a list of a hundred literary agents he'd compiled from Publishers Marketplace. But he quit submitting after forty straight rejections. Only three agents cared to comment on Bullwhip, but the comments came down to no. Disappointed, but determined, Phil, with TJ's encouragement, plus a recent three-thousand-dollar loan from his parents, invested in a comprehensive self-publishing package from Amazon's Kindle Publishing. Four months later, he was able to heft his first-ever published novel. Bullwhip. Its cover carried a close-up illustration of an 1847 Colt Dragoon revolver lying across a coiled bullwhip.

Now, with a drive that was lacking before, because he'd never published a book before, he began to show Bullwhip around. He plugged it on Facebook and every networking site he could think of. He mailed out copies to the book editors of two dozen major newspapers and online literary sites. He submitted it to half a dozen novel writing contests. He did readings that TJ, a playwright as well as an actor, was able to arrange: A spoken-word gathering at a small, non-equity theater in Venice; a coffee shop in West Hollywood; bookshops in Studio City, Brentwood and downtown L.A.

But the buzz that Bullwhip generated was no louder than a gnat's.

Then a Hollywood fairytale actually came to pass. A literary agent, Shelly Hampton, feeling like a grande one evening, happened to catch Phil's reading in a Brentwood Starbucks. Hampton loved what she heard, bought a copy of Bullwhip and read half of it in a single day. Knocked out, she didn't need to read the rest before signing Phil on. She overnighted Bullwhip to an acquaintance at Random House. The acquaintance grokked it as much as Hampton, and passed it around. A Random exec thought enough of it to place it on their Penguin list where it—miracle of miracles—spent twelve weeks on the New York Times paperback trade fiction list, where it rose to No. 7. And damned if it didn't cross the desk of Barry Sonnenfeld himself, who chose to option it, for seventy-five thousand dollars, to produce and direct as an indie film.

Bullwhip, the movie, starred Oscar Isaac as the sheriff who swore never to kill a man until not killing a man was no longer an option. It was shown at Sundance and a critic there compared it to High Noon, the dish being that Isaac Oscar might be looking at a golden Oscar. Isaac didn't receive a nomination, nor did the highly praised film, but Phil was nominated for his adapted screenplay. His cut of the film, back-end though it was, made him a semi-wealthy man. Phillip Adelman was now a recognized name in both the literary and film world.

Tyler Josephus Coe, however, did not fare quite so well as his young friend. He'd been at Phil's side, guiding him, editing him, setting up his first readings, "kicking my ass all the way up the ladder," as Phil put it. But TJ could not deny the obvious. Once Bullwhip made it to the movies, Phil no longer needed TJ's help. At some point, TJ, through some disconnect, came to feel—tried, unsuccessfully, not to feel—that Phil no longer needed him. The long hours he'd spent with Phil had paid off big. But only for Phil. TJ had neglected his own writing to make certain that the glitches in Phil's were not overlooked, and were carefully corrected, leaving only Phil's highly original prose. Phil's voice, amplified by TJ's input, did indeed emerge clear, with its sparse phrasing, its clipped language, its signature, often quirky, turns of plot.

TJ began turning away from Phil in subtle ways that Phil did not pick up on. Attending to his own frantic affairs now, Phil never noticed his friend's mounting ennui. And depression. The two had long since dropped their weekly meetings at the Unurban. And then stopped meeting altogether. But less because Phil couldn't make time to meet than that TJ no longer seemed to be available.

TJ's problem, besides a reacquired drinking habit, was one he'd never faced before: that old curse, writer's block. The good stuff was up there in his head but he could no longer spill it onto the page. He'd always done a crossword every morning as his "mental pushups." Now he found himself doing crosswords all day. Soon enough, he got it into his addled head that he was no longer a writer. Making matters worse, his acting jobs, but for a few commercials, had pretty much stopped coming.

The way he saw it, his nurturing of Phil's writing had, somehow—crazy as it seemed—leeched out his own ability to write. To act, too? Whatever, he hadn't done either in months. Nor, in months, had he so much as talked to or texted Phil. Which, he told himself, had nothing to do with his being jealous. Of Phil, of anyone. Still, it seemed so unfair. Phil had broken through so easily. Hadn't TJ been at this game far longer? For—what was it?—twenty-six years? Was he seeing Phil's success in the abstract? As due to fate, irony, luck, timing, serendipity, but never to the simple fact that maybe Phil was the better writer and deserved his break? No maybes. Phil was better. TJ knew this, had always known it, just couldn't admit it till now. And yet, how bad a playwright was he himself? Why hadn't this happened to him? In twenty-six fucking years?

He finally concluded that he could not fight through this blockage business in L.A. Too busy a town to be so unbusy in. He needed to be alone somewhere. What he found was a six-month house-sit offered him for the fast-approaching winter by an old girlfriend, Claire Scalise, now chief of Paramount's licensing division. Her A-frame in Truckee, just north of Lake Tahoe, was isolated, quiet, the perfect place to contemplate his three-act "Henry in Love," a modern satire about King Henry VIII. "Henry" had been aborning—stubbornly not aborning—for the past year. Including the three months he'd already been in Truckee.

TJ had lived near beaches most of his life. He'd never experienced a Northern California high-country winter like Truckee's; the screaming winds and sideways snow on one side of the wall, a snug fire on the other, which he liked to stoke to a furious burn with logs he'd chopped himself.

What he could not stoke, though, were the fires of his whiskey-tinged imagination. Alone, except for his tiger-striped cat, Max, TJ welcomed distractions. Invented them. Long sojourns on Claire's snowmobile, hiking the woods that surrounded him, emptying the case of Wild Turkey he'd brought with him; anything not to face the unwritten pages of Henry in Love. Maybe Henry wasn't in love. Maybe Henry just wasn't worth writing. Maybe Henry was a piece of shit.

TJ recalled better days, days when the words came easy. His first play, "Elsa" had a three-month run in an out-of-the-way theater on Ventura. The feeling of seeing his work on the boards had been exhilarating. If the play didn't pay the theater's rent, it did get a good, one paragraph review in the Times. But that was years ago. He'd written only one play since, "Turn of the Century," with an apocalyptic theme. But it still sits mouldering on several someone's slush piles. Acting jobs had been all that was feeding him—three feature roles, two for sitcoms, one for a TV movie—but that too was a while back. Residuals were a laugh. His last check was for twenty-eight cents. And if no decent role came through soon, he could lose his SAG/AFTRA medical coverage. He'd already lost his theatrical agent, and no literary agent was interested in him.

Was he kidding himself? Did he even have the rest of "Henry" in him? He had thirty-seven pages. He needed, total, seventy-five. Thirty-seven pages did not a play make. And he still didn't have a third act, an ending. There had to be a better way to make some bucks. His were nearly gone.

Some three years had passed since TJ first stood over Phil Adelman, flogging him to become a better writer. As the trajectory of Phil's career rose, TJ's continued to dive. Phil often tried to reach TJ to offer his help. He was deeply grateful to his friend, offering him cash, anything he needed but never would ask for. When Phil asked TJ to guest-sit the first table reading of his Bullwhip script, TJ turned him down. Turned down a feature role in the film, too. Claimed he was too busy writing his play, though he hadn't written a word in months. Phil kept asking, TJ kept saying no, till Phil, feeling he was putting unwanted pressure on his friend, quit asking. That's when the two lost touch altogether. There was nothing intentional about the parting. Neither would have recognized it as such. But a parting it was.

Phil Adelman was quickly becoming an A-list screenwriter. Didn't matter what a mess he'd been in the beginning, all he'd ever needed was TJ Coe's heavily applied kick in the ass to bring out the skill he'd always had as a writer; of books, movies . . . they were even talking about "Bullwhip, the Musical." Which never happened because Phil was tied up adapting his second novel for the screen. "The Lady and the Bull," part of a planned trilogy, would come out in the fall with Charlize Theron co-starring as the vengeful wife of Isaac's now-legendary Bull Jameson, laid low for half the movie by a bullet that shot off his trigger finger. Theron's character, Amy Lou, limned beautifully by Phil, turns out to be more of a bad-ass than the baddies. "Don't screw with Amy Lou," uttered by a minor character, was to become a classic movie line, used by a man warning of a strong woman.

In September of 2017, "The Lady and the Bull" had a preview showing at the Landmark on Pico in West L.A. Phil, who'd roughed out the third Bull novel, but didn't yet have a name for it, made a guest appearance there to answer questions. The light was poor, even with the house lights up after the showing. The audience wanted to know how Phil knew when he was finished writing, how hard it was to turn a novel into a screenplay, if he had any say-so about actors. Like that. The Q&A ran to forty minutes. "I'll take one more question," said Phil.

"What do you do when the words won't come?" The question came from a vague figure in the dark rear of the theater.

"Are you a writer?" asked Phil.

"Answer the question."

The audience turned to see the source of the rude demand. Phil already knew who the questioner was but didn't let on. His fingers stroked the nub of his chin before he spoke. "You stop and go back and re-read what you've written. All the way to the beginning if you have to. It may give you the momentum to keep writing. Works for me. Does that answer your question?"

"No. What if there's nothing to go back to?"

An uncomfortable silence. "Then you ask a friend to help you. Does *that* answer your question?"

No reply.

People formed a small line after to compliment or congratulate Phil or have him sign one of his books they'd brought along. When they dispersed, he looked out and saw TJ, still sitting alone up top in the rear. "You gonna come down here and say hello, man, or do I have to come up there and drag you down?"

TJ took his time coming down the stairs. His hair and his beard—the beard he'd never worn before—were long and unkempt. His sun-scalded face was blank, his eyes empty and unfocussed. He didn't seem drunk but smelled of alcohol and unwashed clothes. He looked at Phil, not seeming to see him. Then he stuck out a tentative hand. Phil brushed it away and pulled TJ into a hug, an awkward one because TJ wasn't expecting it. Reluctantly, at Phil's demand, he walked with him downstairs to the

Westside Tavern. Over Coca Colas and salted peanuts, Phil coaxed out TJ's recent history.

TJ had found more places to house-sit till there were no more houses to sit. For longer than he could remember, he'd crashed at the few friends he had left. Now—these past three, or was it four, weeks—he'd been living out of his car. No, he hadn't written anything lately. Nothing at all. No acting calls either; he'd become just another middle-aged actor buried in the ranks of the Industry's IMDb data base. Same-old-same-old. Phil listened. Didn't speak except to urge TJ on until he saw his eyelids begin to droop.

"C'mon, let's go," said Phil. He'd recently bought an adobe-style home on 19th off Montana. "Four bedrooms. I rattle around the place," he told TJ. "You're staying with me till we can get you off the dime. No arguments."

"I'd just bring you down, Phil. You don't need that."

"What you need—forgive me, TJ—is a hot shower. I want you to follow me home."

TJ, the erstwhile leader of this two-pack, started to protest but was stopped by Phil's gentle love slap to his cheek. "You're with me now, buddy boy, no backtalk." TJ caved; did as he was instructed. When they arrived at the house, he parked in the driveway as Phil pulled into the garage. But TJ didn't exit his car, a beater Ford. He just sat there, his chin on his chest.

Phil came over and pulled the car door open. "What's wrong, Teej?"

Tears were pouring from him. He wasn't just crying, he was bawling, his narrow shoulders heaving. Phil reached in and put his arm around his friend, who was about to collapse. He helped him out of the car, grabbed the duffel beside him, and got him into the house and into a shower. Then into bed. TJ was asleep in minutes, hardly changing position for the next fourteen hours.

The student would now look after the teacher.

When TJ awoke he looked at his wrist to check the time, but he wasn't wearing his watch. He forgot that he'd pawned it a few days earlier. For food and gas. And for a ticket to see Phil's movie. The only thing he hadn't pawned was his Mac. He still had his phone but its service had been cut off weeks earlier. Still groggy, he stumbled to the kitchen in the way-too-big terrycloth robe Phil had left for him. Phil walked in from his office off the kitchen, said hello and poured him a cup of coffee. "Black with two sugars, right?"

"Morning," mumbled TJ, taking a two-handed gulp. "You remembered. Thanks."

"Not morning. Two-thirty in the afternoon. Any plans for today?"

"No."

"Plans for any day?"

"Wanna talk about it? How we can put you back on your play?"

"What play. I don't have a play. Never had a play."

"Henry? Henry in Love?"

"Never heard of him."

"No play?"

"No play."

Phil's eyes went to the ceiling like he was inspecting for spiders. "OK. Know something? You're right. You say you don't have a play, you don't have a play. Any plans for the rest of your life?"

TJ wouldn't look at him. "What life? No. And I thank you, sir, for your hospitality. Now if I can have a little toast with this coffee, I'll finish my breakfast, or lunch, or whatever you want to call it, then I'd like to do a little laundry if you don't mind. And then I'll be on my way."

Phil replied, evenly, "You're not going anywhere, Coe. You're staying right here for as long as it takes to get you back up and running."

"Charity. Isn't that nice. Well, my friend, I do not need your charity. Correction: I do not want your charity." There was an edge to TJ's voice. "Where's your laundry room?"

"When did you become such an asshole, Teej? I'm not offering you any goddamn charity, I mean to put you to work."

"Say again?"

"Work. W-O-R-K. I don't know what kind. I'll think of something."

"See, Phil? Charity. You're gonna make some kind of work for me. Thank you, my kind and wealthy friend, but . . . no. N-O."

"OK. But stick around for a few days. I insist. I demand it. You look like you could use some R&R."

"You're right. I look like shit, I know it. Two days, max, thank you. Then I'm gone."

Two days later, at 7 am, TJ's duffel was packed, as promised. It sat in the corner of the kitchen as he and Phil sat over their coffee. He'd be gone right after, almost wishing Phil weren't there because it'd be easier writing a note than saying goodbye face to face.

That's when Phil's phone did the first sixteen notes of Lady Gaga's "Let's Dance." "Yeah?" he said, listening for the next ten seconds. His eyes went big. He held a hand up to TJ to apologize for the interruption as he got up and walked into his office, the phone still at his ear. TJ looked at the Times sports. Ten minutes later Phil was back at the table.

"You're not going to believe this, Teej. That was Shelly Hampton, my agent, you remember her? The numbers just came in for the first weekend of 'The Lady.' Twenty-six, six. Ten over what they expected. Sonnenfeld just OKed a third Bull."

"That's good, isn't it?" said TJ, looking up from the paper.

"Yeah, that's good, it's great. But I haven't even finished the novel. Just a first draft. Don't even have a name for it. And the editor Penguin gave me this time sucks. He does not get me."

"And?"

"And? You wanna know the 'and?' Here's the 'and.' And you're gonna edit the book."

"Me?"

"Yes, you, Mr. Tyler Josephus Coe. It just smacked me upside my head. It's what you do best. Editing. Or have you forgotten? Look, I'm desperate. I've got to get this book to press in two months. That gives me exactly one month to put a finished manuscript on Penguin's desk for their editors. So you, TJ, are elected, capeesh? You got a problem with that?"

"Tough guy. Ca-peesh. You're not screwing with me? You really want me screwing up your deathless prose? You gonna trust me with a best-seller?"

"It ain't a best-seller till you make it so. And, yes, I do trust you so don't make me wrong. How's seventy-five an hour sound?"

"Dollars?"

"No, cents."

"C'mon, Phil, I don't know if I have it in me."

"I know what you got in you. Anyhow, I guess we're gonna find out. I got a great little loft above the garage, you can work there."

Phil stopped, reached into a mugful of pencils and Sharpies on the counter behind him, then wrote "10/21" in bright red a foot high in the middle of the sports page TJ had been reading. "Tape this to the wall, it's your deadline. Now empty that bag and get busy."

A crooked smile broke through. The first since Phil had run into him. "Mind if I drink on the job. boss?"

"I can't stop you drinking, TJ. I mind if you miss that deadline."

Phil saw TJ as a born editor. TJ knew it too, even if he'd slowly been losing his confidence about anything having to do with writing. True, he'd done a lot of editing for Phil and a little for a few others. But he understood that this was

serious stuff. He'd allowed himself to fuck up his own life. What if he fucked up Phil's with his editing?

No more time to mull it over. He set up his new writing loft and sat himself at its desk. He thought of doing a crossword, the way he always used to start his day, but was afraid of where that would lead. The only booze he had was a half empty pint of four Roses. He walked it over to the little window in the loft and, after staring at it a moment, emptied the bottle. Then he picked up the rough of Phil's third novel and didn't put it down until he finished it at 3 am, stopping only for some pizza sent up by Phil. By then he had a name for it: "The Sheriff Is No Lady." In it, Bull is killed by a shot from behind, but returns as a guiding spirit. Amy Lou, with her new spiritual sidekick, takes Bull's place as Socorro's new sheriff. Two things became obvious throughout TJ's reading. Phil was still his usual self. Sloppy. And brilliant.

After sleeping for four hours, TJ grabbed a pot of coffee, pulled up the manuscript on his Mac and went right into his edit. He could use some Wild Turkey but, by the end of the first ten pages, was too deep inside his head to even think of it.

He was possessed, finishing the first edit two weeks later. His proofreading was spot on but his comprehensive marginal notes were what pulled the novel together. His completed edits—all five of them, each going a little faster than the other—had Phil losing about ten thousand words, but adding thirteen thousand more. The sagging middle was now pulled taut and the third act called for a long confrontational scene that, according to Penguin's later take, "glowed." The final script would be submitted not just on time, a rarity for a Phillip Adelman novel, but a week early. And Penguin would buy "The Sheriff Is No Lady" as its title.

"Schmuck, you were being paid by the hour. You work too fast," Phil said to TJ the day he placed the final in Phil's hands.

TJ nodded. "I know. But I had to rush the finish. I had other things to do."

"Like what?" said Phil.

"Like paying a visit to Henry."

"Oh? Henry? I'll bite."

"You trying to be funny, Phillip?"

"No, seriously. You back on your play?"

"Yeah, and Henry's back in love. I'm fifteen, twenty pages from a wrap."

"Coe, Are you shitting me?" Phil did not wait for an answer. "I'll be right back." Leaving TJ openmouthed at the table, he ran out of the house. Three stops and thirty minutes later he was back.

With a bucket of Kentucky Fried, a Two Buck Chuck red and a tub of Breyer's Butter Pecan.

The Tarnów Gate

Launching the Ticonderoga

I'm well-settled into my favorite chair, more a leather cave than a chair, sipping and foolscapping new ideas when suddenly the French doors behind me are kicked in so violently they bang against the wall, several of their panes shattered.

This, naturally, causes me to jump, in turn causing my hand to jam my Ticonderoga so hard into the pad on which I'm writing that the pencil breaks in two.

At one moment of the evening I'm enjoying my martini and making notes, and in the next I'm staring at what I immediately recognize as a Glock 9mm semi-automatic pistol. Pointed directly at my forehead. I freeze.

No introductions, none needed. The man holding the Glock gets to the point. "There's a safe or a locked file here that holds something of great value to me." He says this in what I'd describe as a gritty prison-cell-informed voice. At least I think he says this, because he's wearing a black balaclava that covers his entire face except for his riveting, pale blue eyes, muffling his words. "I want it. Now," he mumbles. His meaning is clearer than his words. Curious now, as well as frightened, I believe I'll never come to know how he's come to the information I possess about him. Privileged information, to be sure, but information that could put him back behind bars were it to become known.

"I know who you are," I say. "I recognize your voice from the interview sessions we had at Metro Psych Hospital." The moment I speak these words, I regret them. I've just given him a logical reason to kill me. Did I think I could somehow talk him out of his obsession? What's this going to cost me, my life?

It's obvious from his dilated pupils, bulging with purpose, that he's not just armed, he's on something serious, drugs more likely than booze, maybe both, and it's equally obvious they're about to trigger mayhem. I can still think clearly enough to know that he won't pull the trigger at least until the safe is open and the information is in his hands. After that I'm certain I'll be shot dead.

I know this because I'm a forensic scientist. This isn't his first visit but I recognize a psychopath when I see one. I've seen a thousand, usually across from me in an office and by appointment. What he's after, I surmise, is his file, one among many I've retained as I write my third treatise on criminal psychopathy. He has nothing to be concerned about since I'd never use his name, but, what's there to say, he doesn't know that because, well, he's a psychopath. What he's doing doesn't have to make sense, and that includes murdering me.

Do I really fear for my life? I most certainly do. I find the nerve to speak to him. "Is it your file you want?" He nods his hooded head. "I'll get it for you. You can go with me (as if he needs my permission). But the combination is a long one and I have to write it down because the safe is new and I haven't yet memorized it, the combination, that is."

I'm vamping for time.

"Write it down?" he says.

"Yes, it's in code and it's in the drawer of my desk over there. And I have to sharpen a new pencil, if you don't mind, you made me break the one I was using."

"Get it!" he demands," his impatience showing in his voice. But before I can walk over to the desk, he does, and opens the drawer to apparently make sure it doesn't contain a gun, something, incidentally, I have never owned. The drawer's contents are not incriminating.

I have followed him to the desk. I boot up my computer, open a file titled "Birthdays" but which actually contains all my passwords and such important information as my safe's combination, written in coded characters. I extract a fresh pencil from a coffee cup on top of the desk full of new pencils, while I fish around for and find, in the desk's middle drawer, a plastic pencil sharpener in the shape of a human nose, a humorous stocking filler received just a few days ago on Christmas.

It was a gag gift but it works even better than my electric sharpener.

As my hooded friend watches, I carefully sharpen the pencil, blow away its shavings, turn and drive the Ticonderoga deeply into the just-right spot in his heart, a few inches to the left of his solar plexus.

His gun falls to the floor, followed by his nearly dead body. I stare at it for a moment, remove my pencil, make a call to 9-1-1, then return to my chair to await the police, finish my martini and continue with the notes I was taking when I was so rudely interrupted, minutes earlier.

I have already rinsed off the withdrawn pencil and placed it on my desk.

It looks as innocent as I.

The Tarnów Gate

The Incident at Walgreens

I hadn't visited Papa Del for some time. My wife's father is eighty-four now, ailing but still living alone in his two-bedroom flat up in the Bronx, not far from Yankee Stadium. He's been there ever since he sold his home after Grandma Esther passed twenty-three years ago. I love Papa Del; he's a generous and good-hearted man though he can be something of a trial. That he's concerned mostly with himself and his own problems is something I can handle, but he's been, since I first met him, long-winded and boring.

Still, my Millie would never forgive me if, on my rare business trips to New York, I didn't stop by his place to say hello. On these occasions I do little more than listen to him rattle on about his fifty proud years at Bulova.

Del has one of those large-number flip phones for seniors which I called when I landed at JFK a few days ago. I said I had a long meeting in Manhattan the next day but would like to spend my arrival afternoon with him. He was delighted so from JFK I went straight to his place.

He loves chocolates, so I brought him a box of See's truffles and he offered me his usual cup of cocoa. After inquiring about Millie and the kids, he drifted into a reminiscence about his days at Bulova; mostly stories I'd often heard before. But, as he spoke, it occurred to me that Millie might want to hear his voice for what we all realized could be the last time ever. She loves her Papa Del. So I used my phone to record his entire ramble. I'll skip the first part but the last part, though it starts out boring, is well worth listening to. Here's Del in his own voice. You'll hear mine occasionally too:

"I need to tell you something that happened to me on Wednesday, July 23, 1997, just two years before my retirement. I'll never forget that date. I've never told this to anyone before."

"So tell me, please."

"Well, I was leaving work and stopped by a Walgreens Drug Store near the Bulova offices for an elastic bandage for a sprained ankle I got from tripping over a curb, and for some cotton swabs, which I tend to constantly use for the waxy buildup in my ears. Anyhow, there was this machine outside of Walgreens, one of those amusement devices for kids, the kind you put a quarter in and get a one-minute ride. But this one was different, not a race car or a pony. It was a little booth that looked like those photo booths you used to see in the penny arcades. It was called 'The Time Machine.' I don't know what got into me but, just looking at it, it somehow made me feel almost like a kid myself. No one was around so, what the heck, I sat down in it and closed its folding door. I barely fit in the space because I'm a pretty big fellow, but I was already inside so I dropped my quarter into its slot. A panel lighted up above a round sort of meter. It said 'Select Century.' It was calibrated from 1600 to 2400 in what appeared to be one-year increments. I was a history buff and I was there so I told myself I'd go along with the illusion. I dialed, close as possible, to the year 1963, figuring that if I 'landed' in that year, I might be able to—God knows how—prevent the assassination of President Kennedy. I know, I know, this was just for kids, but the truth is I was enjoying myself. So I pressed the red 'Ignition' button.

"The first thing that happened is that the booth began to vibrate and bounce a little. I didn't care for that very much, nor for the cheesy images of a rocket hurtling through space that came onto a blurry black and white TV screen above the booth's 'joy stick.' I guess this was supposed to lend some realism, but I began to regret that I'd wasted my time trying the silly device. If I could have stopped it then, I would. Then, suddenly, the whole booth seemed to accelerate, pinning me hard against its back wall while the TV screen reported that I was 'Approaching warp speed!'

"I almost blacked out before the damned thing appeared to decelerate and finally stop. My back ached from the ride and I was so anxious to get out of there I practically broke the folding door as I ripped it open. I was stunned at what had just happened, but also felt embarrassed that someone might see me exiting that stupid thing.

"Well, I have to admit that child's ride had seemed so real that I looked around to see if anything had actually changed; to see if maybe I'd been deposited into 1963! But no, I was not in Dealey Plaza in Dallas, I was right there at Walgreens, exactly as I'd entered it for my elastic bandage and cotton swabs, still in the plastic bag in my left hand. Now, I have to tell you that, in that moment, I felt like a complete fool."

Del leaned back then, making me think his little story was ended, as indeed I hoped it was. But it most certainly was not. He went on.

"I did my best to put this absurd experience behind me, buying my late edition Daily News, as always, and boarding my train for my ride home to Yonkers. Settling in, I glanced at its lurid front page then, before turning to sports, I skimmed over stories about a Mafia murder in Flushing, the ground-breaking for a new terminal at LaGuardia and a featured piece about a bus accident in Brooklyn, early that morning, that claimed five lives. Enough of that. The Mets had played the third of a three-game series with the Cards last night and I was anxious to get the details of the game, which I'd had to miss because the damn TV was on the fritz. But the headline said, 'Mets lose opener of 4-game series to Braves, 4-1.'

"How could that be, I told myself, when I knew very well that it was the Cards who'd played my Mets last night. We weren't playing the Braves till the next day, Thursday. Something was wrong. I quickly eyed the date at the top of the page: Friday, July 25, 1997. How could that be? Today wasn't Friday the 25th, it was Wednesday, July 23. I looked at several other pages. Friday, July 25 was clearly printed on every one. I stared out the train window for several minutes until I caught an electric sign over a Wells Fargo Bank: Friday, July 25. And, finally, I thought to look at my Bulova: July 25.

"Then it hit me. It had to be. Somehow that outrageous 'time machine' did this! But what was I thinking? A time machine?! Ridiculous! Still, had I just lost two days of my life? Gone, just like that?

"The train reached my stop at 161st Street. I staggered off in a daze. "Excuse me," I said to a hot dog vender near the exit stairs, 'What day is this?' 'You been drinkin'?' he shot back at me. 'It's Friday, man. You wanna dog?' 'Sure,' I said. 'What's the date?' 'The 25th,' he said, 'you want the year too?' 'Yes, why not?' I said. '1997,' he said, shaking his head as I handed him a ten dollar bill and walked away, forgetting both my hot dog and my change.

"This was no dream. I'd been projected not 34 years into the past but two days into the future! As I neared my flat, I had to stop and sit down on a park bench. I had to think. Re-reading the newspaper for the third time now, I came to the story about the bus crash in Brooklyn that killed the driver, three passengers sitting near him and the driver of the car also involved in the crash. It said that the crash happened just this morning, Friday morning, the 25th. But in my world, I told myself, it hadn't happened yet! I continued home, bewildered. I don't remember eating. The TV was still on the fritz but I wouldn't have watched it anyhow because I thought maybe this whole nightmare would go away if I ignored it. But how could I? I tried to sleep that night but couldn't.

"It wasn't till the next day that it really hit me. The Times at my door told me it was the 26th. A Saturday. So, if that was the case and I was two days into the future, I could possibly go back two days and do something to change what had happened. But how could I change things?Who would believe my explanation? Never mind that, I could at least try to convince that bus driver to take a different route. I would just tell him I had a premonition or something. I had to get back to that machine right away! I had to go back in time to warn that bus driver.

"Anyhow, I immediately rushed over to my station and jumped on the southbound train to Walgreens…"

There was a long gap here before you could hear me say, "And…?"

"And it was gone."

"Walgreens was gone?!"

"No, not Walgreens. The time machine… the booth. I went inside the store, found the manager and asked her what had happened to it. You know what she said?"

"Tell me, please." Del had my full attention now.

"She said, 'Oh that? The dumb thing never worked. Our people came around this morning and took it away. Did you actually want to try it, sir?' She was smiling at me like I was crazy or something.

"'Yes,' I told her. I didn't care what she thought.

"'Well,' she said, still smiling, 'They promised to have it back in two days.'"

The Tarnów Gate

The Interrogation

"What're you having, Dad?"

"I think a pastrami and Swiss. And an egg cream. You?"

"A Cobb salad. So tell me what's going on with you?"

"You really want to know?"

"Yes, I really want to know."

"No, you don't."

"What do you mean, I don't? I most certainly do."

"I met a woman, Mims."

"Don't tell me that. Really? That's wonderful, Daddy. So that's why you asked me to lunch?"

"No, I like your company. Isn't that enough?"

"No. I want you to tell me about her."

"I just did."

"No, you didn't. Tell me more. I mean . . . did you just meet her?"

"I've known her for nearly two months."

"You little devil, you. You never said a word."

"I'm saying now."

"Sounds serious. Please say more. Do you like her?"

"Of course I like her. Why else would I be with her?"

Long pause.

"Don't you go silent on me, Dad. I'm listening."

"OK, OK. She's . . . a very nice person. A—I think she said—a Presbyterian. Or maybe a Methodist, whatever. But a devout atheist and a screaming liberal like me. Was twice married, once divorced, once widowed."

"How old?"

"Seventy-nine. A year older than me."

"A cougar."

"Very funny."

"But, Dad, you've always been attracted to younger women. Mom was twelve years younger. Your last 'girlfriend' was—what?—twenty, twenty-five years younger?"

"I'm done with that mishigas, Mims. Look, I wasn't looking for anyone. I went to the Getty for a lecture on Frank Gehry's architecture. Gehry himself delivered it. He did a slide show. You know how I love that stuff. And I got to talking to this woman who happened to be sitting next to me and I suggested we have coffee afterward so we could discuss the lecture and she says, skip the coffee, let's have a cocktail, which we did. Next thing you know, I ask her to dinner and . . . we're, well, we're seeing each other. And talking . . . a lot."

"Talking? That's it?"

"Talking."

"Sooo . . . are you attracted to her for more than her architecture?"

"Well, Mimsy, I have to admit, she is well built."

"Now who's being funny? What's her name? Does she have family? Is she working? Tell me everything."

"What's to tell. Her name is Christine Abramovitz."

"What? Quite an interesting tag. I thought you said she was . . ."

"She likes Jews. Both her husbands were Yids. She converted, nu? She has four kids, all living back east where she grew up in Manhattan. Nine grandkids. She moved to LA because her second husband got a job here. And died here. She became curator of an art gallery on Melrose, then retired last year as its manager."

"So, Dad, you're an artist, she ran an art gallery. You met in a milieu—an art museum—a place you love at a talk about a subject you both love. You sound like you have a little in common. You love food. Does she? Does she, uh, cook?"

"I've gained three pounds since we met."

"She cooks. Wait a minute, Dad. Are you telling me all this because you're attracted to her in a way that you'd like to, maybe . . . uh . . . uh …"

"Stop uh-ing me, Mims. And thank you for thinking that. Hey, if she's up for it . . ."

"Father mine, I'm talking about marriage. What are you talking about?"

"Uh . . . uh . . ."

"Who's uh-ing now? Are you sleeping with her?"

"Sleeping with her?"

"You are, aren't you? Get that silly grin off your face."

"Daughter mine, it's none of your business."

"You are, aren't you?"

"Sleeping. Cuddling. What's the difference? We're holding on to each other for dear life."

" OK, Dad, I get it . . . I understand."

"But do you, Mimsy? Can you? Can anyone of your tender years understand?"

"Please, Dad, I'm forty-seven. Of course I understand. And I'm happy for you. What does she look like?"

What does she look like? What do I look like? Does it matter? Why don't you ask me what it feels like to be with her? Maybe I shouldn't have told you about her."

"Dad, I'm sorry, I didn't mean . . ."

"I know what you meant. You just wanted to know who she is. Christine is a good person, that's who she is."

"C'mon, Dad, are you thinking of marrying her? I don't want you settling again. You've been through enough pain. I don't want to see you hurt. So maybe you can understand why I want to know more about her. In the end, if you agree that she's right for you, then I will too. Well, I think I will. But it's your turn to understand me. I want to protect you. That's the only place I'm coming from. Don't jump on me for this, Dad, but you've made some mistakes before. They've hurt not just you but me, so maybe I can get to meet this Christine before you go any further? I promise you this, if I see she cares for you, truly cares for you, I know I'll like her. I think if she cares for you, she'll care for me too. Oh, Dad, I love you way too much to see you get hurt again."

"I know that, babe. I love you, too. And yes, I've made mistakes before. Plenty. You remember that last woman, the one I met in the nightclub?"

"I do. And I recall what you said about her. That you were coming from the right place but were looking in the wrong place."

"Right. Truth is, I'm a little scared of my feelings for Christine. Scared that, I may be making yet another mistake. But, you know what, Mims? I really think you'll love her."

"And why is that? Do you?"

"Do I what?"

"Were you not listening, Daddy? Do you love her?"

"I heard you the first time, Mimsy. I don't know if I love her. Funny thing is, I never really asked myself that question. I need to think about that awhile."

"Well, I'm asking now. You don't know if you love her and you're maybe thinking of marrying her?"

"Who said I was?"

"I said."

"OK. Yes. I'm thinking."

"Of marrying her?"

"Yes, I guess."

"You guess?"

"Well, I'm only thinking about it.

"Only thinking about it."

"Yes. I think so."

"You think you're thinking about it?"

"Dammit, Mims, I'm knowing. OK?"

"Knowing? Now it's knowing? What is it you're knowing? I repeat, Father: Do you love her?"

"My God, Miriam, I told you I never asked myself that question."

"So forgive me for repeating myself but I'm asking. Do you love Christine?"

"You're pressuring me. I'm still thinking. Is that OK?"

"No."

"'No,' she says. Then, you know what? I do love her. I do. You know something, Miriam, you can be relentless. But thanks for asking, because if you hadn't . . . I might never have realized it."

"So that's settled. Good. Lunch. Tomorrow. With your Christine Abramovitz. Twelve noon at the Archer Grille on 4th."

"What? What? I can't remember all that. Send me an email."

"A text OK?"

"I don't know how to text."

"Yes, you do.

"So I do."

"Daddy?"

"What?"

"I love you."

"You already said that."

"Yes, but I'm repeating myself again. I love you."

"Yeah, yeah, yeah. Hey, you gonna eat that hard-boiled egg?"

The Tarnów Gate

The Man Who Loved Cigar Boxes

Harmon Terwiliger was a man of deep passion. But almost nobody else cared about his passion. In Europe, yes, but not in America.

Harmon Terwiliger's passion was collecting cigar box art, a subject that generated so little interest that, hard as he tried, he was unable to gather more than three other collectors in Philadelphia where he lived. And, though his passion drove him to then reach out all across America, he still could not raise more than a few dozen collectors.

Ignoring this failure, inspired by it, rather, he went on to write a scholarly treatise on the collecting and cataloguing of cigar box covers, and posted it on Facebook, his fallback medium, where he also began a blog on the subject that so captivated him. This blog eventually generated a following of several hundred other enthusiasts whom he formed into a society he called "La Caja de la Cigarros Aficionados," or the CCA, the "Cigar Box Lovers." But, while he did make progress, he was not satisfied that he'd tapped the depths of the well, shallow though it was.

Those who belonged to the CCA came to learn the backgrounds of the great cigar label lithographers from its golden era, the turn of the 19th Century: Hippenheimer and Maur, Harris & Sons, O.L. Schwenke and the greatest of all, George Schlegel. Age, of course, has always been a yardstick of value but, as with all collectibles, the rarer the object, even if not the oldest, the more valuable it was.

The blog's most popular feature was its cataloguing of cigar box and label values. Here, collectors could compare the prices of what they'd collected. And could, through the site's popular "Trading Post" feature, buy, sell and trade their beloved boxes and labels.

For years, no true market for these objects had ever been established until the International Cigar Label Grading Service was founded in 1982. The ICLGS raised the system of label grading to that of an art itself; collectors now had a respectable and expert archivist capable of placing a well-founded market value on their precious inside and outside cigar boxes, labels, even cigar rings. With this trustworthy pricing source, more and more rare specimens were being uncovered and soon were bringing in, not the usual ten- and twenty-dollar sales, but, for mint condition boxes and labels, three- and four-figure amounts. And as much as $150,000 for one of the art's finest specimens, a Cubano known as the 1861 La Costa del Gordo, a gem of the lithographer's art.

But the single most valuable cigar box label, also a Cuban, was thought to be one of a kind. Called simply "La Evanita," all that was known of its existence was a sepia photo taken in the 1920s, later found in 1987 in the attic of an old vaudevillian, John "Bingo" Benson, by name, a song and dance man whose tenuous fame had faded with the era itself. The ICLGS was able to prove, by careful forensic research, that the box was literally sui generis; one of a kind. And was now worth an estimated $2.5 million. Almost as much as the rarest litho collectible of all, the famed Honus "Hans" Wagner rookie baseball card, currently valued at $3 million. Problem was, the ICLGS, nor anyone else, knew where the box itself could be found.

Harmon Terwiliger, however, did have such an idea. And if "Little Eva," his pet name for La Evanita, could be found, he'd long ago convinced himself that he'd be the one to find it, relying upon a single fact: that Bingo Benson and his family had no idea of how valuable the box and its exquisite lithographed panels were.

Terwiliger reasoned that, first, Benson must have been a cigar smoker. Why else would he take or own a photo of a cigar box. Likely it was so he could show it to a seller simply to replace the box. But, ironically, it was later learned that only one known box had ever been preserved because the last known shipment of the cigars had gone down in a storm off Key West. And no more La Evanitas ever left Cuba again, or were even produced, because the company, due to the loss, was forced out of business. Thus was the provenance of La Evanita's rarity.

Terwiliger further reasoned that no man who loves cigars ever throws away a box he's emptied. So it was logical to presume that, if the photo of the La Evanita box was found in the attic, so too would the box be found there—or somewhere else in the house. It wasn't likely he would ever part with it.

Possessed of this reasoning—convinced of its wisdom—Terwiliger was now determined to not only find his "Little Eva," he was possessed by the idea of owning it as well. No easy trick, as he most certainly did not possess the $2.5 million required to purchase it if he should find it. Therefore, he finally reasoned, he would steal it.

So now he must find Bingo Benson's old house—if it still existed—and make a thorough search of it, a prospect that, frankly, thrilled him. He was never happier than when searching out a rare cigar box or label.

His research uncovered old Bingo's obituary in the New York Post. It stated that, after retirement, he'd lived out his last days in the family's red brick Victorian mansion in upstate Utica. "Mourners," the obit said, "will be received at the family home, 211 Clinton Street, from noon until 6 pm next Sunday, following the interment." Now Terwiliger knew the address. The very next day he was on his way, due north, to visit the Benson family manse in Utica, praying all the way that it was still there and he could gain access to it.

And Terwiliger's prayers were answered. He arrived to find that, not only was the 211 Clinton Street home still there, it had a Century 21 realty sign visible just above the long, un-mown grass of its expansive front yard. Forthwith, he headed for the realtor's office where he learned that the Benson family still owned the place and had often used it as a summer getaway, but now found it to be a high-maintenance white elephant that could not even be rented at a reasonable price. Thus, no one had lived in it or rented it for the past sixteen years.

Terwiliger told the agent that he was interested in looking at it but was in town only for the day. She apologized that she was very busy today but saw no reason why he couldn't look around for himself. She gave him the code for the lockbox and he was back at 211's dilapidated doorstep fifteen minutes later.

The musty odor that met him as he entered did not deter him. The home was a shambles, mostly empty of furniture. After a cursory search, it was obvious that the few chests and other furnishings still remaining, some, muslin-covered, were ready for the scrap bin. He wasted little time in its main rooms, and even less on the second-floor rooms, barer than the first. He'd almost skipped both in his anxiety to inspect the attic. A mystical feeling came over him, making him feel almost certain that the precious box resided there, tucked away into some forgotten corner, perhaps in the rafters.

But his heart sank when he saw the attic. Much of what had been there had also been removed. Had his Little Eva been removed with it? Twenty minutes later, still on his hands and knees, sweating profusely in the attic's stifling early August heat, he finished fine-combing every square inch of the place, even reaching under loose floorboards for the box that just had to be there. But he could find nothing resembling the treasure he so eagerly sought. The home had good bones and would make an excellent residence again with extensive refurbishment, but even a second-hand store wouldn't want the chattels left behind.

He took a moment to lower himself gingerly onto a rickety rocking chair with only three of its eight back spindles remaining. Mopping his forehead, he pondered the mind of Bingo Benson and his heirs. This was a wonderful house in which to hide things. Even he who did the hiding might never find what he hid. The thought was not encouraging. Terwiliger felt defeated.

Descending from the attic, the deep disappointment consuming him, he tripped on a loose step. But the near accident struck a new thought in his troubled mind. The stair tread he'd just tripped on belonged to a still very solid staircase. Why was it loose? Lifting the tread, he could see nothing in the semi-darkness beneath it. But the treads both above and below this tread were loose as well. He was easily able to pry up the upper one, yet, again. Using the flashlight app on his iPhone, he could see nothing beneath the tread. However, when he did the same with the lower tread, he detected something tucked behind the left corner of its riser. His heart jumped as he grasped it, realizing, as he pulled it out, that he might very well be holding . . . La Evanita!

Made of thick tagboard, the box was about seven by ten by two inches high; the typical dimensions of an earlier type. But it was covered in some sort of cloth with a garish, now-faded pattern of green-stemmed red poppies. The cloth was cemented over every square inch of its outer surface. A rusted nail sealed its lid. Carefully prying it out and preserving the nail, he found that the inside was covered with green felt, glued to every surface. The box contained a sheaf of individual notepapers, each with a small picture of Snow White at the top. Written on them were messages scrawled by what must have been a young girl, their i's dotted with circles, their words, misspelled practice forms of the heartfelt thoughts they expressed: "I love you Tommy and I will forever and if you want me to be your girlfriend I will be." And "Yes, Tommy, I would love to go see the Wizard of Oz with you. Maybe we could get a malted afterwards." Terwiliger judged these to have been written by, perhaps, a daughter of Benson, around 1939 or 1940 when The Wizard of Oz first came out.

But if Harmon Terwiliger was touched by the ardor of the girl's words, he was quickly brought back to the sickening reality of what she had done to the box itself. Was this truly his Little Eva? He wanted to rip the ugly cloth off the box but dared not lift even a little corner for fear of harming the perfection of what lie underneath.

Was there maybe another La Evanita hidden under another step? And in perf condition? Likely not. All the other steps were still tightly nailed down. He searched the attic again for an additional hour, then scoured the rest of the house, but to no purpose. He could find nothing more. It did not matter. Not if he already had what he thought he had.

Wrapping the box in some muslin, he carefully placed it in a cloth supermarket bag he'd brought for the purpose, then called the agent, telling her that the house was unsuitable for his needs and he'd get back to her next time he was up looking.

Not trusting the limited resources available in Philadelphia, he then headed straight for Manhattan. There he would put the cigar box in the hands of what he knew to be the finest art preservationist in the country, Anton Petrovich & Sons. Only Petrovich could be trusted to restore the pristine beauty of Little Eva.

James Petrovich, Anton's grandson, looked disinterestedly at the box then asked to be excused so he could examine it closer in his office. He was there for nearly twenty minutes while Terwiliger anxiously waited out front, reading a magazine on antiques that his eyes refused to focus upon. Anton Petrovich's verdict: The box could be valuable but it would take at least three weeks to properly remove its offensive covering; that's how old and encrusted the glue had become and, even then, he could not guarantee that he could save what was beneath. The box was not unlike an impastoed old master. The cost for this service would be seven hundred and fifty dollars.

Terwiliger's gulp was audible. "Seven-fifty?"

"Mr. Terwiliger, people bring me valuable objets d'art. You have brought me what you believe possesses a high value. So does the service I provide. If you wish to take this objet to a lesser firm, you certainly have the right to do so. If you wish Petrovich to oversee the preservation, we will require half payment now and the balance upon completion of the restoration."

"Is there any way of knowing beforehand what lies beneath the covering?" asked Terwiliger.

"I'm afraid not" was the answer. Petrovich, for someone asking a lot of money, sounded like he could care less if Terwiliger walked out the door.

Terwiliger considered the words Petrovich has just spoken. The man represented the best in the art. Never mind if he was the snootiest, too. "All right," he said, sliding his Amex Gold across the mahogany counter. He hadn't mentioned the likelihood of the box being La Evanita because he didn't want Petrovich to know its true value. God knows what the man would have quoted if he had known! This was an announcement Terwiliger would make to the world himself.

It was a full month before he got the call. "Please come in, Mr. Terwiliger, your treasure is ready for viewing. The operation was a success." This latter remark was said with a twinkle in Petrovich's voice. He must have cracked the same poor joke often.

Though it was the next day, it seemed like another week before he could drive up to Manhattan. He wanted to see his exquisite Little Eva immediately on arrival. But Petrovich insisted upon making a show of presenting it. He was wearing white cotton gloves. He'd actually set the box upon a velvet cushion and had draped a satin cloth over it, removing the cloth with a flourish worthy of a toreador. And there it sat, a perfectly preserved cigar box, so expertly restored that it looked factory-new.

Terwiliger, his heart beating wildly, had never seen a finer specimen. It was as if it had never been defaced by the glued cloth. It was much finer than the nearly identical one he'd seen just yesterday. Where? On eBay. A Heidefeuer Habanos, easily worth . . . forty dollars.

Terwiliger, devastated, tried not to fault fate. If he'd been a fool, he'd had only himself to blame for chasing such a crazy dream. The odds had been stacked ridiculously high against him. Slumped, he began to exit the shop. But before he could open the door, he heard Petrovich say, "Just a minute, Mr. Terwiliger."

"What is it?" said Terwiliger, testily.

"I regret that your object is obviously not what you expected it to be . . . but I do believe you owe a balance of $375."

Terwiliger returned, glared at the man without saying a word, laid his Amex on the counter and, after the transaction, spun around and stomped out. But not before dropping the Heidefeuer to the floor and stomping on it.

As soon as Terwiliger was gone, Petrovich, a cigar aficionado and box collector himself, slipped into his office, sat down at his desk, lit up a Havana and stared benignly at the object lying upon it.

La Evanita.

The one and only.

The Tarnów Gate

The Waverly Tontine

If word of it had ever spread, Father's tontine would most certainly have become the most famous in history. And it may yet. But it had been held the darkest of secrets until I learned of it just this past week. Outside of its participants, I may be the only one to know of its provenance. And its stunning conclusion.

My name is Colin Townshend Waverly. My Father—God love him, he was a good one, but I hardly knew him—Richard Townshend Waverly, Dickie to his friends and colleagues, was the creator of the Waverly Tontine. Thus its eponymous name.

Tontine? I presumed you understood. It's, well, a cross between a wager and a life insurance policy which, after all, is nothing more than a wager. But a tontine is an insurance policy by which you deign to be the sole beneficiary.

What informed me of the Waverly Tontine was a wax-sealed, handwritten letter from Father, which the tontine's solicitor and trustee, an up-and-coming young man by the name of Henry Jamieson, was instructed to deliver to me upon Father's death. The letter explained the intent of the tontine and listed its ten distinguished members. Each had belonged to Boodle's, the exclusive gentlemen's club founded in 1762 by the future PM, Lord Shelburne, in St. James, London.

Boodle's, named incongruously for its first headwaiter, Edward

Boodle, was formed almost exclusively of peers, upper house MPs and, later, captains of industry. Males only until 1982. Churchill was an honorary member, and Beau Brummell made his last bet at Boodle's before fleeing to France. Among Boodle's notoriously eccentric members, Father was seen to be, perhaps, the most eccentric. But all had one trait in common: uncommon wealth. If the Boodle's name strikes a familiar note, it's because it was taken, in 1847, by the famous British maker of dry gin.

But back to Father's secret Waverly Tontine. As all of its participants are with us no longer, its secret can now be revealed.

It was Father's idea to arbitrarily hand-pick a group of nine other Boodle's members, most of them retired, and suggest to them what he presented as an investment scheme. He did this during a lavish dinner behind locked doors at a private meeting salon in Mayfair's Connaught Hotel. When all were full of rare roast beef and Yorkshire pudding, and partaking of their VSOP and Upmanns, Father silenced them by tapping his knife on his near-empty snifter, then toasting to "friendship and long life." After a chorus of *hear, hear*s he at last laid out his clandestine scheme.

"Gentlemen, we, gathered here, are certainly the best of friends. And so it is to you, and only to you, my friends, that I make this unique proposal. Or call it, if you will, a friendly wager. I propose that we, as a group, purchase an insurance policy of sorts on our collective lives. The amount of the policy—the wager—shall be ten million pounds. That is, we shall put up one million pounds sterling per man."

Father paused here to survey the faces around the table and allow the number to register. Bemused looks were all he saw. "This amount," he continued, "would be invested in a trust, an interest-bearing and/or capital gains scheme that would hopefully produce perhaps multiples of our investment, our wager. Who shall be the single beneficiary of this sacred trust? Why, the last man standing—the last to die—that is who, simply put. And that, my dear sirs—and you are not only dear, several among you are sirs—is the entirety of my scheme. May I hear your comments?"

The room went silent for a long moment as the peers and KBEs and business titans pondered what their ears had just heard. Clouds of cigar smoke mingled with clouds of thought. If they were fazed, it was certainly more by the concept of the scheme than the poundage called for.

"Dickie, old chap, I do believe you're suggesting a tontine, rather illegal, mightn't you say?" This from Colonel Alfred Demingworth, A Korean war hero, now head of the Royal Bank of Winchester.

"And when," Father replied, "has a little illegality ever stopped any of us from whatever we damn well please to do, Alfy?" The good colonel was Father's best friend.

Through the laughter, came another remark, this from the staid Sir Reginald Schreiberman, who owned half the newspapers and TV stations in England. "I've been running some numbers in my head, Richard. You seem to have selected us for the relative sameness of our ages. We are, I suspect, within two, three years of each other, are we not? Was that the key factor in your selecting us?"

"That, Reggie, and the fact that none of you serfs would miss a million or so. It would hardly be cricket, of course, if I'd selected anyone ten or more years younger, would it now?"

Lord Cyril Pemberton—Baron Pemberton—next. "My good fellow, I must commend you for the most interesting scheme any Boodles fellow has proposed in years. Frankly, I'd love to have such an extra incentive to extend my years. And it would be but a small hardship to lay out a million pounds. But, while it would be a most welcome windfall to collect ten or even twenty million if one were to be, as you so neatly put it, 'the last man standing,' I frankly doubt it would build the estate of anyone here more than perhaps ten percent. Furthermore . . ."

"My dear Lord Baron," interrupted Father, "you're being more upper- house windy than usual. Please, man, do get to your point."

"All right, Dickie, here it is. I welcome, if not your unkind wit, your scheme. I believe it a sound one. Only, in for a penny, in for a pound. I motion that we make it truly interesting; that we each put up five million." Murmurs circled the room. When they subsided, the good baron asked, "Do I hear a second?" All looked grim except Father who stood his place smiling, arms crossed.

"Seconded," Abel McLemore chimed in, almost without hesitation, picking up upon the parliamentary turn the discussion had taken. As head of one of Britain's largest hedge funds, he was a man accustomed to making quick decisions; to investing millions within seconds. More murmuring. A bit of grumbling as well.

Father then held up his hand for silence and said, "Gentlemen, the motion has been made and seconded to enter our scheme at five million pounds sterling per man. But before we take a vote, it would behoove us to open the floor for further discussion."

Minor points and objections were raised. Then, a half hour and another round of cognac later, Father clinked his glass again, repeated the motion and called for a vote. Nine hands slowly rose, along with his own. The one that didn't belonged to Amos Feather, Esq., a noted barrister to the film industry and owner of a small but highly profitable chain of boutique hotels. He had dozed off after his third cognac. Awakened and informed of what the rest were up to, he added his yea and returned to his stentorian slumber. Three days later, with all transfers of funds made to the private trust created and overseen by Jamieson, the Waverly Tontine was afloat. The year was 1998.

Not three days after the tontine's founding, Thierry Ames, who'd amassed three long distance trucking companies and a garbage hauling firm, a man whose speech still revealed his cockney upbringing and who still insisted on calling himself a lorreyman because that's what he'd been for the first sixteen years of his working life, sustained a sudden massive heart attack while watching a championship football match between Manchester United and Arsenal at Wembly Stadium. He was dead before the ambulance arrived.

Nothing more happened for over a year until Cyril Pemberton, he who'd upped the stakes to five million a man, was taken with pancreatic cancer and was gone within seven weeks. Two years later, in 2001, Sir Conrad P. Bailey-Hobbes, a Nobel laureate in Economic Sciences and husband of the reputedly richest and meanest woman in all of Wales, was killed, along with a woman, not his wife, in a five-car car crash while misreading the hills above Biarritz.

No deaths occurred for another three years. The odds of anyone winning his wager on longevity, now worth £91.6 million, had dropped to 7 to 1. But in that year, 2004, two more died, Abel McLemore, from acute diabetes, and Sir Donald Schreiberman, also from a heart attack.

Half of the tontine members were now gone.

Upon the third Thursday of each December, the survivors of the Waverly Tontine, anxious to keep their "rather illegal" scheme under wraps, had been meeting secretly at the Connaught to dine mightily and assess their burgeoning £50 million "investment." By the oddest of coincidences, at the seventh-year dinner in 2005, land baron Simon L. Ramsay IV, unable to dislodge a pheasant bone from his throat, perished from asphyxiation on the way to hospital. In his absence, and after a minute of silence to wish him the best, the meeting continued. The tontine's balance sheet indicated a net worth now come to £92.3 million and climbing.

Only seven years had passed. It was now 2006. The survivors, including Father, numbered only four, their ages ranging from 78 to 80. Father, though in excellent health was—it's difficult for me even to say this—the very next to die, and in a most shocking fashion. He and his companion, Madame Elyse Borcheron, a lovely French woman—my mother has passed several years earlier—and two other couples were sailing on his yacht off Ibiza when a squalling rainstorm suddenly arose. As Father joined his crew in battening down, his foot slipped, he fell overboard and was drowned. Search crews sought unsuccessfully for a week to find his body.

So Dickie Waverly—my father—was the scheme's seventh victim. But the Waverly Tontine was still quite alive. Seventeen months later, Amos Feather, who had fallen asleep at the tontine's first meeting, sustained a traveling blood clot which caused a lethal stroke, thus making him the eighth member to die. Only two now remained: Colonel Alfred Demingworth, Father's best friend, and Thomas "Tommy" Atherton, arrogant successor to his father as chairman of Atherton Airways, a company that leased jets to the semi-wealthy who couldn't quite afford their own. Two years after Father's passing, Alfy came down with what at first appeared to be a simple flu, but which quickly escalated to a double pneumonia and his lamented death a week following. Hardly lamented by Tommy Atherton.

With the demise of its ninth member, nearly ten years after its establishment, the Waverly Tontine had come to its own demise. The tenth man, the last man standing, Tommy Atherton. profligate that he was, had never worked a day in his life until given daddy's airplanes to play with. Atherton Airways, under his misguidance, had been about to go under when Colonel Demingworth conveniently contracted his pneumonia, leaving Tommy the tontine's winner.

Then a most unlikely thing occurred.

Our Tommy boy was accosted by a thief who emerged from an alley off of Eaton Terrace in Belgravia. Before Atherton could hand over his wallet, he was shot dead, murdered just a day before he was to collect his windfall, topped off now, in spite of the 2008 crash, at a neat £102.2 million. Such things do happen, but now it was Jamieson's duty—he had no choice—to inform Atherton's heirs of the secret tontine's existence and to distribute its substantial funds to them. This was the thought on his troubled mind as he was walking to his chambers to make his first contact with the heirs on a gloomy, foggy Monday morning in November, two days after Atherton had been interred.

But into Henry Jamieson's mind crept another thought, a most devious one. He did have a choice. What if— just what if—he were to keep the Waverly Tontine a secret? What if he were to keep the Waverly Trust altogether? After all, wasn't he the only one who knew of it, and had access to it? And hadn't he overseen its rise from fifty to over a hundred million pounds? Didn't he deserve something more than a paltry few million for his services? He would, of course, have to devise a highly clever, undetectable method of draining the trust and passing its funds to himself. Of laundering it, as it were. But he prided himself on being a highly clever man. This was Jamieson's distracted manner of thinking as he approached his offices.

Where a yet more unlikely thing occurred.

A man, wearing a Burberry raincoat and a felt hat draped low over his face, was standing next to the door. He was unrecognized by Jamieson. Looking much older, adorned by a long grey beard and still very much alive, there stood my father, Richard Townshend Waverly.

Without so much as a handshake or how-do-you-do, and to make certain that Jamison would know exactly who he was, Father grabbed the solicitor's hand, slapped his identification papers into it, then, on the spot, declared his legitimate claim to the Waverly Tontine funds. Jamieson, had no choice but to forget his own avid hopes and honor Father's claim. And his demand that—unknown to me—the funds be placed in a new trust with myself as the sole beneficiary on Father's death. Forthwith, the shocked solicitor prepared the transfer papers and collected his £2 million commission.

By now you may have wondered about the convenient timing of Father's reappearance.

A substantial landowner and housing developer, Father had had several reversals prior to his supposedly accidental death. Among the last was the unfortunate discovery of extensive toxic waste deposits under the parcel of land on which he had nearly completed development of a 3,000 home, gated community of rowhouses on Hampshire's shores. Its forced closure forced him to contemplate a declaration of bankruptcy, as he was unable to repay imminently due loans. The shame of impending bankruptcy—of his ruination—was driving him to madness. That's when he sought to at least temporarily escape his woes by taking his little yachting sojourn on the Mediterranean.

He saw the storm as a gift from God. When it came up, as one often did at that time of year, he took advantage of it to slip overboard. He swam to a dinghy tied abaft of the yacht, untied its painter line and hung on to the dinghy's side as it was quickly blown adrift. The storm was such that no one spotted him doing this. Paddling to a secluded cove on Ibiza, five nautical miles off, he quickly disappeared from his debts, from me, from the world, taking himself, by tramp steamer, to Australia's outback where he was known as Henrik Coover, an eremitic, sheep-farming emigré from South Africa. What kept him alive during those lean years was his covetous desire to outlast the remaining two members of the tontine and collect what would then be due him.

He followed their lives closely on the Internet. When his dear friend, Alfy Demingworth, succumbed to pneumonia, and the trustee, Henry Jamieson, was about to declare the insufferable Sir Thomas Atherton as the sole survivor of the Waverly Tontine, he knew he must make his move. He flew back to England the very day he learned of Alfy's death, dispensed of Atherton with a Walther Special, and got away with it by immediately fleeing back to Australia.

I of course had not known of the Waverly Tontine. Nor could I know that Father had survived his "accident" until Jamieson, just yesterday, flew over to Paris, where I am now living, to stun me with a cheque for the trust's ending value: £124.6 million.

Garrote

It was the late '80s, a time when certain New Jersey cops, even a mayor or two, could be bought cheap, and Lupo "Wolfman" Marchesi was just the man to do the buying. Lupo had made his bones with the Mob twenty years earlier and was now pretty much running the show in Atlantic City. Lupo had a lock on the unions that manned the casinos rapidly rising along the Boardwalk. Nobody worked in a casino without Lupo's oversight. If trouble arose over wages or working conditions, Lupo's word would send the workers walking. Any scabs who dared to show would feel the Wolfman's wrath. Cooperate with him and things would run smooth. One tough guy who'd crossed the picket line after laying out a union worker wound up in pieces inside a garbage truck manned by workers also overseen by Lupo.

Lupo Marchesi was not a big man in the physical sense. He was short and wiry and always wore well-pressed suits, usually of gabardine, and different suspenders—his signature—every day. There was something about him, a certain cocky way he had of bouncing on his toes as he walked, that few cared to challenge. In his soft-spoken way, he preferred to out-talk his enemies but, on the rare occasions when he failed to do so, he would fall into a rage and resort to sterner measures. His preferred method of dealing with those who "deserved"—his favorite verb of condemnation—to be murdered, was the garrote. The hammer to the head, the foot to the gut, the everyday maiming, he left to his henchmen. But, if he deemed a man worthy of death, it was the Wolfman himself who most often would carry out the sentence.

The garrote is the simplest of killing devices, consisting of no more than a three-foot length of, usually, woven wire anchored at each end to the middle of a four-inch hardwood dowel. Surreptitiously looped from behind over a man's head, and pulled with sufficient strength, it could kill a man almost instantly by slamming shut his esophagus. Manipulated with even greater strength, it could cut through a man's flesh right down to his neckbone, effectively beheading him. Lupo had gained his love of the garrote's efficacy

after watching, as many as fifty times, the garroting of Luca Brasi in the first Godfather movie.

Fear of sudden death from the man kept Lupo in charge. By garrote or by any other method, killing came easy to him. Getting away with it was another story. Normally, with enough undercover money being spread around to crooked cops and legislators, Lupo had little to be concerned about. But, in his corner of New Jersey, there were a few good apples in the barrel. These days, the good cops, the smart ones, were on to checking the waste plant—the Boneyard they called it—for human remains when, say, someone who couldn't pay the main or even the vigorish on his debt, went missing.

It was getting so that Lupo was running out of places to dispose of the "deserving." His hit list of the still alive had recently risen to three, and he was itching to try out his latest killing machine, a garrote with mother-of-pearl inlaid handles and scaled down razor wire he'd fashioned himself in his shore-side Longport mini-mansion, just south of the Boardwalk. He'd have put it to its test by now if only he'd known what to do with the body. Even the old cement shoes routine was out because of the wary ever-present trawlers of the Coast Guard, headquartered nearby.

Captain Harry Brubaker was the 4th Precinct's top cop, an untouchable whose forensics people were the best in the business. He knew all about the Wolfman, his nemesis. He'd never met him personally, but the Wolfman's image popped up often in Brubaker's dreams. Harry Brubaker, a thirty-year man on the force, wanted nothing more than to take Lupo down before grabbing the pension he'd so well earned. The IRS boys were working on it too but the only way he knew to do it was to nail Lupo for Murder One. And to do that he'd need a body, a corpse that would put Marchesi away for good.

Five Mob-related murders had taken place in the last eighteen months alone. Par for the AC course. But these men could not be reported as murdered because no bodies had been recovered, they had to be listed merely as "missing." And missing men told no tales. Brubaker was certain these men were murdered, and just as certain that the murders were done by Lupo or his thugs. But none could get solved until a body could be turned up. Brubaker suspected a cover-up coming from the level just above him, but there was less he could do about that than he could do about Lupo.

A snitch had spilled that a body had been dumped into the furnaces of the Egg Harbor trash plant. It had been hinted to him from upstairs that he'd find nothing there. He investigated anyhow, and did find what appeared to be human bones, but the commissioner ordered them to be confiscated by main forensics downtown, and that was the last they were heard of. Brubaker desperately needed a body, preferably a whole one; his own forensics would take it from there.

It's not unusual for murderous men to possess a working brain. The solution to Lupo Marchesi's quandary came to him in an aha! moment on a blustery spring day while attending his father's interment at the Greenwood Cemetery in the AC suburb of Pleasantville. As Marco Marchesi's casket was being lowered into its concrete vault, a vision came to Lupo. He could see the body of Mauricio "Pickles" Panettieri lying atop the casket.

Pickles ran the plasterers and drywallers local 341, a crook who'd been known to steal from his own union. This, Lupo could understand and possibly forgive. What he could not forgive is what he suspected: that Pickles had fingered one of Lupo's men after a holdup at a high stakes poker game in Ducktown. The icing on the cake was that Pickles' son had stood up the daughter of Lupo's right-hand man, Robert "No-nose" Azzolini, practically at the altar. For these transgressions, large and small, Pickles Panettieri was a marked man.

What better way to make a body disappear than to rest it atop another body to be buried forever? You bury someone in the woods, it never seems to be deep enough and they always seem to discover it. But in a cemetery? What better place is there? Who'd ever look there? Why hadn't anyone thought of this before? It was hard for Lupo to concentrate on the burial proceedings at hand.

Lupo's wife, Lena, and his five children had lovingly sprinkled holy water, provided by the priest, on Marco's coffin after it had been lowered. He was the first to toss a shovelful of dirt on the coffin. The dirt made a heartrending sound as it hit and bounced off the lid. Others followed, first sprinkling, then shoveling.

With the Pater Noster, the graveside service came to an end. Lupo spent the limo ride home in contemplation of the best way to carry out the very excellent plan his gracious God had presented him.

The Wolfman kept his eye on the obits in the Press of Atlantic City. He needed a fresh grave, obviously, because its freshly laid earth wouldn't attract attention. Which led him, for the entire week following his father's burial, to pore over the obits as carefully as he did his racing form.

Lily D'Amico's name caught his eye. It was a name he recognized as he'd once spent an evening with her. She'd been sodomized at fourteen years of age by her father, a blackjack dealer at the Golden Nugget until he was fired for "taking off"—skimming—chips. Lily, now twenty-three, was tall, slim and make-up beautiful, and had what all men agreed was a perfect body, one that was for rent at a thousand and up per night, depending upon what was required of it. But what must her perfect body have looked like after a fall from the 23rd floor of Trump's Castle? Suicide? Nobody knew for certain.

But never mind that, Lupo was looking for a far more nondescript stiff, one who'd died a natural death, someone more assured of forever resting in peace. Almost anyone would do, so this would not be a difficult task. Edward C. Morgan, Dorothea Colangelo, Oscar R. Diemert,

Raymond Kovacic, D'Antoine Williams, Yetta Wasserstein, Sonya . . .
Wait a minute. Yetta Wasserstein? If Lupo was going to plant an Italian, it
had best not be in an Italian garden, the first place the law would be likely
to look. And, more often than not, it was Italians Lupo was offing.

He read further. "Yetta Wasserstein, 87, beloved wife of the late
Morris C., cherished mother of Loretta . . . blah, blah blah . . . Graveside
services will be held 10 am Sunday at Beth Israel Cemetery, Northfield . .
." Perfect, thought Lupo. They bury the nice, unassuming Yetta
Wasserwhatever on Sunday, we plop Pickles Panettieri right on top of her
that night.

Lupo had three days to put his master plan together. He'd been
scoping out Pickles whereabouts ever since he'd devised the plan.
Inquiries were made and paid for. What he learned was that Pickles liked
to hang out and stay late, drinking and playing poker, at his union
headquarters up in Philadelphia. And he'd be there Sunday evening. And
so would Lupo, with two of his goombahs, when Pickles exited the hall
around midnight. As Pickles approached his Sedan DeVille in the
adjacent parking lot at 12:16 am, Lupo's thugs confronted him. Before he
could utter a word, Lupo stepped out from the shadows and approached
Pickles from behind. In seconds, as his men watched with bored looks on
their outsized faces, the razor wire of Lupo's garrote, with its gleaming
mother-of-pearl inlaid handles, was slipped over Pickles' head and
looped around his neck. No sound had time to leave Pickles' wide-open
mouth. Less than a minute later, the Plasterers and Drywallers boss, his
eyes wide open and popping with dismay, lay dead next to his Caddy, his
severed jugular spurting a three-foot stream of blood from the depths of
the sharp garrote wire's deep penetration.

Before the sun came up the next day, his mutilated corpse lie splayed
on top of the modest, $1,800 Isaiah model poplar, crepe-lined casket in
the dug-up and re-filled grave of the late Mrs. Morris C. "Yetta"
Wasserstein in Beth Israel's Northeast Quadrant, Plot No. 1359, not a
thousand yards from the first tee at the posh Atlantis Country Club.

And that is where the remains of Mauricio "Pickles" Panettieri
remained for the better part of the next year. Remained, that is, until the
hierarchy of the Atlantis Country Club finally convinced Beth Israel to

relocate its ancient cemetery to a quieter location nowhere near as close to a major highway as their old one. That way, the ACC could offer a spa, a much-needed driving range and additional parking to its burgeoning membership. Logic was used in the convincing of Beth Israel's people, the logic being an $8 million donation to its relocation fund.

It should come as no surprise that, during the requisite exhuming of bodies, Yetta Wasserstein was found to be sharing her hallowed grave with the rotting, bug-riddled corpse of one Mauricio "Pickles" Panettieri.

The reign of the Wolfman was over.

Dendrick and the Living Dead

His friends had never called him anything but Dendrick. And they were few.

Gaunt, painfully so, Dendrick Tipton's most notable feature was his height of six feet, seven inches, His poor posture made him resemble a question mark. In his middle-forties, he was peculiarly bald because his only remaining hair was a wispy tuft up front which he attempted to comb into a preposterous pompadour. Along with the problem of the tuft, he had a poor complexion due to rampant acne in his youth, and his skull was not one of those rare ones that look better bald. Instead, it protruded to the rear, giving his profile that of a bicycle helmet. His mouth, except when he thought to close it, tended to hang open as if he were always about to ask a question. His teeth protruded, and his chin receded into a too-long neck with a prominent Adam's apple, giving him the appearance, generally, of a turkey vulture. And his voice, due to overactive polyps, had an unpleasantly raspy quality. These features, taken together, gave others an additional reason to avoid striking up a conversation with him.

Dendrick, dedicated to the company he worked for, had, after twenty-two years, made his way up from stock puller to chief line inspector of furniture at the Walmart Distribution Center in North

Platte, Nebraska. At Walmart he earned $17.15 per hour plus a year-end bonus which last year topped $1100.

He lived alone with a fourteen-year-old cat named Ezra on the Blue Star Memorial Highway just south of town, in a two-bedroom, one bath, shotgun-style home he'd purchased six years earlier for $67,500.

Dendrick, never intending to be a bachelor, had come to accept himself as one. Though not an unfriendly person, he was on the shy side. He believed it would be nice to be married, but he'd been warded off in his few attempts to become so. Women tended to not see him at all or look past him if they did. He had conversed occasionally, in the Walmart employees lunch room, with Maryellen Dornberger, a wide-bodied troll of a woman over in Dispatch. But

what he meant to be a conversation leading to perhaps a date, she treated as small talk, and often ended the conversation by saying how busy she was and she had to get back to work.

Maryellen did finally give in and accepted his invitation to take her out for dinner, but the date wasn't much, consisting of overdone country-fried steak at Marie's Roadhouse and a movie, "Daddy's Day Camp," at the Carmike Six on S. Dewey, so bad that she asked if they could leave an hour in, which they did. When Dendrick asked for another date the next week, she turned him down, and when she did the same for each of the following two weeks, he quit asking.

But that was all right with him. On weekends he was satisfied to hang out with his only friend, Ed Turnblood over in Maintenance, and sometimes with his old high school friend, JJ Englander, a long-haul truck driver. On these occasions Dendrick and Ed and went for some beers at Marie's or bowled a few lines down at the Cedarbowl. Dendrick saw a lot of Walmart people at these places but they didn't much acknowledge his presence.

Now, Dendrick did love his television. Not sports so much, but movies. He particularly favored vampire and zombie movies, which he liked to call "flicks." This movie watching took up a good deal of his free time, but that was all right too because he had plenty of it.

Where Dendrick spent many of his summer weekends was at Lake

Maloney, just six miles due south of North Platte. He'd recently purchased, on time, a small, partially wooded lot on its less desirable, but more affordable, eastern shore, and hoped to put up a one-room prefab cabin there someday. He'd build a pier too, and perhaps would dock a rowboat with an outboard motor there so he could go fishing, which was something he'd never actually done but thought he might enjoy doing. He once spent an entire vacation week there, living in a tent, roasting hamburgers over a bricked fire-pit he'd built himself, and watching the sun set across the lake, a sight he never tired of. Ezra loved these outings too, because there were plenty of field mice and sparrows to chase, though he hasn't caught one yet.

The years passed slowly for Dendrick. They always seemed to. He was now in his mid-fifties, having been part of the Walmart team—as the company liked its people to call themselves—for twenty-seven years. Ezra had passed too, having been replaced by another rescue cat, Helen, whose antics Dendrick enjoys observing. He was a salaried floor manager now, making upward of $48,000 per year. And he was still, and was certain he always would be, a bachelor. By now he'd put up his prefab at Lake Maloney, along with his pier, and had his boat, a used Lowe V-Hull Classic, for which he'd paid nine hundred dollars including trolling motor. Though he never took much to fishing, he liked to putt-putt around the lake just to take in its lush, fir-lined shoreline.

One lonely evening, Dendrick, drinking a beer in front of his cabin's fireplace, decided to do some soul-searching. He'd lived in North Platte all these years. This was where the North and South Platte Rivers meet. It was a satisfying place to live. He'd never thought of living elsewhere. But he was getting older and the winters were getting harder to cope with, and he was tiring of the care required to maintain his home. He planned to retire at sixty-two, just eight years off, at which time he could take early Social Security. His 401(k) would then amount to well over $175,000. Having led a frugal life, he figured that, if he sold his home at retirement, along with his 401(k) and his other savings, he could buy one of those condominiums he'd been reading about, on the West Coast of Florida, at Cape Coral, a place he liked because of the way its name rolled off his tongue. There'd be no maintenance to speak of and there'd be a swimming pool and sandy beaches to walk on all year round and maybe get into some serious shell-collecting. What's more, he could keep this cabin on Lake Maloney and, if he chose, spend his summers there. The picture he painted began to look better and better.

But, after two more beers, his daydream took on a little tarnish. He'd never been to Florida didn't know a soul there. What if he made the move and came to regret it, where would he be then? What if it was the worst move he ever made? If he couldn't call himself completely happy about his life in Nebraska, he was, at least, comfortable in its surroundings. He was established here and did have some friends. And his Walmart team would always be here, even in retirement.

So maybe he should stay, sell the house in town, and build a real house on the lake to replace the cabin; a house he could live in for the rest of his life. But just what would he do there for the rest of his life? He hadn't done much so far, had he? He hated to admit this to a mirror that now reflected what he had to admit was not just a homely middle-aged man, but a bored homely middle-aged man. He needed to make a decision about his life. But could he? He'd sleep on those troubling thoughts.

And he did.

The very next morning, a rainy Saturday, Dendrick was awakened the same way he'd always been awakened: by the thunk of the North Platte Bulletin landing on the front porch just outside his bedroom window. He arose, dressed, hauled in the paper, fixed his usual apple juice and raisin toast and coffee, and slipped the paper from its plastic sleeve.

The front-page headline, seven words printed extra-large, jolted him:

"Netflix to shoot 'Night of the Living Dead' remake in N. Platte"

The story filled most of the page and was continued elsewhere for another whole page, with pictures of the director and the actors who were signed to lead parts. It went on to say that over thirty movies had been filmed in Nebraska—in Omaha and Lincoln, and in Fremont, Kearney, Hooper, Ogallala and some towns with smaller populations—but never once, in the 150-year history of North Platte, pop. 25,117. Not even a documentary.

The crew and actors would soon arrive and "virtually take over North Platte for six weeks to shoot this third remake of George Romero's revered classic zombie thriller, "Night of the Living Dead," once considered, according to the article, "the *ne plus ultra* of gore."

Dendrick reckoned this to be the most exciting event ever to happen in his home town. He read, with growing interest, every word of the article, even stopping to look up the meaning of *ne plus ultra*. Every citizen of North Platte who still read newspapers must have been reading along with him. But it wasn't until deep into the story, on page five, that a boxed paragraph jolted him again: It was sub-headed "Will cast locals as zombies" and went on to say, "Living Dead casting director Elizabeth Sherman will arrive next Saturday to audition the local populace for the film's forty non-speaking zombie roles. Those extras hired will be paid a flat rate buyout of $125 a day for up to two weeks of shooting. Open auditions will be held at 10 am the following Tuesday at the Oak Tree Inn on Halligan Drive. Acting experience is not required."

Dendrick got goose bumps just thinking about that. He refilled his coffee cup and re-read the entire article. He did some arithmetic in his head. At almost as much as he makes per day, that would be $2250 for two weeks of work. He had a lot of sick days coming. Could he do this thing?

He returned to his oracle, his bathroom mirror, and stared at it. He saw the same downright homely man he always saw. Ugly, even, no doubt of it. But what he saw, for the first time ever, pleased him. He saw the makings of a perfect zombie. He contorted his face into one he felt would impress this Elizabeth Sherman person. Then he placed his hands, with their long knobby fingers, beside his head, palms toward the mirror and turned them into claws as he rocked slowly from side to side. Not having shaved for three days, he liked the grizzly stubble he saw. He'd never acted in his life, not even in an elementary school play. He was always more of a stage crew person. He could not believe he was even thinking of auditioning, but, as he stood there, he resolved that, yes, indeed, he would do this thing. And then, with his deepest rasp, he let out a bloodcurdling gnarl. And then another. He was already rehearsing.

Immediately, Dendrick rushed to his computer and punched up the original 1968 version of "Night of the Living Dead" on Facebook. For the rest of the day he watched it, studied it, sat through its 98-minutes four straight times, hardly moving, not stopping to eat, except for a bowl of Orville Redenbacher cheese-flavored popcorn. That night, lying in the darkness with his hands behind his head after turning off his bedside lamp, he vowed he'd become the most fearsome zombie ever to lurch through a wheat field in quest of a satisfying human meal.

Elizabeth Sherman was impressed at first sight of him. Upon auditioning Dendrick, she selected him for her first phalanx of zombie extras. "You have the look," she told him with a straight face. He offered a snaggle-toothed grin and thanked her. He couldn't wait to rehearse his role. It would be one among the hundreds (accomplished by use of a green screen) of flesh and brain eaters closing in, stiff-legged and famished, on Bill Connors' dilapidated Victorian farmhouse where the film's seven humans are barricaded at the climax. Old Bill would be taking in $1500 a day for the rental.

A week later, when the actual shooting began, Dendrick found himself no longer one among many. His rehearsal performances had been so spot-on, so "authentic," that the director singled him out to become the leader of the zombie pack. As he approached the farmhouse, the camera would come back to him again and again. And stay on him as he smashed through the window of the rear door, then through the door itself. Other scenes were spliced in, but the camera returned to find him gnawing on an arm he'd torn off one of the feature characters. His insane grimace and his rumblings of satisfaction were recorded, placing him in the role of a voice actor for which he would now be moved up to the minimum $375 per day, and would list him by name in the crawl at the film's end.

Finally, at the height of his barbaric assault, the camera rested for fully half a minute on his singular face, made even more disgusting by oozing prosthetics, as he gorged himself, blood and brains pouring from his grinning mouth.

But this did not end his role.

He was so convincing that the director insisted he, not a stunt double, be the key zombie to attack the lead actor's character in the final scenes. The scene, beautifully choreographed and rehearsed for an entire day, had Dendrick's zombie cornering the character and struggling with him until he, the zombie, could be dispatched. Three cameras filmed the scene from different angles for six horrific non-stop minutes but Dendrick had long been ready for his close-up. When the director yelled Cut! the other actors, and all of the crew not otherwise occupied—everyone within eyeshot—roared their approval of Dendrick's singular performance.

And a zombie star was born.

"The Night of the Living Dead" was released two months later. It was no better received than earlier remakes. One reviewer claimed that the zombies' acting came off better than the leads'. Dendrick, taking this remark personally, seized it to define his new career path. Dendrick Tipton would no longer be bored by life because he meant to spend the rest of it in, yes, Hollywood. As a professional actor.

Not finishing out his planned last years at the Walmart Distribution Center, he left the city of his birth. However, before leaving, he visited Cape Coral just in case his new career didn't work out. But the city disappointed him; a strange city in an even stranger state. It did not occur to him that his disappointment was colored by his newborn confidence in his own success in a different city. He returned within three days.

Hollywood, then, did not in any way disappoint him. There, through the auspices of Elizabeth Sherman, he found immediate and steady employment in what are known as "creep" films. But few of its characters were creepier than the persona that Dendrick had created for himself as a zombie, vampire or otherworldly alien creature. One critic doted on Dendrick, whose signature tuft was still in place, and dubbed him "the new Lon Chaney."

The roles kept coming. In nine years Dendrick compiled a filmography of thirty-six feature films. These paid him well, even if most were of the B or lesser variety. A few gained cult status, more for being so bad that they were seen as being good.

Dendrick was now sixty-seven. He'd retired from his second career, worn out by the roles he had worn so well. Done, at last, with the madness of the life he'd taken up, he returned, the conquering hero, to North Platte, Nebraska. Not to his house—he'd sold that long before—nor to his cabin on the less desirable east side of Lake Maloney, but to a $1.3 million mini-mansion on the more desirable west side of Lake Maloney, where he was thereafter held in high esteem as North Platte's first citizen; its most famous citizen since Glenn Miller and Buffalo Bill Cody.

Getting to Miami

He'd had it with Detroit. For forty-two years Ivo Lukins, the only child of Andris and Rasa Lukins, had suffered the damn city. He grew up on 12th Street in the old section mixed with poor whites and ethnics like him and even an enclave of Chinese.

His love life was just about all that was going well for Ivo. His blond good looks made him attractive to women. Was it the cruel, blond mustache, cut close to the edge of his upper lip, that did the attracting? He was rarely seen without a fine-looking woman on his arm, their conquest just about the only pleasure he had left to him.

But everything else seemed to go poorly for Ivo. It wasn't that he didn't try to improve his lot, it was the stumbling block of his father who prevented him from doing so. Ivo never made it out of high school. Might have if he'd tried but, at his father's insistence, he dropped out in the tenth grade to apprentice at Andy's Shoe Repair, Andris's cluttered shop downstairs of the two-bedroom flat where they'd lived since long before Ivo was born.

Ivo's mother had died of "accidental trauma" when he was only twelve. He wanted to believe anything but the truth he knew: that Rasa Lukins died from the latest drunken beating by her hirsute and wordless husband; a beating that combined fists with the repeated administration of a thick, wide, studded belt the disgruntled shoemaker had fashioned out of boar's hide.

Ivo didn't measure up to his father's hulking size, but he was just as sturdy. He knew that Andris had made the dreaded belt for the sole purpose of striking human flesh. He'd felt its sting himself, more often than he could remember but too painful to forget.

Ivo's day would come. At age seventeen, he wrenched the belt from his father's hand during such a beating and pounded his father's face to a bloody pulp with the buckle end of it. To overpower him physically was the only way to escape the old man's tyranny.

Escape? He was banished from his home, never again to exchange a single word with his father, never even showing up for the old bastard's funeral eighteen years later.

Self-made, of harsh necessity, Ivo bootstrapped his way, over the years, into the proprietorship of three "luxury" shoeshine stands, one on each concourse of the Detroit-Wayne Airport. But in no time, it seemed like everyone was wearing either suede desert boots, Birkenstocks or sneakers, and business fell off so badly he had to sell out at a loss. He sunk the $17,000 he netted into a greeting card franchise. Within a week his rented garage was crammed with thirty huge cartons of the cheesy cards. But no leads were provided and no sales guidance offered from the fly-by-night franchisor. He managed to discount two cartons worth, going from drugstore to drugstore, before the combination of a wicked thunderstorm and a badly leaking garage roof wiped out the entire balance of his inventory.

Making matters worse, Ivo, a hard drinker like Andris, had a lawsuit hanging over him for a quarter million dollars he didn't have and never would have, any more than he had insurance that might have covered him. He'd been driving drunk one night and caused an accident that took a young man's leg, and put him, Ivo, in the lock-up for ninety days on a third offense DUI conviction. Which is when his girlfriend left him. And, because he was not available to deal with anything on the outside, his beater car managed to collect forty-one parking tickets before being hauled away to a storage lot where it was eventually sold for charges.

Nor did his woes stop there. During his incarceration, his shotgun shanty slipped under water and was snatched from him for non-payment of its third mortgage, long before the term "under water" had come into vogue.

So it wasn't much of a stretch to describe this broke and broken man as someone who truly did have it with the Motor City.

On February 23, 1969, the frigid and blustery day Ivo Lukins was released from the Wayne County Correctional Facility, he possessed exactly twenty-seven dollars and forty-three cents, a maxed-out Diners Club card and a battered suitcase of well-worn clothes now a full size too big for him, that's how badly fed he was at the facility. Having no siblings, no friends either anymore, and feeling like the ex-con he was, he made a quick and easy decision. He would leave this godforsaken town.

He set out from prison on foot through the bitter cold of a blizzard, heading for the Greyhound bus station on Howard Street, barely avoiding frostbite getting there. His only stop along the way was a liquor store where he bought a pint of Old Overholt rye for four dollars. Evening was approaching and the station was nearly empty. He had to wait five minutes at the counter till his

teeth stopped chattering long enough to ask the man behind it how far twenty-three dollars would take him.

"Pretty much anywhere this side of the Mississippi," was the man's reply. "You look pretty darned anxious to leave this lovely weather we're having. I'd go south, I was you."

"Give me some prices."

The man took his time looking up the fares. He quoted Atlanta, Savannah, Miami and Orlando.

"Miami." Grunted Ivo. He knew little about it, but he liked the sound of the word.

"Good choice, fella. Nineteen dollars and twenty-five cents. You'll be there in forty-seven hours, give or take. Bus leaves 8:20 sharp tonight. That's exactly . . ." He pulled a pocket watch from his blue vest and studied it. ". . . two hours and thirty-two minutes from now. Leaving town for good, are you?"

Ivo ignored the question, paid the fare, decided it was too cold to leave the station, plucked a Miami brochure from a rack next to the counter and fished out yesterday's Detroit News from a trashcan. Seating himself in a booth at a beanery attached to the bus station, he ordered a cheeseburger, fries, a slice of cherry pie and a cup of coffee, his first real meal in three months. Two hours and thirty-two minutes and three cups later, during which he practically memorized both the brochure and the paper, he was on his way to Miami, meaning—swearing—never to set foot anywhere near this damned burg again.

With what money he had left, he could feed himself until he got to what the brochure called "The Magic City." Like he'd done all his life, he'd worry about money when it was gone. Steal it if he had to, fuck it.

Exhausted from imprisonment and from the downhill slide of his life, he slept long, if fitfully, as the bus rolled through the blustery night and into the next day down U.S. I-75 through Ohio, Kentucky and Tennessee, making stops in Dayton, Lexington and Knoxville, among others. He dreamed one of those incredibly real dreams in which he pulled into his driveway and walked into his home to find it occupied by strangers who screamed at him to leave, then began beating him with boar hide belts. He could almost feel physical pain.

The first thing Ivo saw on awakening were the loblolly pines and sycamores of southern Tennessee. And not a flake of snow in sight. By this time tomorrow, he figured, he'd be in Miami, a place he'd never been. Hell, he'd never been south of Cincinnati. There was sunshine in Miami, year-round. So

what if he was broke, he was making a new start. He was excited and his spirits, for the first time in months, were rising.

Under threatening skies, the bus made a rest stop at a roadhouse on the northern outskirts of a Georgia town called Macon. "Pop. 73,420" was what the green roadside sign had said. He broke his last bill, a fiver, and ordered a container of chili to go, loading up his pockets with free saltines. It would be his last meal before his money ran out.

While he waited for the chili, he felt a sudden and powerful urge to empty his bowels, last accomplished in the Greyhound station in Detroit. At this vital task, he took his good old time. Afterward, he washed up good, picked up his container of chili and hurried out to the bus.

But there was no bus.

The sonofabitch driver had left without him. And with his suitcase. What the hell was the matter with that asshole, did he mean to strand him for being a few minutes late? But stranded he was in—what was the name of this stupid town?—Macon. With no clothes except those on his back. And no booze either since he'd left his nearly empty bottle tucked under his seat.

Ivo was pissed, for certain, but, even more, he was utterly flabbergasted, his head ready to burst. What the hell could he do out here under these rainclouds in the middle of a nowhere cracker state like Georgia? He didn't feel this miserable the day when, three months ago, they slammed the steel doors on him. At least there he got fed and housed. He was confused and consumed with fear for what lie ahead.

Stumbling away from the roadhouse, he came to a bridge a few hundred yards south, perched over the Callahoochee River, forty or fifty feet below. There was no more than a trickle of water flowing over its wide shale bed.

The thought snuck into his troubled mind that he could easily jump the railing and be done with this madness. But the thought merely flitted. Ivo Lukins made himself believe that he was made of better stuff than that. Not that anyone would give two shits if he was gone. He sat down on the bridge's railing, put his head in his hands and squeezed it, as if to squeeze out a solution, a way out of this bottomless hole he'd fallen into.

"Maybe if I hadn't gone to the crapper," he said to himself. The thought—blaming his downfall on taking a crap—suddenly set him to laughing hysterically at himself.

Aw, the hell with it," he said, out loud. He couldn't think of anything else to do so he began walking south again. Toward Macon's city limits. And, sure enough, it started to pour, almost like the rumbling skies were weeping for him.

Or pissing on him.

It was now well past dark. Ivo could walk no farther. His four hour, twelve-mile, trek took him into a rundown neighborhood like he'd left back north. It was still raining and he was so soaked he might as well have swum the distance. Cold and totally spent, it dawned on him that he was without a place to sleep. And flat out homeless.

It was a Saturday. The downpour had left the streets nearly deserted, leaving the town looking about as friendly to him as a prison yard. A feeling of loneliness, close to despair, now crept over Ivo. His only hope for shelter was a small, paint-chipped church he noticed on a street called Progress. Its lighted sign read "Good Shepherd Evangelical Baptist Church." On its letter board was an announcement "Spaghetti Dinner tonight! 6 pm, $4. All are welcome."

Ivo hadn't seen the inside of a church since he was nine. His family was Lutheran. His mother had attended services, only sporadically, and always without him because his father made him spend Sunday mornings cleaning up the shop. But he was desperately tired now and getting hungry again, and so he walked right in, thinking maybe he could cadge a meal and maybe they'd even let him lay his head there for the night.

It was 9:15 pm. The chapel was dark, lit only by a dim light over the altar, but he could see light coming from under the double doors of a room off to the right of the chapel. He peeked in and saw only one man there, probably a janitor or cleaning man, clearing away what must have been the remnants of the spaghetti dinner. The man, a tall, lanky, slightly bent negro, was of an indeterminate age, late sixties maybe. He wore a starched tan shirt and blue khakis, and a full-length blue apron with white stripes. His face, with its high cheek bones, was so black it was almost purple, making his too-perfect teeth look even whiter than they were.

The man turned toward Ivo. "Well, who are you?" he said, his hooded eyes widening at the sorry sight of the dripping visitor.

"Uh," started to say Ivo, "I must have missed the dinner." He knew it was a stupid thing to say right when he said it.

"Well, I guess you did," said the tall man, his startled features softening. "But come in anyway, I guess I could scare up another plate.

You must've been a long time in the rain."

A puddle was forming around Ivo's shoes. "You sure it's OK? I don't have any money."

"Yes, it's OK, it's on the church. Now you just relax and dry yourself off." The man tossed him a fresh dish towel. "I'm the pastor here," he said, offering his hand to Ivo. Ivo looked at it tentatively before taking it. "Porter Underwood's the name," the man said. "What's yours?"

Ivo stared at the pastor, as if dumbstruck by the simple question. He took a long time in answering it because, in those few silent seconds, something strange was going on inside his head. He couldn't name it because he didn't know the word for it, but he was having an epiphany. He would reinvent himself on the spot. Starting with his name. "Ivan. Ivan Liggins," he replied, with firmness.

"Well, sit yourself down, Ivan Liggins, and welcome to the Good Shepherd Evangelical Baptist Church. If you don't mind my asking, are you a Baptist?"

"Uh, yes . . . I mean no. But I'm thinking of becoming one."

The pastor looked at him sideways. "Well, never mind that. You don't have to be one to get fed here," he said, grinning at Ivo. "You don't sound like you're from these parts. Where might you hail from?"

"Toledo." It was the first name that came to him. He'd been there twice, once to pick up two cases of Cat's Paw rubber heels for his father, once just to get away from him for a few days. It was close to Detroit.

"Holy Toledo!" said the pastor. Catching himself, he added, "Not much of a joke, was that? Anyhow, wait a few minutes I'll heat you up a plate of spaghetti."

"Thanks. And, uh, I seem to be catching a cold. Would you happen to have a touch of something to warm me up?"

The pastor's face lost its false-toothed grin. "Will you settle for a cup of coffee?"

"Sure," said the disappointed Ivo, glancing around the hall. He saw a row of photos on the wall nearest him. Members, he guessed, or church officials. Then he heard himself ask, "Is your whole church negro?"

"Why, yes, it is, Ivan. Pretty much the whole town is. It's called Cottontown. White folks hereabouts didn't much want it to be a part of

Macon around the turn of the century, so it became a township, unincorporated. Why do you ask?"

"Well, isn't it a little unusual for an all-negro church to have a spaghetti dinner?"

"What'd you think we'd be having, hog maws and chitlins?"

Ivo had heard of those things but wasn't sure of what they were. "No, I'm kind of happy it's spaghetti."

The pastor erupted with laughter at this joke Ivo didn't mean to make. "You just hold on, Ivan, I'll be right back," he said. "In fact, I'll get you something to throw over yourself before I fix your dinner so's you can hand me your clothes to put through the dryer." A few minutes later, Ivo was sitting alone wearing nothing but two red and white checked tablecloths, one wrapped around his waist, the other, around his shoulders.

Ivo Lukins knew an opportunity when he saw one. In the pastor's absence, he snuck back into the chapel where he spotted a pair of slim crystal candlesticks on the nearby altar. Grabbing them and sticking one inside each side of the waistband formed by the tablecloth, he hurried back to the dining hall. He'd stolen stuff when he was a kid, but that was for the thrill of it. This was a desperate time and desperate times call for desperate measures. He needed traveling money. For Miami.

Minutes later, the good pastor reappeared with a tray heaped with a bowl of spaghetti, two slices of garlic bread, salad and a large cup of black coffee. Then he sat with Ivo, drinking his own cup and questioning him as he ate, asking him what he was doing in town, what his plans were as a newcomer, did he have a place to live, even to stay at tonight.

Ivo spun out a story, most of which he didn't have to make up. He related the Greyhound incident and explained that he was a skilled but out-of-work shoe repairman now looking for not just a place to live but a job as well, and, no, he didn't have a place to stay tonight. Or any night, he thought to himself.

At this, the pastor suggested the homeless shelter downtown but, "Never mind, it's a good two miles away and it's too nasty a night to buck, Ivan, so why don't you just sleep on the sofa in the alcove off the kitchen tonight and we'll see what tomorrow brings. Our church has always served as a sanctuary and you are welcome here."

"You get a lot of white guys here?" asked Ivo.

"You're my first, young man. But you look OK. Now, you won't make me sorry I did this, will you?" he said, smiling his white-toothed smile.

Ivo smiled back and thanked Pastor Underwood and told him he appreciated his helping hand.But he was now beginning to feel more than a little guilty about the candlesticks which, incidentally, were sticking painfully into his sides under the tented tablecloth. At the same time, he was feeling a little foolish because he realized that he needn't have taken the candlesticks had he known he could now, in the middle of the night, steal half the church, hit a pawn shop and be off for Miami before the pastor awoke in the morning. But the pastor's comment, about Ivo possibly making the pastor sorry for his kindness, did give him pause.

Not, however, for long. Ivo Lukins, a.k.a. Ivan Liggins, after his massive dinner, fell into a deep sleep, made dreamless by his aching weariness. Before he dropped off, he'd told himself that tomorrow would be a better day. How could it not be after today? Especially not with the major overnight plans he had for it.

From long habit, Ivo awoke at 6 am. The church was still pitch dark. Half asleep, he lay there, allowing himself to peek into and dream of his future, immediate and long range. He'd load up his pillowcases with whatever of value he could find in the chapel, hit a pawn shop in Macon soon as it opened, buy some clothes and a backpack, get to a Greyhound station and be in Miami by the next morning. With cash in his pockets.

He saw himself on a beach where he'd pop a cold one and just lie there. Later, he'd find some work, maybe at a shoe store. Not in a repair shop; never again in a repair shop, never mind that he'd come to know everything there was to know about repairing shoes. He could make a pair if pressed to, maybe even become a shoe designer. Those people make real money. Bruno Magli. Then he could live in one of those high-rises they showed in that brochure. They were right on the beach. Miami Beach!

Time to get moving. He found a bathroom, washed up, put on his dried clothes, grabbed the pillowcases and cautiously opened the door to the chapel. He listened for any sound of his host. It was quiet as—he smiled to himself—a church mouse.

He felt his way in the darkness to the altar where the tiny light was still on above the rostrum. He could make out the large gold crosses affixed to each door of a cabinet behind the altar. He popped them off and jammed them into the first pillowcase with the candlesticks. Wrenching out the cabinet lock, he liberated a set of silver-gilded plates, two gold cups, several silver and gold crosses on chains and two large bibles with hinged, silver filigree covers.

The pillowcases were now full. The cabinet also contained a cedar jewelry box with a wooden handle attached to its side. Ivo ripped off the box's flimsy lock to find cash inside, a lot of it. Had to be the collection box. In the dim light he could make out mostly ones, but some fives and tens too, and some change. Well over a hundred bucks. He scooped out the paper money, jammed it into his pocket and headed up the center aisle to freedom . . . the main doors at the back.

And that's when he saw him. His father, Andris.

In three hours the church would be Sunday-jammed but the sun wasn't yet fully awake. In the semi-darkness it was only that the man appeared to be his despised, long-dead father. But the image quickly morphed into that of . . . the good pastor Porter Underwood, sitting perfectly upright in the aisle seat of the last pew. He was looking directly at Ivo. Apparently had been, throughout Ivo's dedicated thievery.

"Going somewhere, Mr. Lukins?" said the pastor, his voice soft but menacing. Nowhere near as friendly as it had been last night.

"You been sitting there all this time?" replied Ivo, his voice shaky and his heart pounding as he heard his real name. He shifted his eyes to seek out another exit, to think up some lies that would get him out of this.

The pastor answered his question with a nod.

"Well then, you'd better stay where you are, Pastor, I'm carrying a gun."

"Not likely, Ivo. But I am carrying one," the pastor said, lifting his right hand above the pew in front of him. In it was an old Colt .38 Police Special aimed at Ivo's heart. There was enough light in the chapel now to reflect the rising sun off the noses of the bullets nesting in the revolver's chambers. "Ever hear of baptism under fire?" said Pastor Underwood.

"What's that supposed to mean?"

"I think you know what it means. You're about to get yours. Now just set those pillowcases down nice and easy on the pew next to you."

"Well, I guess you got the upper hand here, Pastor," said Ivo, doing as he was told. "How'd you know what I was up to?"

"The tablecloth."

"Tablecloth?"

"It slipped while you were eating last night. Pretty funny sight, those candlesticks sticking in your sides." But the pastor wasn't smiling.

Ivo's head began bobbing. "And how'd you happen to know my real name?"

"Looked in your wallet while you slept."

"Isn't that against the law?"

"Around here, I am the law, Mr. Lukins." He was speaking very slowly.

"But you're a pastor."

"I am that, young man. And the police chief of our little Cottontown enclave."

"Ain't it kind of unusual to be both?"

"In Detroit, maybe. Not in Macon. At least not in Cottontown."

"So what happens now, Pastor? Or should I call you Chief? You bust me, right?"

The pastor sat there, not saying a word, just staring at Ivo.

"Why did you take me in last night?" asked Ivo.

"Nothing wrong with being charitable, is there?"

"To a man who might rob you? You coulda shot me just now."

"In Detroit, maybe. Not in Macon. A black man shoot a white man here—even a black policeman shoot a white thief like you—where you think that would get me?"

"So what now, Chief?"

The pastor/chief sat silent another few seconds. "Good question," he said, absent-mindedly slapping the side of his revolver against the palm of his left hand. "Sit down on the floor where you are. Let me think on that a while."

Ivo sat.

The rainclouds had cleared overnight. The two sat there as the sun's rays slashed through the church's arched windows, pasted over with ruby-colored cellophane to imitate the stained glass the church could hardly afford.

The pastor tightened his lips. He inhaled deeply before speaking, "Here's what I'm going to do, Ivo Lukins, may the Good Lord understand and forgive me. I'm going to take a chance on you. You said you need a job. That part I believed. So I'm going to give you a bucket of hot water and a wet mop and put you to work scrubbing out my dining hall, which is a mess after last night's dinner. Then I'm going to get the sleep I missed because I chose to look into the likes of you all night. If you're gone when I wake up, you're gone, don't forget to leave me a thank you note. But, if anything is missing, Ivo—so much as a bookmark from a bible—I'll put out an APB on you first I learn of it. And I promise you will go to prison. But . . . if you remain, and you've made my dining hall sparkle, I may just offer you a job as our janitor. What we really need is a good handy man and general factotum. So I figure if you can repair shoes—if that's what you really did—you can probably repair anything. Any questions?"

"What happened to the janitor you had?"

"He's in jail."

Ivo asked no more questions. He could only make his head bob up and down.

Pastor/Police Chief Underwood, his hand on the back of Ivo's shirt collar, marched Ivo into the dining hall and made him stand awhile before presenting him with a bucket of hot, soapy water and a wet mop. Then he went off to the rectory attached to the church.

Ivo sat himself down to think. He sat so long that the bucket's water turned cold. I can take a chance and split and make my way to Miami . . . but I have no cash . . . then again, I could clean up the hall and maybe get hired for doing it . . . that way I could actually get to Miami after my first paycheck . . . with no cops on my back.

But another thought struck him. Another epiphany. No one, not one single person in his whole entire life, had ever done anything like what this negro pastor was doing for him. And something else happened to Ivo Lukins that had never happened before. Out of the blue he started sobbing. And kept on until he had no more tears inside him. Empty, he became filled with light.

And refilled the bucket and got to work.

The Tarnów Gate

Amnesia

"All you ever do is read," she says. And she doesn't say it nice. She hasn't said nice to me since I can't remember.

"I read so I can write, Ginnie," I mumble over my shoulder as I stare at the near-empty screen of my dilapidated Mac.

"What the hell is that supposed to mean, Howard? I'm sick of your sanctimonious crap about a writer being what he reads. All you ever do when you're not reading is write. Or read when you're not writing. I don't want to hear any more about the 'marriage' of reading and writing. What about our marriage? Your nose is 24/7 in a book or your fucking computer."

God, I do not want to be in another one of these unilateral conversations. Nor, come to think of it, in this joke of a marriage. But what have I done to begin the ending of it? I just want to write. If only I could replace the hours I spend eating, sleeping, even having sex which we no longer have anyhow, by writing, I'd do so. But here's Virginia, my lovely wife of eighteen years, telling me, while I'm in the middle of crafting a perfect sentence, that I have to pay heed to the life I have, not the life I'm trying my damnedest to put on paper.

I spin slowly in my chair and look at this whining pile of flesh, my onetime "Virginia Slim," now doubled in every dimension. And I reference God once again, this time thanking Him for not giving us kids who'd likely be there right next to her, demanding their own share of me.

But demanding my time is only half of why I so detest this hellion. She's constantly on my case for forgetting everything. Amnesia. She keeps throwing that word at me. Her fucking mantra. "You lose your keys, your glasses, you don't remember what you've just told me, you forget to buy more syringes when I'm running out. Amnesia's what you got, Howard. Can't remember shit. Amnesia. What are you good at, Howard? What are you good for?"

Well, screw that, Ginnie. What am I good at? I am good at writing. I think. Maybe that's the only kind of good that's in me, woman. And just yesterday she starts on me for the "quality" of my writing, reminding me incessantly of my being dropped by my agent and my failing to sell anything but a few magazine articles this past year. Jeezuz!

"You're a lousy writer, Howard!" This from a half-literate sow who can't write a proper grocery list and whose nose is always in People or one of those vampire romance novels.

Anyhow, I've been thinking about self-publishing. But that would take money I don't have and, worse, would steal even more time to promote. I've never doubted that I have another novel in me. Maybe a book of shorts. Maybe just a book of shorts. All I need is to write it. But I need time to do that, Virginia, dear, without your big mouth screaming at me and your fat ass hovering over me.

No wonder I'm beginning to doubt my work, my very worth as a writer; something I've never had reason to doubt before. Especially not before Ginnie began sticking pins into me every damn day. Doesn't every writer go through this when his words dry up a little? Maybe. But every writer isn't shackled to the likes of my lovely Virginia. Damn that woman!

And that's when the idea freezes me right between key taps. What was I thinking just before? Something like she won't let me lead the life I'd kill for. I'll get rid of her non-stop nagging and criticizing. I'll get rid of her. Not by divorce, either. Too costly, too time-consuming. No, I'll kill the bitch! That's it. Virginia. Dead. No, seriously, I mean really dead. *Dead* dead.

Hey, you're the mystery writer, Howard, figure out how. What the hell, there may be another story in it. Like "Wake Me When I'm Dead." That sucker sold 6500 copies. Nine years ago. Just make sure you get away with it because prison time isn't quite the kind of personal time you're looking for. And then there's the bonus: her $200,000 life insurance policy. It won't look like the motive because you didn't just take it out, you bought it twelve years ago when you still had the bucks. See, Howard, you're already covering tracks you haven't yet laid out. Time to do so, Howard. Step to the line. Step over it.

So I step. Can't let this get complicated. Tangled web and all that. Got to be in and out, badabing! Need a method, an alibi. Wait! The old Twilight Zone.

What I come up with is beautifully simple, simply beautiful. My lovely, since she turned herself into a porcine poster girl for Type 2 diabetes, takes insulin twice daily. So she leaves a suicide note stating she's despondent because the goddamn disease is killing her, then she snuffs herself with an overdose of insulin. That simple.

So I start the process.

The suicide note is the hardest part. I tell my beloved I need such a note to illustrate the cover of the mystery I'm working on, "The Suicide Note." Does she have any thoughts? Would she write one for me so it looks like it's in a feminine hand. If she'd like, I can write it for her and she can copy it in her hand. Before telling me I'm wasting my time with such trash, she goes along with it, joking that I'd better not use it against her.

Oh, the delicious irony of it.

After explaining her hopeless predicament, she writes the note. Which concludes, ". . . the only way out of this miserable, hopeless life is for me to take it myself. "That's beautiful," I tell her. "Couldn't have done better myself."

"I agree," she says.

Alibi? I take in a late movie I've seen before so I know its plot if asked about it later. I make myself seen when I enter the theater. Spill some popcorn or something. When the movie starts, I slip out an exit, tape the door lock open for reentry, head home, do the deed then hurry back so I can discuss the movie with someone while walking out. That gives me a witness, covers me. Then it's back home to find that my poor wife, my beloved Virginia has taken her own precious life!

I run the scheme over and over in my mind, do two practice runs and time it out at exactly fifty-two minutes from first entering the theater to the time I return to my seat. An hour to spare if anything slows me down.

So I execute the plan. I go to an apocalypse film and slip out just when the earth is ending due to an attack from some fourth dimension something or other. I arrive home, find Ginnie in bed watching TV, and offer to inject her, something she taught me long ago to do. She's preoccupied and doesn't notice I've tripled her dosage. Enough to kill a mastodon. Then I tell her I need to go back out for some cigarettes. Sure enough, I'm back in my theater seat with an hour left of the movie. Worst movie I ever saw. But I see enough of it to repeat its best lines, of which there are none.

When I return home, Ginnie is lying in peaceful repose . . . stone cold dead, incapable of speaking another vile word. I sit on the bed for a few minutes, admiring my work. This is easier than writing. I set the note on her bed table and place the syringe I'd used in her hand, making sure her prints, not mine, are all over it.

I call 9-1-1 to blurt my hysterical report. When the police arrive eleven minutes later, I'm shedding alligator tears, suicide note in hand, sobbing uncontrollably over the loss of my beloved soul mate whom I discovered dead upon returning from the movies.

I'm a pretty good actor. Better than I am as a writer?

The detective, Lt. Roberts, informs me that an autopsy will be performed and an inquest made, S.O.P. for suicides, and I'll be required to attend. I tell him I'll cooperate in every way. He offers his condolences and leaves.

At the inquest I'm surprised to find a coroner's jury convened. For a simple suicide? The coroner has me tell my story. Then Lt. Roberts is called to the stand. He tells the coroner that my whereabouts at the time of the injection have been checked out; that the suicide note appears to be in Virginia's handwriting, that he concludes the suicide is exactly what it appeared to be. The coroner then requests the opportunity to depose me under oath.

Before he questions me, he addresses the jury. "I have convened you," he tells them, "because of a rather strange circumstance that has arisen.

You'll be made aware of that as I question Mr. Vanderveer. Now," he continues, "Mr. Vanderveer, on my own I have taken the time to read many of your short stories. Call it research. You might say I wanted to know how the mind of a mystery writer works. I find you, incidentally, to be quite an accomplished writer, sir."

"Thank you," I say, flattered, but wondering where the hell he's going.

"Mr. Vanderveer, are you familiar with a short story, a mystery called But I Was at the Movies?"

I reach into my mind but find it momentarily empty. "I don't recall it, Lieutenant."

"You should, Mr. Vanderveer. You wrote it exactly . . ." He stops to consult a yellow pad on the table in front of him. "fourteen years ago." It tells of a writer so nagged by his sickly wife that he plans her murder by walking out of a movie to return home to overdose her with her medicine. After, he returns to the movie to establish his alibi. He then comes home to find her dead, a suicide note in her handwriting next to her. Then he . . ."

"You can stop right there, Lieutenant," I say, in half a whisper. By now, the jury's collective mouth has dropped.

"Please speak up, Mr. Vanderveer. Are you saying that you now do remember writing that short story?"

My eyes are downcast. I nod my positive reply.

"Quite a coincidence, your little story and the murder of your wife, wouldn't you say, sir?" This mention of murder audibly draws the air from the room.

I nod again.

"Well then, Mr. Vanderveer, can you explain it?"

"No. I guess I just forgot about the story."

"Do you have a problem with your memory, sir? Never mind that, Mr. Vandeveer. Allow me to come to the point. Did you, in fact—not just in fiction—murder your wife much as you wrote about it fourteen years earlier?"

I look around helplessly and nod once more. "Amnesia," I mumble.

"What was that, sir?" replies the coroner. "I couldn't hear you."

"Never mind," I say, nodding my head a third time.

The Tarnów Gate

Blues for Bluester

(for Coralie Mia Harris)

Pacifica. The word means "tranquil." Pacifica is the name of a perfect little town nestled at ocean's edge in Northern California. That's where Coralie lives. And that's where this story begins.

Coralie's house is on a corner in a regular neighborhood with regular houses on every side. But her house is a bit irregular. It's the only one with a big chicken coop nestled behind it. In which something happened that was not the least bit tranquil. We'll get to that in a while.

Coralie's chicken coop was built by her mom and dad and big brother, Julian, whom she called JuJu. They built it so they could have pretty little chickens to look at, and fresh eggs to eat every day because no egg is tastier than a fresh-laid egg.

Coralie visited the chicken coop every day because she loved its feathered residents, so much so that she named each and every one. There were Bessie and Elizabeth and Wanda and Noodles and Delmar and Wingy and Selma and Turtle (she was very slow) and Rachel and Scratch. And I almost forgot Thomasina and Dingbat and Cranky and Eleonora. There was maybe no one better in the world at naming chicks than Coralie because she had an amazing imagination. The roosters she named Oscar and Boris.

Coralie adored the little chicks the brood hens were allowed to hatch, and especially liked watching them bravely peck their way free of their shells when being born. She never tired of watching this miracle occur.

Came one rainy day in January, she was sitting inside the coop watching a special egg hatch; special because it wasn't white or brown or speckled like eggs almost always are, it was striped with shades of blue and green and red and orange and yellow and violet just like the colors of the rainbow. This baffled her because the only way an egg could look like that was when it was painted for Easter, and Easter was a long way off.

Coralie's mom and dad, and JuJu, too, saw the egg but they didn't think anything of it. They thought Coralie had colored it with her crayons. And Coralie didn't say otherwise. The truth would be her little secret.

She was pretty sure that no matter what color an eggshell is, the little chickie inside will come out yellow. But she wondered about this special egg because of its rainbow-striped shell. Her mom, who'd read whole books about chickens, had told her that some chicks, like Rhode Island Reds, often came out a reddish color. But the chick, when it lost the down it was born with, would then grow up to have feathers that were usually white, but sometimes brown or red or black and white mixed together, or even speckled like some eggs.

The brood hen Wanda, had been sitting on this, her special egg for a whole month, which was about ten days longer than it usually took an egg to hatch.

It was almost like the chick didn't want to leave the egg.

Three weeks had come to pass during which Coralie rushed home from school each day just to be there when the chick in the rainbow-striped egg hatched. She'd sit right next to the coop where Wanda sat the egg. And there she would stay for hours making beautiful drawings of what she thought the chick might look like when it pecked its way to daylight.

Then, on the thirty-first day, a cold and breezy Saturday, while Coralie was at the coop coloring, she heard a soft tapping from the egg. She dropped her crayons and snapped her head around to see the egg crack a bit as a sharp little beak came through the tiny hole it had made.

She was so wrapped up in watching that she couldn't tear herself away to let her family or her best friends, Theo, Xander and Kaiyah know of it. Oh, well, she'd surprise them after it hatched.

A few more pecks and the hole began to grow and, suddenly, a big chunk of shell fell away and quicker than you can say frangipani, out tumbled not a yellow chick but a little blue chick. A true blue chick, brighter than the brightest blue crayon in Coralie's box, so bright it almost glimmered like the neon Pepsi sign at the 7-Eleven store.

Coralie could hardly believe it. In all her five years, she'd never seen a chick this strange color. But then she'd never seen a rainbow-striped egg either. Though her mom said some chicks could be red, she never mentioned blue. So Coralie was absolutely sure there'd never been a bright blue little peeper like this before.

Never, ever.

She watched the freshly hatched chick stumble about, hop a bit, then bump into a wall, then scurry around in circles. Just before Coralie rushed into the house to inform everyone, the blue chick turned to her, looked up into her eyes, cocked its tiny head to one side and spoke. Maybe not in the way you and I speak, but in a way that Coralie somehow understood. Was this her active imagination or was this really happening?

What the chick said—Coralie clearly heard it—was, "Hey, I'm hungry. You have anything to eat?"

Coralie wanted to ask how the chick could possibly speak, not being a person, but she was so surprised at hearing its words that all she could say was, "What would you like?"

"Whatever you got," said the chick. Then it asked Coralie her name.

"I'm Coralie," said Coralie, still not knowing quite how to speak to a chicken, never having spoken to one before. "How about some corn?"

"Whatever corn is, I'll have some. And I'm thirsty too."

"Corn and water, coming up," said Coralie. She was already more comfortable about talking with a chicken. Quickly fetching the corn and water, she watched the blue chick eat. "You know, chickens will eat almost anything," she said. "Sometimes even pebbles."

"Pebbles? Yuk," said the chick, "But, what the heck, throw in a side of pebbles." Coralie watched in amazement as the chick ate, then ran into the house to reveal the hatching of the rainbow-striped egg.

Coralie's mom was reading "Raising Chickens for Dummies" in her favorite chair in the living room. Her dad and Julian were eating Funyuns and gummy worms and leftover samosas and tacos while watching a football game.

Coralie's words spilled from her mouth, "Mommy, Daddy, JuJu, you gotta stop whatcher doing, I have something wonderful to tell you." They could see how excited she was, so they gave her their full attention, even muting the TV's sound.

"You know that rainbow-striped egg?" she said, jumping up and down. "Well, it just hatched out a blue chick. A bright blue chick."

"Hatched?!" said her mom, snapping her book shut.

"Blue?!" said her dad, almost falling off his chair.

"Bright blue?!" said JuJu, flipping over the back of the couch.

"Yes," said Coralie, "and that's not all. "It can talk!"

"Whaaattt?!" they all shouted together.

"You mean peep, don't you?" said JuJu, laughing as he braided green and red and orange gummy worms together before stuffing them into his mouth.

"No, I mean talk," squeaked Coralie.

Three pairs of eyes rolled up to the ceiling. But they knew that Coralie was not one to fib about such things. And, since she didn't sound like she was joking, they all raced out to the chicken coop. JuJu and her dad, running next to each other, got stuck for a second in the doorway to the deck.

They found the little chick, eating. Their words, all talking at the same time, ran together. They, like Coralie, could not believe what their own eyes were seeing.

"Wait a minute, please!" shouted Coralie. They got quiet. "Why don't just one of you speak? Ask the chick a question."

They nodded their heads in agreement. JuJu, feeling a little foolish talking to a chicken, spoke first. "What's your name, little chick?" As he said this, he winked at his parents.

The chick said nothing.

"Would you like to come in and watch the ballgame with us?" asked Coralie's dad, kidding the way he often did.

No answer.

"Are you happy to join our family?" asked Coralie's mom.

Again no answer. And again, JuJu winked at his parents.

Coralie noticed the wink. They didn't believe her. The blue chick had let her down. "Please, little one, talk to my family," she pleaded.

But the chick remained silent.

Coralie's mom said, "That's OK, Coralie. Maybe it'll talk when it's finished its dinner." Being the family's chicken expert, she picked up the chick to inspect it. "I believe we have a little rooster," she said. What are we going to do with yet another rooster? As soon as she said this, tears came to Coralie's eyes. Her mom, regretting her words, said to Coralie, "But of course we'll keep it. It must be the only blue rooster in the world."

A smile quickly replaced Coralie's tears.

"So does he have a name?" said JuJu.

Without thinking, Coralie, the family's naming expert, blurted, "Bluester!"

"Then Bluester, it is," said Coralie's mom. They all bobbed their heads in agreement. And that was that. Bluester, the bright blue rooster, was now a member of the family.

The others went inside, but Coralie remained at the coop. She would call her friends to come and see this little miracle, but first she'd have a talk with this suddenly silent Bluester, the rooster. "OK, mister," she said, doing her best to look angry, "what's up with you? You talked to me but you wouldn't talk to my family?"

Bluester had a funny look on his cute little face. "I'm sorry, Coralie," he peeped. "I didn't mean to make you look bad. But it seems that the only one I'm able to talk to is you. I'm not sure why that is or why I'm able to talk at all, or even why I'm blue, but I sure know I'm different from every chicken here, even from my brothers and sisters."

Bluester was way too cute to even be angry with. And too sad-looking. Coralie shrugged her shoulders. "That's OK, Bluester, I understand," she said. "I guess my mom and dad and JuJu will think your talking was just my imagination. They say I have a pretty good one."

"Well, I think your family should believe you. Or believe in me. Or believe in you the way you believe in me.

"Maybe," said Coralie, thoroughly confused. She wasn't sure what Bluester meant. She was only five years old.

Half a year went by. The chicken coop and its population had grown. A small room had been added to give the coop an L-shape. There were now twenty-eight chickens, four of them brood hens, still just three of them roosters, including Bluester, who was no longer a cute little chick but a handsome, nearly full-grown rooster himself. The rest were very busy layers.

Bluester, because he was so very blue, was made, by the other chickens, to feel very blue. No hen would come near him for the very reason of his blueness. Nor would Oscar and Boris, the other two roosters. He was so different-looking that they wanted nothing to do with him.

And so Bluester, as friendly a fellow as he was, had no friends. I guess if you had no friends, you'd be pretty blue, too.

Well, Bluester did have one friend. A wonderful friend. Coralie, of course. More than a friend, she was almost like a mother to him because not even Wanda, his real mother, accepted him. Theo, Xander and Kaiyah liked him just fine, as did, of course, Coralie's family. But he truly did wish for some chicken friends as well.

This family was nice, and he certainly loved his Coralie, but the entire flock acted almost as though he weren't there. So Bluester wasn't able to father any chickens, that's just how it happened to be since it takes a rooster and a hen to make a chick. What the hens were afraid of was that if Bluester fathered their chick, it might come out bright blue. Or worse, green, or maybe heliotrope, and be as strangely different-looking as Bluester himself, not at all like the rest of the chicks.

Would Bluester ever have anything to crow about?

How would you feel if no one wanted to be near you and you couldn't have any kids? Bluester had no choice but to roost at the far end of the coop while the rest of the flock roosted as far away from him as they could.

One day, Bluester walked over to Boris, Bluester's head bobbing like chickens always do. He tried once more to be friendly and say hello. But Boris sneered at him and pecked at him and spit at him, and they got into a terrible fight that Bluester lost because, although he was bigger and stronger than Boris, he didn't want to hurt someone he was hoping would someday, somehow become his friend.

Bluester, the bright blue rooster, was now bluer than ever.

It was shortly before Christmas that a red fox, a chicken's worst enemy, found its way into Coralie's chicken coop. This was a mean old fox who lived in the wooded hills not far from Coralie's home. And who doesn't know that foxes like nothing better than to steal chickens and eat them? The chickens, as expected, panicked when he broke in and, before any of them knew it, he snatched up, of all chickens, Bluester's mom, Wanda, and carried her off to his den.

Bluester, though fully grown, couldn't hold back the tears he felt coming for his mother because, even though his mother, like the other chickens, didn't want him, she was still his mother. But, sad as he was, he was also very angry. He vowed that, if this loathsome fox returned, he would find a way to stop him from ever wanting to steal another chicken. Coralie was sad too, most of all for Bluester. She begged her parents to let her move into the coop to protect the other chickens, but, of course, they wouldn't let her. Still, naming the fox Ferocious, she meant to be there when and if this Ferocious returned.

Foxes, we've come to know—especially big nasty red foxes like this one—are very clever and can always find their way into a chicken coop. This one, who was extremely clever, had done it quite often. They can jump over or dig under fences or find holes in them to slip through. It's said that no fence can stop a determined fox that means to breech it.

And, sure enough, one blustery moonless night threatening a rainstorm just before Christmas, the favorite kind of night for a wily fellow like Ferocious, there he was, digging his way again under Coralie's coop while everyone in the house was asleep. The chickens, as soon as they felt the fox's presence, were all astir, hopping from roost to roost, doing their best to find safe spots when, really, there were none. None safe enough to escape the ferocious Ferocious. Oscar and Boris crowed an alarm and the rest of the chickens cackled their lungs out, but the wind was howling so loud that no one in the house could hear them.

Bluester, during this hullabaloo, was silently tensing himself, waiting for Ferocious to burst in. He knew he'd be the only one willing to deal with this vicious fellow because Oscar and Boris were simply, well, too chicken to fight him off. If still quite young, he was strong and brave. But he'd never learned how to fight because, as we've learned, he'd never wanted to fight. Till now. He swore to himself that he'd give up his life to protect the other chickens.

And, in seconds, he might have to because Ferocious had just cleared the underside of the coop's southern wall, and was now inside, slowly slinking around, selecting the chicken he would attack first. The hens and chicks, Oscar and Boris too, were all the while running and flapping around, frightened out of their wits.

And now Ferocious made his choice. His evil eye fell upon a plump leghorn name of Sylvia, the best layer in the flock. Crouching low, he took a tremendous leap toward her as she cowered in a corner. The red fox—his long, pointy claws extended, his mouth wide open, his lips curled back—now hung in mid-air, about to sink his razor-sharp fangs into the neck of the unfortunate Sylvia.

But just then a figure came flying out of the darkness directly across the arc of Ferocious's leap.

It was Bluester, who else? Who else would dare?

The bird and the fox slammed into each other at the top of their flight paths, knocking each other to the floor. The fox could not believe its beady red eyes. He, the meanest, nastiest fox in all of Pacifica, was here to attack chickens, and now a chicken was attacking him! But this was no ordinary chicken.

This was Bluester, the bright blue rooster.

The two circled each other, Bluester's head bobbing left then right, looking for an opening to strike his enemy. He didn't know if he could survive this battle for his life and the lives of the other chickens. He'd never been in a fight, except the one with Boris. But Ferocious fought this way every day. So Bluester would have to let his instincts take over and do whatever came to mind. He could not, would not, allow himself to fail. He would save his fellow chickens from this murderous fox who had carried away and killed his mother.

Or he would die trying.

For a while, the two continued to circle each other like middleweights in a boxing ring. The fox was the first to lash out, catching Bluester's right wing and knocking out several feathers. The injured rooster hopped out of the way of Ferocious' other claw and in time to escape his sharp, bared teeth. Before his antagonist could set himself for another thrust, he half jumped up, half flew up and landed squarely on the back of the fox's neck, digging in his claws to let him know he meant business. The shocked fox shook Brewster off violently. They went at it again, keeping at it for many minutes, Ferocious, clawing and biting, Bluester pecking and scratching, until both were near collapse. But it soon became obvious: Bluester was no match for Ferocious.

The red fox stepped back to recover some strength. In a low crouch again, he leaped upon Bluester, throwing him onto his back. Three quick clawings, administered by Bluester, held Ferocious off for a moment. But not long enough to prevent the fox from having his way with the gasping rooster. Though he'd fought a superior opponent valiantly, it looked like the brave and willing Bluester was done for. The vicious vulpine was now licking his lips in victory.

Was our brave rooster truly done for?

Suddenly, ignited by Bluester's heroic example, all the other chickens, including the newly bold Oscar and Boris, swooped down on Ferocious like a raging army. They swarmed all over him, pecking at him and clawing at him, blinding him with their flapping wings until the hapless fox was forced to crawl, whimpering, limping, and perhaps mortally wounded, back through the hole he'd made under the coop. Bewildered, and nearly frightened out of his black socks, there was no way he'd ever return to this coop again.

Oscar and Boris congratulated themselves on their newly discovered bravery, but the hens ignored them, surrounding Bluester to thank him as they gently carried him off to a bed they quickly made from their nests. And there they tended to all the scratches and cuts and bites that had been dealt to him by Ferocious.

But it did not look good for Bluester. His bright blue feathers were now fading a little. He was sinking fast. Could he possibly survive the terrible wounds inflicted by the ferocious fox?

Coralie's family, having at last heard the hub-bub in the chicken coop, rushed out to see the tail end of the fight and the white-tipped tail of Ferocious as he limped off into the woods.

When they saw Bluester, lying near death in his makeshift bed, they understood what had happened and how very courageous the bright blue rooster had been to fight this coop invader. They couldn't know that Bluester had fought alone until the last-minute help from the others.

But something else shocked them every bit as much as the fox invasion. They had never seen, in all the days since Bluester's hatching, the entire flock crowding around him, tending to him like he were the most loved chicken in the flock. Which he now apparently was. It no longer seemed to matter that he was of a different color. And from that day forward, he would become more than just their beloved friend, but their respected leader as well.

If he could stay alive.

Every chicken in the coop remained awake that night, maintaining a vigil in hopes of keeping him alive. Oscar and Boris stood guard against any possible return of Ferocious while the hens lay next to Bluester, keeping him warm throughout the windblown night.

If he'd been alone before, and friendless, he'd be alone and friendless no longer.

Coralie's mom and dad would not allow her to spend the night in the coop with her dear, dear Bluester. In tears, she would only go to bed after seeing all the hens caring so lovingly for him.

Later that night, when everyone was asleep, Coralie had a dream in which Bluester was calling to her as he arose from his nested bed to float up into the clouds. That had to mean that he was saying goodbye to her. She was certain that, if she did not immediately rush to his side, he would be lost forever. The dream, worse than a nightmare, felt so real, so troubling that it woke her up.

Lightning cracked, whip-like, across the sky. A huge rumble of thunder shook the house. Torrents of rain came down, blown almost sideways. But Coralie did not care. With her favorite blanket wrapped around her, and her favorite stuffed animal, Skye, under her arm, she crept down the stairs and ran barefoot across the rear deck to the coop to hold Bluester in her arms. Even with the hens doing their very best to keep him warm, he was losing his body heat. He didn't seem to be breathing very well and his eyes were closed. Would they ever open again?

Coralie was afraid she was about to lose him. She continued to hold him closely, wrapping him tightly in her blanket to keep him warm. And all through the night, though he didn't appear to hear her, she kept telling him how wonderful he was and how much she loved him.

"You've been the bravest rooster anyone's ever seen," whispered Coralie. "You know how much I love you so you'd better not die on me, do you hear me?" Her tears were spilling onto the faded feathers of his blue head.

Then, abruptly, it was as if Bluester had heard her whispers because he opened one eye and let out a soft cluck. And, once again, he spoke to Coralie: "Would you mind loosening that blanket a bit. It's a little too tight."

Coralie had no words to answer him. She was crying too hard. But now the tears rolling down her cheeks were tears of absolute joy.

Bluester, when fully recovered, thought long and hard about what had happened to him. He said to Coralie that it shouldn't have taken an attack by a fox to be accepted by his fellow chickens. They should never have shunned him for being a different color. Why hadn't they accepted him for who he was, same as Coralie accepted him, and loved him from the beginning? But he understood that, sometimes, that was the way things worked out. He finally decided to just be thankful they worked out in his favor. You had to take chickens for the way they were, he concluded. Maybe it was that way with people, too.

Coralie, listening carefully, agreed with Bluester, even if she didn't fully understand him. After all, she was only five years old.

Anyhow, inside of a few months, with all the hens liking him now just fine, a lot of rainbow-striped eggs started showing up in the coop.

The Superficial Wound

"Look again, Tom," said the doc, after a cursory glance at the body we'd just brought in. "That's no bullet hole. The opening is slit-shaped not round. I'd say this old fellow was stabbed by a knife. You testing me? Give it up."

I was testing him. Sheepishly, I hand Doc Hamilton the baggie with the knife we'd found on the floor of the vic's car. "But what do you make of the slit being just half an inch wide? The blade's width is more than an inch. And there was hardly any blood."

"The wound didn't kill him. It's superficial. Half an inch deep as well. But the tortured look on the man's face? That's a clue as to what did kill him."

"What's your guess, Doc?"

"I don't make guesses, Tom. You want the answer, wait till I've completed my autopsy. Testing will take at least two days. Now beat it, I'm busy."

Warren Hamilton, our medical examiner and coroner elected for eight straight four-year terms, has the formidable reputation of never having made an incorrect finding. His nickname, "Doctor Right," is no misnomer.

He likes to play the curmudgeon though everyone knows he's a pussycat.

At eight, off-duty, I hit Jake's Bar, around the corner from the station. My partner, Ed Torgeson, has beat me to our roundtable. A few other detectives from the 18th are there too. I catch the end of Ed's story, but he never finishes one because they always break him up first.

"What are you so ebullient about?" I ask him.

"I'd tell you if I knew what aboolyant means. You look troubled, pardner."

"No, Ed, just baffled about what snuffed that old stiff we found on Halworth today. Got to be murder. He was stabbed in the thigh, though that couldn't have killed him. Before you ask, Doctor Right needs two days to tell us what really did him in." I hardly finish my sentence when Sally, Jake's gorgeous wife, tending bar, who might have been my wife if I'd had the nerve to ask her ten years ago, slaps down my usual double Manhattan with its usual three cherries.

Mike Milligan pipes up. "What makes you so damned sure it was murder?"

"Well maybe it's not a certainty. He was found face down in the gutter about a dozen yards from his car, the driver's door open. I'm guessing he was stabbed then dragged out for some reason. He's old so, who knows, it could have been a heart attack due to the physical attack."

Two days later, I get the call from Doc Hamilton. "That rictus on your vic's face, Tom? That's what asphyxiation looks like. He was poisoned. And, by the way, he had cancer. Pancreatic. Final stage."

"Wait a minute. Stabbed, choked, now you're saying he was poisoned? What's the connection with the stab wound? I don't get it, Doc."

Doctor Right has an odd sense of humor. He's thoroughly enjoying my confusion. Makes me wait several beats before he delivers his verdict through what must be a smug smile. "The old gent died of suffocation as the result of poisoning by curare, a highly lethal toxin. The knife blade was tipped with it."

"Curare? In Detroit? Isn't that the stuff South American Indians used on their darts and arrows to kill warthogs and unfriendlies?"

"Yeah, Tom, but it's still used today, principally by homeopaths. Ingested in small quantities, it's seen as a general remedy and muscle relaxant in treating pain. It's only lethal when injected by a needle. Or a knife tipped with it."

I know Doc Hamilton so I know there's more coming. "When it enters the blood stream it causes instant weakening of the skeletal muscles, leading to asphyxiation due to paralysis of the lungs. Your vic died at about 8:45 pm, approximately twenty minutes after he was stabbed. From the angle of penetration, he might have stabbed himself. But that's for you to determine."

"Thanks. Now that I know the how and the when and maybe the why, I need to know the who."

"You're the dick, Tom."

"Just how did you mean that, Doc?"

So if there was no assault, our victim, one Charles Atherton, age 73, likely committed suicide. Ed starts checking out area drugstores and homeopathic practitioners. It could take some time and yield nothing, but it's S.O.P. Meanwhile, I call Atherton's widow, Emily, to request an interview. I can hardly understand her through her tears but she's willing to see me. Atherton's body has been released to the funeral home so I can stop at the house this afternoon.

The Atherton home is a modest, nicely-kept Prairie-style bungalow in Morningside, an old but still upscale Eastside neighborhood. Emily Atherton is being attended by her half-sister, Frances Tunbridge, a top-heavy woman a full six inches taller than Emily. Turns out, Frances has been living with Emily these past two years after her own husband died. Frances, maybe ten years younger than Emily, hovers above me like I'm a burglar who just broke in. I do my damnedest to ignore her.

I offer my standard apology to Mrs. Atherton "for intruding at a time like this." Then I'm obliged to tell her we're treating this matter as a homicide until and unless it proves otherwise; a suicide.

Frances glares at me as if I've been reciting the Kama Sutra. "How dare you suggest Charles killed himself," she says. "He was not that kind of person. He was a lot of things, that man, but he wouldn't harm a flea so he couldn't harm himself. Some terrible person out there did this to him. That's who you should be looking for!"

"We are looking, ma'am. And now I must ask you to leave us so I can speak with Mrs. Atherton privately." Scowling, Frances marches out and clumps up the nearby stairs, her feathers badly ruffled.

"Mrs. Atherton, again I apologize for troubling you but did you ever know your husband to have brought home substances with which he could harm himself?"

Emily Atherton wipes her eyes, blows her nose into her lace-edged handkerchief, tucks it into her sleeve, then answers. "My Charley never brought home anything more damaging than a bottle of rose hip wine. He was a gentle, loving soul but was beginning to show signs of dementia."

"How so?"

"He was afraid they'd soon take away his driver's license so he liked to drive around the neighborhood, but when I'd ask where he'd been, he'd look at me strangely. Once he said he hadn't been anywhere—hadn't been out of the house—when I knew he'd just been out driving around for almost an hour."

"Any other odd behavior?"

"Well, lately he'd become—how shall I say it?—suggestible. And he said he'd been hearing voices."

"What kind of voices?"

"Never said. Just voices. Said they'd told him he'd be better off dead. I told him it was just a bunch of nonsense but he seemed to take those voices of his seriously."

"He was paranoid."

"I guess. But everyone loved Charley. Must have all been in his mind. I told you he was showing signs of dementia."

"Had he mentioned anything about taking his own life?"

"No, but he was very depressed. Still, my Charley would never take his own life. Before the depression, he loved life. He was as happy playing Scrabble with me of an evening as if he'd been king of England."

"What do you think caused his depression, his paranoia?"

"Don't know. Wasn't like him. Oh, I wish you'd known him, sir. He was such a sweet man."

"Were you aware he had cancer?"

"I suspected something of the kind, I did. But it was like him to hide that from me. That's what must have caused his depression."

"Was he seeing a homeopathic practitioner?"

"A what? Never! Charley stayed away from doctors as much as he could."

"One last question, Mrs. Atherton. Did he or you purchase drugs for him recently?"

"No, absolutely not. He didn't like taking drugs any more than he liked seeing doctors."

As I'm thanking her, Frances comes rumbling down the stairs, glaring at me for "abusing" her sister. I'm sure she's heard—and disapproved—of every word we've said. She'd have shooed me out with a broom if she hadn't been riding on it. I'm beginning to wonder where her deep interest comes from.

So I'm sitting at my desk a day later, still troubled by Emily's revelations about her husband. They told me everything . . . but nothing, really. Probably suicide, maybe homicide. Then my phone blurts Springsteen's Born in the USA. It's Ed Torgeson. Our men have visited every drugstore and homeopath within a five-mile radius. Only three scrips for curare were filled in the past month. Rare call for the stuff. Two went to homeopaths. One, to an address in Morningside.

"You ready for this, Tom?" Ed, says, laughing like he's about to deliver a punch line. "The address belongs to a Charles P. and Emily R. Atherton, and the stuff was ordered by a Frances Tunbridge. Mean something to you?"

It means something to me. It means that Charles Atherton attacked himself because he knew about the curare! But did he procure it? Did he apply it to the knife? Did he talk himself into killing himself? Was he capable of that? Then it hits me. Jeezuz! A quick trip to the judge for a search warrant and I'm off to the Atherton home . . . after telling Ed to collect the pharmacy's copy of the receipt and to meet me there, stat.

I brake to a sliding-stop on the Atherton's gravel driveway and ring the bell three times. Ed is right behind me. Frances Tunbridge pulls the door open with a "What the hell do you want?" look on her long, mole-spotted face.

You, Frances, I want you, I say to myself. I hold the warrant up to her horse face and back her up while we walk in.

"Who is it, Frances?" I hear Emily call from another room.

"It's those nasty detectives."

"Well, invite them in, for heaven's sake," says Emily, as if we'd been invited for lemonade. We gather in the front room.

I don't waste time. "Frances Tunbridge, I must inform you that you are under arrest. You have been implicated in the murder of your brother-in-law, Charles Atherton." Before she can react, I spit out the rest of her Miranda rights, then indicate to Ed that he can take her in without cuffing her. No need to stir up the neighbors unnecessarily.

Frances screams with angry disbelief as Emily drops into shock. Ed, at a nod from me, pulls Frances into another room to vent her rage. Emily looks up at me with pleading eyes. She deserves an explanation and I offer her one. "Mrs. Atherton, we believe we can prove that your sister was responsible for your husband's death. He died of curare poisoning as a result of stabbing himself with a curare-tipped knife, and . . ."

"But what does carara—she mispronounces the word—have to do with Frances?" she interrupts, one hand over the other on her chest.

I show her the pharmacy receipt. "Your sister ordered that poison. We've checked the signature and know it to be hers. We believe it's been her all along who's taken advantage of your husband's dementia by urging him to kill himself. Remember the voices? It wasn't paranoia that drove him to do what he did, we believe it was Frances. And in his state of mind, he was so suggestible that he finally took the knife we believe she handed him, the knife coated with curare that she bought and applied to the knife. He then drove away from home and, with her suggestion clogging his mind, stabbed himself in a way that caused his death. Suicide, yes, but murderously abetted, we believe, by the suggestion and with the purposeful aid of your sister."

Emily's state of shock grows as I watch her. Her head is now draped over the back of her armchair while her eyes are closed and her mouth hangs open. She then speaks in a stunned monotone. "I'll confess something to you, sir. Frances did not much like my Charley."

"Go on, please," I urge.

"Truth be told, she actually hated him because she felt that he came between us. She often said she could take better care of me than ever he could. Or would. She may have wanted him out of the way but she could never do a thing like what you described. Never. With all her faults, she's a decent person."

"Well, apparently she could do such a thing, ma'am, and we have proof of her actions in that direction. The receipt is a damaging piece of evidence. I'm truly sorry for your loss, Mrs. Atherton, but we must act on our findings."

Frances Tunbridge was indicted and tried two months later on a charge of aiding and abetting the death of her brother-in-law, Charles Atherton, by, knowing of his suggestibility, suggesting that he kill himself, then giving him the weapon she herself poisoned with which to do so. The signed receipt for the curare was damning evidence, indeed. Her demeanor and surly attitude whenever her brother-in-law's name came up, did not help her case. Additionally, the prosecutor elicited from Emily the fact that Frances resented Charles for coming between her and her sister. After a short deliberation, the jury found Frances guilty of manslaughter—murder in the second degree—and sentenced her to 10 to 15 years imprisonment at the Women's Huron Valley Correctional Facility in Ypsilanti, Michigan.

Did the case end there? After serving three and a half months, Frances was released with a full pardon exactly one week after Emily Atherton died of what her niece, Samantha Turner, said was a broken heart.

Why the pardon?

After Emily's death, her diary was discovered by Samantha. The diary explained, in great detail, what had actually transpired at the Athertons in the weeks leading up to the death of Charles Atherton. The diary, as it turned out, was a confession of murder.

Emily Atherton had allowed Frances to live with her because her sister had nowhere else to go, and because Frances had practically demanded it. Emily had long harbored a hatred of Frances who had repeatedly nagged, browbeaten and occasionally abused her physically throughout her life. And lately, Emily detested her even more for disrupting the tranquil life she'd always led with her beloved Charlie.But, just prior to his "self-inflicted murder" as the trial defined it, Charles was diagnosed with the cancer that told him he had only weeks to live. So he begged his Emily to help him die. And that is what she did.

However, careful not to implicate herself, Emily decided to kill two birds, one with heartfelt mercy, the other with no regrets. It was she who ordered the curare by phone, using Frances' credit card and claiming Frances to be a nurse-practitioner. The pharmacy bought the ruse and delivered the curare along with a delivery receipt signed for by Emily but as Frances, who knew her sister's signature down to the last flourish. Especially since she'd been practicing it for a month.

So, for the best of reasons, it was Emily who tipped the knife with the poison, Emily who gave it to Charles and sent him off to do the euthanistic deed, informing him that the merest jab of the knife would grant him his release, his wish to die.

Emily's was one of the critical "voices" Charles last heard.

The Ombudsman

Nathan Sokoloff was a hard man. He lived hard and was hard on those who lived with him. He was a secular Polish-Russian Jew, the only member of his family to survive the Sobibor death camp in Poland. Emigrating to Israel in 1946, he fell in love with a Jordanian woman named Fatima al-Abbadi and married her in a civil ceremony in Jerusalem in the winter of 1947. The next year they had a child, a boy that Nathan, though a Jew in name only, insisted on naming Abraham over the ignored objections of his wife who preferred, well, a little less Jewish-sounding name, perhaps Mark or Matthew.

Nathan would hear no talk of religion in his home. Fatima would have practiced her fading Muslim faith there but Nathan would not acquiesce to even discuss the matter, and she could not practice it in her parents' home because she was no longer welcome there. Her father, in fact, considered her dead the day she married Nathan.

Abraham loved his father and respected him—to a degree—and would have feared him and his harsh ways if he had even the semblance of fear in his emotional makeup. It was his mother, the gentle and loving Fatima, whom he was to hold dearest throughout his life. Her quiet wisdom, her stubborn insistence that he treat all people—Jew and Arab alike—equally, is what he came to respect the most and emulate.

There was, understandably, a rivalry growing between Nathan and the son he liked to call "Abe." Its provenance was the vitriolic criticism that Nathan constantly spewed upon his wife and son for seeming to defy his commands, however passively. Young Abraham resisted his father's diatribes mostly by ignoring them but could not ignore the demeaning words lashed at the put-upon Fatima. The son knew exactly where he stood when first he saw his father strike his mother.

And Fatima knew that her beloved Abraham, though not yet of majority age, was ready to defend her from the toxic behavior of her husband; physically if necessary, as he was now taller and even broader than Nathan. But the equanimous Fatima urged Abraham to be patient, to at least consider his father's side of things.

Nathan, not a man of reason, would hear an argument from no one, however well put, especially one from his son. All would have come to a head if he, a construction worker, had not died from complications of a fall off scaffolding he'd just erected at a development of Jewish homes he was helping build on the West Bank.

Abraham, after a brief period of mourning and consoling his mother, found himself in an odd position. He was half Jew, half Arab and felt little of either. He was, nominally and legally, an Israeli citizen, but was not accepted as one religiously or socially because his mother was not just a non-Jew but a Muslim. Thus, at eighteen, Abraham Sokoloff, without a father to guide him, without a religion he cared to call his own, was deeply confused. He had arrived at a critical nexus in his life.

An avid reader, hungry for knowledge and, like many people of his age in the '60s, Abraham became enamored of the German author Hermann Hesse. When he read Hesse's gripping novella Siddhartha, about the travails of a young man searching for enlightenment, for the meaning of existence, as had Buddha, also known as Siddhartha, he was so at odds with himself and so taken with what he'd read, that he set out in search of himself, as had Siddhartha.

But first, Abraham wished to honor his beloved mother. He did this by changing his given name, legally, to the Arabic Ibrahim. To this he added his mother's maiden name as his middle name. He was no longer Abraham Sokoloff, he was now Ibrahim al-Abbadi Sokoloff. Why, he reasoned, shouldn't the rest of the world be just as confused by his name as he was by himself?

Inwardly, he knew he would somehow discover himself. And perhaps the world would discover him. And he could then give back to the world that which his mother had given him, but which his father had not: a love for his fellow man and a way for him to teach his fellow man to love one another.

Ibrahim Sokoloff, a bright fellow and no fool, realized that, to fulfill this desire, he would require a formal education. And so, with the meager funds left him by his father, and already possessed of fluency in Hebrew, Yiddish, several Arabic dialects and a growing knowledge of English, he was accepted by American University, in the heart of Washington, D.C., in a country he had never even visited. There he minored in languages and world history, and eventually took an M.A., with honors, in International Relations.

But Ibrahim, a secularist with boundless curiosity, knew that his search for himself had not yet even begun. Upon graduation, and with his mother's blessings, he began this search by backpacking his way along the very path of Siddhartha, one that led him to a Buddhist monastery in Thimpu, Bhutan. There he became a studious acolyte for three years until the day he was forced to decide upon giving himself to monkhood for life. At this troubling point, however, he had an epiphany. He interpreted his sighting of a single shooting star going the opposite way of others during a meteor shower, as a sign that he must return to the secular world and serve it as his very calling. Did he believe in God? At that propitious moment, all he believed in was the message of that star.

With his consummate skill at languages, his training in world affairs, his mother's balanced approach to life and his Buddhist ways, he was readily accepted into the diplomatic corps of Sweden, a country known for nurturing world diplomacy. There, seen as an honest man with a knack for cutting to the heart of matters, he rose quickly. He also possessed an innate ability not just to see both sides of a given question, but an even greater ability to convince each side to see and agree with the other.

His dedication was such that he never got around to marrying. His life was a private and lonely one. Little of it was known because, in his Buddhist modesty, he rarely revealed it.

For years, he appeared at the diplomatic tables of disputing, even warring, sides in Kenya, Niger and other sub-Saharan countries. In Afghanistan and Armenia, too, and the Middle East. There and elsewhere he was able to bring fighting factions to agreement through the double-edged sword he wielded best: compromise.

And so, Ibrahim, now recognized worldwide for his unique talent, was given the name, by the world press, of "The Ombudsman." His friends and fellow diplomats began calling him, simply, "O." Neither he nor anyone who knew him and dealt with him had a cause any longer to be confused about just who Ibrahim al-Abbadi Sokoloff was.

But some degree of confusion was yet to arise within him. Inevitably, he was called upon to sit, for his first time, at the head of a table at which sat the Jews and Arabs of Israel. And Americans and Russians. He was not certain he was ready for this. All eyes, with a mixture of hope and skepticism, were upon "The Ombudsman," not just because of his reputation for fairness but for another compelling attribute: he represented no country and thus was seen to have, in the vernacular, "no dog in the fight." It was thought that, if anyone could settle matters, that would be Ibrahim Sokoloff. It was now 2015 and the bone of contention—there was always such where Jews and Arabs were concerned—was the weighty matter of Iran's burgeoning nuclear arms threat.

The first thing "O" accomplished was semantic; an agreement to call Iran's nuclear enrichment program anything but a threat. That was the easy part. It was now, per Ibrahim, a "bargaining chip," one of low denomination. Getting all parties to agree that Iran was sincere in its guarantee to stop its nuclear proliferation and allow unlimited inspection? That was a more difficult task. To the world powers involved, trust of an enemy who had sworn death to them over and over again, the trust of the free world would not be easy to come by.

Israel and America, if staunch allies, were by no means agreed upon an approach to the problem. President Obama and Prime Minister Netanyahu were at strong odds. If they could not trust one another, how then could the Jews trust an enemy who repeatedly promised to destroy them?

How? Ibrahim unsheathed his well-worn weapon. He insisted that trust could only come with compromise. A giving before any taking. But, it was argued by the allies, what if trust were extended and breached? Would it not be too late to stop the full development—and use—of a nuclear bomb? Yes, argued Prime Minister Netanyahu, but no, argued the doves, seconded by Ibrahim and President Obama and the Russians.

Trust could be gained, even if only by inches, but trust must first be given. And ironclad verification would, of course, have to be included in any agreement. More than once, the combatants threatened to leave the table. But Ibrahim's consoling words brought them back each time, and an agreement, however tentative, was forged; one that took a full three months for all minds to meet and ultimately ratify. It was an agreement marked with the imprimatur of Ibrahim's hand.

Throughout the process of ratification, outrage was expressed on the right side of the aisles in America's congressional halls and in Israel's Knesset. The 2016 presidential election in America might well turn on successful adherence to Ibrahim's words. But the outrage was overcome and the historic document was signed by all parties. Both hawks and doves then lined up on their country's fences to observe its outcome.

At this juncture, not only was there strict adherence to the agreement, Iran soon came to be seen as one of the more peaceful nations in the Mideast, no longer any open talk, at least, of "Death to the infidel!" And it came to be a richer nation, as well, for the prosperity brought about by its new capitulating and capitalistic ways; ways soon followed by other Arab nations fed up with being chronic have-nots.

Ibrahim Sokoloff, the Ombudsman, was given the full credit he deserved for his prominent part in the making of peace with a war-faring nation. And thus he earned the additional sobriquet, "The Peacemaker."

Relations between Israel and its neighbors, of course, continued to simmer, if not, at times, boil. But Ibrahim was, if a peacemaker, hardly a miracle worker.

Exhausted by his lifelong diplomatic duties, Ibrahim al-Abbadi Sokoloff, né Abe Sokoloff, retired at age seventy in 2018. He now resides in the Bhutan monastery where he first began to discover his true self.

The Star of India

I'd been living alone in my garden apartment in Santa Monica for only a few years before I smelled it. Curry. Its inviting scent wafted in from the kitchen window of my new next-door neighbor. He—a well-fed-looking Indian man of, I'd say, near 50—and his grown son had moved in several months earlier, but I had yet to meet either as they were reticent sorts who managed nothing more than a nod when I offered a hello in passing on my way to the laundry room or carport.

By the second time I sniffed that compelling fragrance I was salivating. I'd never smelled Indian food like it. I knew absolutely that, withdrawn though they were, I must find a way to sit at my neighbors' table. But, not even knowing their names, I could hardly invite myself. So I devised an obvious plan. I would introduce myself and invite them to my place for dinner. If they accepted, they'd then be obliged, I was certain, to invite me to theirs.

A slight problem remained. I do not cook. I'll retract that. I cook a little. But my repertoire is extremely limited. I cook up pasta and pan fry steaks, burgers, chops, that's about it. I can toss a salad but not very far beyond lettuce and tomatoes. But I had gained something of a reputation for my baked spare ribs which I first rub with cayenne pepper then coat by dumping them into a paper sack filled with flour, onion, garlic powder and other usually years-old spices dug up from the back of my cupboard.

So I settled on the ribs, along with oven-baked, frozen French fries and coleslaw imported from KFC. Would this meal elicit the curry I was after? The next day I rapped on my neighbor's door. It was opened by the son who spoke not a word, looking at me as if I were handing out religious tracts.

"Hi," I said, sticking out my hand. He eyed it like it was a rotting fish. That didn't stop me. "I'm Ned Cort, your next-door neighbor. I see you moved in recently and wanted to welcome you to our little community."

Still not speaking, he did not take my hand. But nor did he slam the door in my face. "Amit," he said, aiming the word at the rear of his apartment, "please come to the door." With that he walked away, soon, but not very soon, to be replaced by his father who, though wanly smiling, looked at me quizzically as had his son.

"Yes?" said the father, peering at me with suspicion, his face revealing nothing that resembled a greeting. I repeated my little speech. He repeated his blank look, blinking at me all the while. Then, slowly, a smile began to grow on his florid face.

"Ned Cort, you said your name was?" I nodded. "Then I will tell you that my name is Amit Subramaniam and this—Raj, come here—is Raj Gadhavi." Raj approached, still saying nothing. Amit went on. "I was beginning to think everyone here was unfriendly, but I'm very pleased that you have come by to say hello. This is a first since we arrived in America three months ago. Excuse me if I seemed to doubt your purpose here."

"Well, then," I said, "I'm certainly glad I came by. I didn't bake you a cake, Mr. Subra . . ." I stumbled over the name.

". . . maniam," he offered, "but please call me Amit."

"Well, Amit, I would like to welcome you to America by inviting you and Raj to dinner at my place. Would you be willing? Let's say, sixish this coming Friday?"

Amit and Raj looked at each other. Using their eyes to communicate, they indicated they were pleased with the invitation. Amit turned to me and, with a slight bow, said, "We would be delighted to accept your invitation, Nedcort."

I didn't correct him for saying my name as a single word. From that moment forward I was to be Nedcort. "I'll look forward to your coming," I said. Do you have any dietary restrictions?" Again, the quizzical look. "Is there anything you can't eat?"

"None, nothing," he replied, with another big smile. "Oh, I must tell you, Raj is not my son. We are looking forward to Friday . . . at sixish. What is sixish?"

The word came out as "seexeesh." I had to explain. Odd, since he spoke nearly perfect, rather formal English, even if with a strong Indian accent. So Raj was not his son? Whatever, the plan was working.

Friday arrived, along with Amit and Raj promptly at six. As I opened the door, I said to them, with my own little bow and my hands in prayer position, "Namaste!" I felt a little foolish but they seemed pleased that I did so, offering their greeting in return as Raj handed me a six-pack of ice-cold Kingfisher Beer, supposedly, India's best.

The dinner was a huge success. Amit and Raj loved my ribs, devouring nearly a full rack apiece, and said they'd never had better salad than the KFC slaw. I didn't reveal its provenance or the fact that I'd kicked it up some with Stubb's, the same hot sauce I'd drowned the ribs in.

Raj, I learned, was not Amit's lover but his nephew, the only son of Amit's sister who'd recently died back in India. Amit, a bachelor from New Delhi, had invited Raj to join him in pursuit of their fortunes together in America. Amit was a systems engineer, Raj an IT specialist trainee.

The two, who seemed never to talk, never stopped talking that night, their conversation being oiled by my overly-poured martinis followed by two Kingfishers apiece. By the end of the evening you'd think we'd been friends for life. As they walked out, Amit confided that this was one of the best homemade meals he'd ever tasted anywhere, India included.

My plan did indeed work, right down to the curry whose scent had so enticed me. Two days later, when I bumped into Amit in the laundry room, he invited me to join him and Raj at their place for a Saturday dinner. Would it be all right if he cooked a curry for me? It most certainly would. I could almost smell it and taste its complex flavors already.

Came Saturday, I presented Amit with a bottle of Hungarian Debroi

Harslevelu, a fine white that Trader Joe's assured me would go perfectly with any curry.

One dish after another came out of Amit's small kitchen. Exquisitely crisped potato samosas along with miniature lamb kebabs. A basket of crisp papadams and warm naan followed by Amit's self-declared "specialty of the house," his rogan josh, a spicy lamb curry made with yoghurt, saffron, ginger and cardamom. I over-ate then struggled to make room for the dessert of gulab ramun: golden, deep-fried milk balls dipped in sugar syrup.

We exchanged our life stories over postprandial snifters of Courvoisier VSOP, Amit's "special occasion" cognac, which he was saving "for the first person who invited him to dinner in America." I was thankful I had only twenty steps from his door to mine. Two weeks earlier we'd been strangers to each other. Now we were breaking bread together as friends.

Of course, this called for a replay at my table. Trouble was I had nothing more to offer. But I'd somehow convinced Amit and Raj that I was some kind of fabulous cook. A new plan was called for. What I couldn't cook, I could buy.

The day of the dinner, I picked up three monstrous king crab legs, forty bucks a pound, if you please. I'd never spend this much on myself but now I had a reputation to uphold. The fish market fixed me up a wonderful Manhattan clam chowder to go with the pre-cooked legs which required nothing more than a two-minute zap in the micro. On my own, I managed to melt butter dusted with garlic powder, and mix a cocktail sauce of chili sauce and horseradish. And my "homemade" Jello, laced with canned peach halves and maraschino cherries, drew laughing appreciation. Again, my dinner was a huge if slightly drunken success, enough to elicit another dinner invite from Amit. I'd made a good investment.

This time, Amit offered up a delectable, perfectly finished tandoori chicken preceded by a platter of momos, a Northeastern Indian variation on dim sum, accompanied by a fiery red chutney. And another platter of scrumptious pani puri, small, crisp, hollow rounds of bread filled with tamarind paste, potato, onion and chickpeas which I devoured like they were Oreos, again having to nearly roll myself across the walkway to my apartment. On this heavenly night I dreamed I'd died and gone to New Delhi.

Naturally, I invited them back for a brilliantly conceived, Jewish-themed dinner of juicy brisket and farfel preceded by a hearty mushroom-barley soup, finished with a dessert of chocolate-covered halvah and teiglach, crisp dough-balls boiled in honey syrup and covered with shredded coconut; "a recipe passed down to me by my beloved Aunt Eva." The superb meal, every course, of course, purchased from a deli, Izzy's on Wilshire, concluded with the last of Amit's special-occasion Courvoisier, which he'd gratefully brought along. Would they like a hit of my special grass, a remnant of my recent trip to Jamaica? They certainly would. Laughing all the way, we were no longer just friends, we were brothers for life.

And, of course, Amit, not to be outdone, invited me back for another of his Indian extravaganzas, this one consisting of a to-live-for dal soup and more of his samosas, these babies stuffed with ground lamb, plus a simple, utterly delicious butter chicken over basmati rice and his own version of gin-infused mango lassi, India's sui generis of all smoothies. All, followed by a large dollop of kulfi, Indian ice cream that's, well, more than ice cream. With three—or was it four?—Kingfishers in each of us, we wound up sitting on Amit's balcony sipping small—several small—glasses of Ouzo. "Isn't that Greek?" I asked. "Yes," Amit replied, "and these Santo Domingo cigars are Cuban. You got a problem with that?" he added, grinning his huge grin. He'd latched on to several Americanisms by now.

I was more than a little high. But these were my new dear old pals and I was unable to contain the truth I was dying to spill. I'd realized, in my pleasantly foggy state, there was no way I could—or could afford to—keep up this ridiculous charade. I was no great cook. Take away my "famous" spare ribs and I was no cook at all. It was time to spill.

"Amit, my dear fren," I slurred, through a swirling garland of cigar smoke, "got a confession to make." Amit looked at me a little cock-eyed. "Those great meals I been making? Those ribs, the crab legs, the brisket and farfel? Didn't cook one damn thing but the ribs. Not one. Brought 'em all in from restaurants. I'm a fraud, nothin' but a fraud, you know what I'm sayin'?"

The two stared at me throughout my wobbly speech of contrition. Amit, his face growing redder as I spoke, was so frozen by what he was hearing that his Domingo went out. Pointing it at me like it was a laser pen, he roared, "Nedcort, how dare you tell me this. I have been cooking my heart out, making you my very best rogan josh curry, my tandoori chicken and my butter chicken, my pani puri and gulab ramun, and you sit there and tell me you served me restaurant food? You ordered your meals, you didn't make them yourself? What kind of a friend, what kind of brother, what kind of a man are you?" If we hadn't been sitting out-of-doors, he'd have, by now, sucked all the air out of the room. Though I expected some form of rebuttal, I was too stunned by his attack to speak. He stopped abruptly, holding his head and shaking it in disbelief. The silence that followed was deafening. Raj, his head shaking too, turned the other way.

Amit looked at Raj, his face growing redder yet. Raj looked back at Amit. Their eyes and their general demeanor told me they might be about to throw me off the balcony. Then, in unison, they burst out laughing, so hard that Amit literally fell out of his chair, his cigar stub flying over the railing.

I was stunned. And devastated.

Containing himself at last, Amit arose, pulled me off my chair, stood me up and . . . hugged me. "Thank you, my friend, for telling me this because I was about to make the very same speech to you. I have never cooked anything but my silly curry in all the years of my life. All of this: the chicken, the samosas, the pani puri and kebabs and momos and gulab ramun . . . all of it, everything, comes from Star of India, right around the corner. I was too—how do you say?—embarrassment to tell you this but you have relieved me of that awful task. You have shown me that, in lying, at which we both have become so expert, we have become closer. For this, my brother, I thank you."

And that is how it went down on that memorable evening of confessions. A pair of one-dish guys conning each other. Brothers in deceit. We haven't cooked for each other since. The three of us dine together once a month now.

At the Star of India, if not Izzy's.

The Tarnów Gate

The Trouble with Max

Their lives ran in parallel so they never met. Max Foret and Beth Dellinger. Until their lines somehow crossed at an Al-Anon meeting in Culver City on the west side of Los Angeles. His first, dragged there by friends who knew the remorse he never stopped feeling over the loss of his wife, Sofia.

For Max Foret, Al-Anon was a long time in coming. His Sofia had been gone twelve years now, succumbing to addiction swiftly after the sudden and inexplicable onset of her non-stop drinking. This was in Boston, where they lived at the time. Nothing could deter Sofia from the disaster she recognized she was facing. Not a month at a renowned rehab just outside Boston, not long stays at other rehabs, not by attending AA meetings. At her last one, she showed up drunk.

Living with Sofia's alcoholism did not destroy Max's love for her. Nothing could do that. But seeing her destroy herself went a long way to destroying him. He threatened her: Stop drinking or I'll leave you. She didn't stop, he left her. Divorced her, then did what everyone told him was an incredibly brave thing. He moved cross-country to Los Angeles to start a new life alone as a writer for a documentary production company. He was OK until a year later when Sofia was found lying dead in a pool of her own vomit, sprawled among empty vodka bottles and empty cat food cans. Her cat, Tiptoe, was sitting next to her, hungry and crying.

And then Max was *not* OK.

After first discovering Sofia's hidden bottles, Max had visited an Al-Anon meeting at the urging of a friend. Beset with anger, he had to vent it; anger at Sofia for not quitting, and anger at a god he could not bring himself to believe in, a god he blamed for shattering his once idyllic life. But he slipped out of that meeting in disgust because, to him, it was nothing more than a bunch of miserable people talking about their miserable lives living with an alcoholic. Which, of course, was the meeting's very purpose, but he never got that. Later, he came to understand that alcoholism was a disease that some—well over half—of all alcoholics couldn't beat. What he didn't understand was that there

was nothing he could do to stop Sofia's drinking, to save her. Only she could do that. Instead, she quit trying. And he quit Al-Anon.

He would deal with his loss in his own maudlin way. Each evening he'd play the jazz tunes of their almost perfect marriage, and he'd drink to her, in devotion to her, in devotion to his sorrow. Too many fingers of bourbon but an effective catalyst to the self-pity and self-loathing that emerged from the simple fact he'd never seen himself as others saw him, as a "hero" for embarking on a new life. The way he saw it, he'd abandoned Sofia when he might have chosen to stay with her and maybe have found a way to save her. Co-dependency they called it, but he abhorred the very word. Nothing could convince him otherwise.

Picking up the pieces, Max did make a go of things. When his loneliness became unbearable, he met a woman and convinced himself he loved her enough to marry her. But the marriage was a disaster, lasting less than a year. She did not care to share her bed with the specter of Sofia.

So Max found himself alone again. There was his work occupying his head during the day; and Sofia occupying it at night. This was the life Max Foret chose to live.

Beth Dellinger's ex had been a denier who refused to own his drinking problem. Not entirely true. He often owned it, climbing on the wagon only to fall off again and again and again until Beth, like Max, gave her ultimatum. Off, permanently, or divorce. It came up divorce but she did not grieve as Max had. For her this was freedom from the abuse—mostly mental—of a disappointingly childless marriage that had never really worked.

Beth had her own powerful feelings of guilt that she'd contributed to the failure of her marriage as a co-dependent. But she became disabused of this notion when she discovered Al-Anon, quickly taking to it, realizing that, regardless of where the "blame" (she was urged not to use that term) lay, she had to accept herself and move on. Alcoholism belonged to the alcoholic. You can start them but you can't stop them. Once she understood this she became, within a year, a sponsor to two other women. For her, Al-Anon worked.

Beth and Max, that night after the meeting, were introduced to each other by the mutual friend who had brought Max there. The discreet friend left them alone to talk with one another. Beth did most of the talking. Max, during his two minutes in the meeting, had barely managed to mention Sofia. Wordsmith though he was, he'd struggled when called upon. For years he'd tried to write their story as a play, a novel, a poem, but couldn't. He'd spelled it out on paper halfway but couldn't bring himself to speak it aloud.

It had been mentioned in the meeting that newcomers might wish to seek out a sponsor. So Max, based on their brief earlier conversation, asked Beth if she'd consider taking him on. She'd looked at Max, liked what she saw and had been touched by his words, few though they were. But she had to tell him he needed a male sponsor. The intimacies revealed during the working of the twelve steps made it so. She also said that, while she could not be his sponsor, it might be fine if they'd simply meet for, say, coffee or lunch. Just to talk.

Max, blinking, looked at Beth and said, innocently, "Wouldn't that be sort of like a date?"

"I didn't think of it that way," she replied, flinching at her lie, "but now that you mention it, maybe it would be 'sort of like' a date. Still want to meet?" An imp was hiding behind her reddened face.

"Yeah," Max heard himself say. "Sure, I'd like that."

"Good," said Beth. "Tomorrow's Sunday. Brunch OK? Back on the Beach, you know the place? That OK?"

"Yeah, sure," said Max. And the "meeting" was on. The date. He hadn't been on one in years. He told himself he wasn't nervous about it but, not meaning to, he put his pajama bottoms on inside out that night, and almost broke his toothbrush working it too hard the next morning. Beth was, he had to admit, a nice-looking woman. And there was something right about her, something more than looks. He wondered what Sofia would think of her.

To Beth this was a date. What was wrong with that? She was interested in his story, never mind that he was a nice-looking man. Needy. But aren't most men? Was that part of his attraction?

At Back on the Beach Cafe next morning Beth spotted Max waiting for her at a table on the sand next to the low fence that surrounded the beach dining area. He's feeding scraps to his dog tied to the fence next to him, she thought. He brings his dog on his first date? . . . the dog has to be his focus—live and learn.

She had approached from behind so he didn't notice her until she said, "Nice boxer, Max," at which he popped up to greet her, knocking his chair over backward.

"Uh, hi, Beth. Good morning," he said, righting his chair. "It sure is. Wish it was mine."

"Right," said Beth, reddening as she had the day before.

Beth had asparagus quiche, Max, a Western omelet. And they talked. And talked some more. Though Max, for once, wanted to talk about himself, he was more comfortable getting Beth to talk.

Beth, since her split, lived alone in what Max took to be a nice home because she said it was north of Montana, the priciest part of Santa Monica. She was a lighting director for both films and the stage and was apparently in steady demand. In the two years since her divorce she'd met many men, most through eHarmony and Tinder, but never through Al-Anon. Nothing serious, though. She asked Max to talk about what brought him to Al-Anon but he said, no, he just wanted to talk about her.

Beth had heard such before as a ploy to impress, but somehow, coming from Max, it rang true. So she went on talking. And Max was hungry to listen, especially to this woman.

Beth, wondering what kind of crowbar could open this man up, stopped abruptly in mid-sentence to say, "OK, Max, your turn."

It took him a moment before he spoke. She listened, he spoke some more. When they finished their meal, an hour and three cups of coffee later, Max, realized he didn't want this date, or whatever it was, to end. He suggested they walk across the wide expanse of beach down to the water's edge. Beth thought it an excellent idea, it being such a perfect day, which pretty much every day in Santa Monica is. Carrying their sneakers, they walked down to the lapping water. continuing on into the gentle waves all the way up to their knees.

It was only noon but, with more to say, they found themselves strolling south nearly two miles along the water's edge, all the way to the Santa Monica Pier where they bought custard cones and never stopped talking all the way back to the Beach.

Max got into his personal history, his oft-times quirky ways and more of the thing he didn't mean to talk about, Sofia, although, with this woman, he suddenly did want to talk about Sophia. Was it right to do this? Wasn't talking about his woman to another woman a major turn-off? But Beth was drawing Sofia out of him. She invited him to say more.

And he accepted the invitation.

"Sofia and I had fifteen years of what I saw as bliss. She lived most of her life in Poland where she was born, but never seemed to talk about our happiness though I was certain she felt it.

"We'd have a glass of wine before dinner, usually in front of the fireplace. These were the best moments. We'd talk on and on and almost forget that dinner was on the stove. These were the moments I cherished, the ones that made me the happiest. It was that way for years. It was perfect.

"Then one day I discovered some near-empty vodka bottles hidden in the back of a cleaning closet. And more of them were stuffed into the backs of cabinets. That was my wake-up call. And then it was over almost before it began. She hardly tried to hide the empties. Overnight—it seemed to me—she went from being a casual drinker to. . ."

Max had to stop. His jaws were clamped shut. Tears were welling up in his eyes, which he had to clear with an embarrassed swipe of his sleeve. He went on. "The rest—the ER runs, the stomach pumping, the stitches after the falls—is too ugly to talk about. Everyone said I was the last to know about her 'little drinking problem.' That's what I kept on calling it. Little drinking problem. But it was too late. Way too late. And then—as they say—she died."

Max had never revealed this history to anyone. Till now. And now he couldn't stop. When he finished, Beth's soft gray eyes stayed locked on his. Neither spoke for several minutes. Then they continued walking along the sand. He wanted to hold Beth's hand; wanted to hold her and be held. But he held himself back. From the set of her face, he could see questions welling up in her.

"What one thing's troubling you the most about Sofia, Max?"

"Troubling me? Not one thing, two things. First, I abandoned my wife. I divorced her and left her to die. I knew she was going to die and still I left her. And she died. And I'm still thinking maybe, if I couldn't stop her drinking, I could at least have kept her from dying. If I was there."

"Kept her from dying for how long? Only she could do that. Your leaving her didn't kill her, Max, alcohol did. Sofia killed herself. You're feeling guilt you needn't feel." Beth meant this but did not mean to say it. It was the truth but she was way out of line for saying it. She hadn't known this troubled man for more than a few hours but her strong feeling for him had got the best of her. How stupid could she have been? Why, she said to herself, had she said this?

Walking back to their cars she started to apologize but he held up his hand and stepped away from her. He was literally biting his lip before stating, in slow angry words, "Where do you get off telling me how I should feel? That I'm not guilty? You can't tell me how to feel. I know what I did and I don't need you or anyone else apologizing for me. I don't even know why I told you all this. My mistake. Sorry. I'll see you around." He sped to his car, slammed its door and drove away without looking back.

Beth stood there, stunned, mortified. And angry. At herself, of course, but at Max too, because, she told herself again, whatever she'd said, dammit, she'd spoken the truth. Would she ever see him again? Wait a minute. He'd said there were two things that were troubling him. Two questions he had. But he only spoke of the first, the abandonment. She'd find out. She sensed he'd get over it, then she'd see him again, hopefully soon. But she didn't see him again. Max didn't call. No second "date." And he never showed up at Al-Anon again. Months went by.

Then years.

The outcome of their sole "date" and the time elapsed since, would suggest they'd forget about each other. Which they pretty much did. Until a few weeks after the second anniversary of their chance meeting.

*   *   *

Max Foret was now writing and directing for a different production company. He was in New York this evening directing a biopic on Steven Sondheim at the theater on East 43rd named after the famed playwright. While standing on stage, waiting for Sondheim himself to arrive, a small klieg light came crashing down from the fly loft, landing near Max, who was to interview Sondheim.

A woman came rushing down from her control box at the back of the theater. "Jeezuz, I'm sorry," she shouted, as she approached the stage. "Were you hurt?"

Max stared at her. Not missing a beat, he replied, "Yeah, a couple years ago, by you. Did you do that on purpose?" he said. But he was smiling when he said it.

"Max! Max Foret? Oh, my God. I'm so sorry. I am really sorry. I've been hanging lights for fifteen years and that has never ever happened before. Not once."

"It was an accident, Beth. Forget it. Can we talk after the shoot today?" And they did talk. At the Blue Bar in the Algonquin around the corner from the theater. They talked about the coincidence of bumping into each other like this in New York; then about what a small world their world was. And about what happened two years earlier.

"I'm the one who should be apologizing, Beth. I can hardly

remember what you said that upset me so much back then. After I blew up though, I thought you'd never want to see me again. And I guess I just let it all slip away, and went back to being me. To being sorry for me. Shut in, shut away. But you know something, Beth?" Max looked left and right before he spoke again. "I was an idiot."

"You were an idiot."

"Yeah. What have you been up to?"

"Me? Very little. Mostly working, which is what I do best. But you know something, Max? I thought for half a second we had something good going."

"We did."

"You think?"

"Yeah, we did. Any chance of, uh, getting it going again?"

Before answering, Beth played with her cocktail napkin, twisting it around the stem of her glass. "Did you ever get back to Al-Anon?"

"No. And you're asking because—?

"Did you ever resolve your abandonment issue?"

"Still working on it."

"There's something I remember, Max. Something you said. Don't know why I remember it, but I do."

"What's that?"

"You said there were two things troubling you. One was the abandonment of your wife. You never got around to mentioning the other. You recall what it was?"

Max took a long pull from his Heinekens before answering. "Yeah, I do. It was a question: 'Why?' I know what Sofia did, I know she couldn't stop doing it but I have never been able to figure out why she did it. She could never say why. And not knowing why, she committed suicide by drowning herself in a bottle. That's what's troubled me and always will. I've never found an answer."

They sat silently for a while, Beth waited till Max's jaw unclenched. Leaning toward him, her hand now on his, she said, "Maybe there is no answer."

"No answer," he said, repeating her words. Then he asked a question. "How can there be no answer? I know I left her but, in a way, she left me.

She gave up. Maybe she didn't know why. But she sure as hell never said why."

"I'm sorry, Max," said Beth. She wanted to hold him. He looked so empty. She wanted to pull his head to her shoulder.

"No answer," he repeated.

They were silent again, her hand still in his, his head hanging. Then he lifted it and said, "You still in Santa Monica?"

"Yeah. You?"

"Yeah."

"Feel like dinner?" he said.

The Tarnów Gate

Hermes Is Missing

Bertha Sam Norris had been with the Neudeckers going on thirty-two years now. She wasn't the best washer of floors, even she'd have to admit that, and Eleanor Neudecker never let her forget it. But Bertha Sam could make up a bed so's you could "bounce a quarter off the sheets," something Connor Neudecker had never stopped noting, him having once been in the Army from whence the phrase arose.

Bertha Sam, by now, family to the Neudeckers, was eventually "willed" to their daughter Melanie and her husband Charles when the empty-nester Neudeckers downsized to a condo in West Palm. Which was fine with Bertha Sam as she'd practically raised Melanie from birth, treating her far better than Melanie's mother ever had.

But the loving care supplied by Bertha Sam was never quite appreciated by Melanie, who tended to take after her irascible mother. Particularly in the way she ignored her own daughter, Dana, whose upbringing she tended to leave to Bertha Sam.

At this point of her life, the arthritic Bertha Sam could no longer care for Dana to the degree she once had for Melanie. The long walks in the park she'd taken with Melanie were now nothing short of torturous with Dana in tow. So much so that she'd had to beg off them, much to the annoyance of "Miss Melanie," the appellation by which Bertha Sam always addressed her.

Bertha Sam was no longer the excellent bedmaker she'd once been either. Nor the excellent cleaner. Though she always did her best, her best couldn't touch what she'd once done for Melanie's parents.

Now, you'd think Melanie would have understood Bertha Sam's shortcomings, cut her some slack for her age and for the obvious fact that Bertha Sam had devoted the best part of her life to the Neudecker family. But such understanding was simply not there.

These days, everything Bertha Sam did drew a snide reproof from Miss Melanie. It was, "I hope you noticed the crust you left when you cleaned the stove, Bertha Sam." Or, after little Dana was bathed, "Who's going to clean the ring you left in the tub, Bertha Sam?" When Bertha Sam had trouble dusting the top shelves in the kitchen, Miss Melanie had no trouble spotting this discrepancy and putting her down for it.

Bertha Sam did not allow her simmering anger over Melanie's off-putting behavior to surface. She desperately hoped to retire in a few years but was not at all certain that Melanie and her oblivious husband Charles would ever consider a proper settlement. She'd been working for them six years now and the man had never once used her name. Probably didn't even know it.

Bertha Sam would have quit by now had she been able to. But her $27,000 yearly income hardly allowed her to set retirement funds aside. She'd once loved her job but frankly, for many years now, she detested it.

And it was then that the Hermes incident occurred.

Melanie, rushing to dress for a formal dinner, could not find her beloved Hermes Birkin evening bag. Frantic, after searching through the oversized Victorian home her parents had bought her as a wedding present, she had to settle for the Louis Vuitton that hadn't cost a tenth of the Hermes. This had discomfited her no end at the dinner. Searching again the next day, she still could not find the Hermes, gifted to her by Charles on her thirtieth birthday. The thought now entered her mind that, impossible as it seemed, it had to be Bertha Sam who had taken it. Stolen it. There was no way Bertha Sam would ever do such a thing, Melanie told herself. Or would she?

Sleeping on it, Melanie had an incredibly realistic dream in which she saw Bertha Sam walking in the park with Dana, and the Hermes was boldly hanging from her left shoulder. Next morning, upon awakening, she was convinced that Bertha Sam had indeed stolen her Hermes handbag, the very best in her closet.

Still not fully trusting her instincts, she made yet another careful search of her home, even scouring the attic where it could not possibly be. The bag was gone. Not lost. Stolen. And who else could have stolen it but . . . Bertha Sam? Unlikely as it seemed to mistrust this longtime family retainer, it was now time to confront her. Melanie's doubts resolved, this had to be done.

Bertha Sam was scrubbing the master bath toilet when Melanie walked in on her. The caretaker immediately noticed the ominous tight-jawed look her employer was giving her. "Bertha Sam," said Melanie, "please come into the bedroom."

Bertha Sam did as she was told. "What's wrong, Miss Melanie?" she said.

"I won't mince words, Bertha Sam. Did you or did you not steal my Hermes handbag?"

Bertha Sam did not reply. Not for a long moment. An incredulous, open-mouthed look replaced her normally benign one.Her reply was choked. "No, ma'am, I did not. I could never . . . How could you . . . No, Miss Melanie, no. I did not steal your purse."

"Well, I believe otherwise, Bertha Sam. That handbag cost $28,000. I have every reason to believe that you did indeed steal it. You are fired, Bertha Sam. I want you to leave right now, this minute. And if that bag is not back here by tomorrow, other consequences will follow. The police will be informed. Do you understand me?"

Bertha Sam, still looking stunned beyond belief, dropped her scrub brush, smoothed down her crisp white uniform, and left.

Three days later, searching for her Bottega Veneta carry-on, Melanie spotted her Hermes birthday bag tucked away behind it. exactly where she must have placed it. On sight of it she slammed the luggage closet door, not wanting even to look at the costly bag. More than embarrassed, she was mortified. She'd told everyone that Bertha Sam had stolen it, had been dismissed as a result, and would be prosecuted. And now she'd have to apologize to the blameless woman and reinstate her.

Or would she?

Perhaps she would just forget about the whole thing. The matter was ended. But a new scheme snuck up upon her. She would hide the bag, report it as stolen and collect a full payout from the insurance company. Brilliant. So that was that.

Or was it?

Bertha Sam, later on the day of her firing, sat in her kitchen staring at Miss Melanie's precious bag perched on the table before her. The irony of its being worth more than a year's wages wasn't lost on her. Smiling, she poured herself a celebratory glass of iced ginger ale, added a few fingers of Canadian Club, and continued to both smile and stare.

The Hermes "retirement fund" was worth many times more than what she might have received had she actually retired; even when you deducted the $28 she'd paid for the knock-off she'd bought from the trunk of a Boyle Heights seller's Chrysler 500. She was certain the bag would fool Miss Melanie who always tended to see what she expected to see. Or would be too embarrassed to even look at when she found it.

Bertha Sam knew how Miss Melanie's mind worked, guessed that she'd report it stolen. She could just see the look on Miss Melanie's face when the insurance company informed her she owned a fake, a cheap phony.

And Bertha Sam could only wish she could be there to see Mr. Charles' face when Melanie confronted him about his precious goddamn birthday gift.

The Pitch

Chris Sinclair and Mickey Greenbaum, growing up together in West Los Angeles, were practically one person. Best of pals at Fairfax High, their pet names for each other were Chris's "Salami" for Mickey, Mickey's "Ham" for Chris.

Mickey was the Lions' trainer to Chris's star fullback, stage crew boss to Chris's star turn as Lennie in the senior play, "Of Mice and Men," and an ad salesman on the school paper, The Colonial Gazette, edited by Chris. Hell, Mickey was happy to snag the stray coed who hadn't made it upstream, those four years, into Chris's arms. Chris graduated with highest honors. Mickey

. . . graduated.

That was then, now is thirty years later and things, they have changed. Both work at Fox Searchlight. Mickey's name pops up often now, high on the credits crawls while Chris's name appears low. Preceded by the legend, "Story by," which is Hollywoodese for doing the idea but not the heavy hauling, the writing.

Now don't read this wrong. Chris is a more than decent writer. If he's having a Sahara of a dry spell, it's because he hasn't been dry one day in the past ten years. A little problem they used to call dipsomania. But now, it's a tocsin call to quit that Chris seems unable to hear. Without Mickey,

Chris would be history at Fox. So why does Mickey still have Chris's back? Because, well, they're still . . . Ham and Salami.

Today, we find Chris at a door whose brass nameplate reads "Michael C. Green, Vice-President in Charge of Production." No one knocks on Michael C. Green's door because one must be buzzed in by Mary Ann Phister, Mickey's personal assistant, who's as friendly as a gallows hangman. Chris has always had an open invitation to enter Mickey's inner sanctum, but the invitation is beginning to wear a little thin.

So Chris enters. Reeking.

"Hiya, Salami," says Chris, tripping slightly over the effects of his last two bourbons and the two-inch height of the dead bear pelt that fronts Mickey's football field of a desk.

Mickey's nose scrunches up. "Jeezuz, Chris, I can smell you from here. Are you drunk?"

"No, Michael, my friend, I am not drunk. OK, had a small one at lunch, but . . ."

"You're talking to me, Chris. You been drinking lunch. Look, man, I love you to pieces but you are killing yourself with your fucking booze and you're killing your work and, if you tried a little harder, you could kill the longest friendship both of us have ever had, I am not shitting you. Now, what's on your mind?"

Look, Mick, I've been working—I mean really working—on a killer script. Best work I've ever done, believe me. Please, gimme your ear for a minute. One minute, all I ask."

"Do not beg, Christopher. Do not do that with me. Look, you caught me at a bad time. I'm having lunch with C.K. in half an hour. We're looking at the new season, polishing a power point next week for the boys upstairs. I'm sorry, Chris, but I just don't have time for your pitch today. Maybe next week . . ."

"No, no, Mickey, this is a perfect concept for your 'boys upstairs.' Feature film all the way, no straight-to-TV crap. I swear, you hear this, you are going to fall down weeping for joy. While you're pissing your pants laughing, promise. It's got pathos, suspense, humor, belly-laughs, tears; it's poignant, it's heartbreaking, it's . . . it's good, Mick, I swear it, it's good."

A long silence follows during which Michael C. Green, Vice-President, Production, his teeth grinding, glares at his oldest friend. After he lets out an exasperated breath, he rolls his eyes up to his wood-paneled ceiling, shakes his tonsured head, leans back into his six-thousand dollar Herman Miller Eames Executive Work Chair, throws his Ferragamo alligator skin elevators up, with difficulty, onto his desk, folds his hands over his fifty-two inch belly, shakes his head again, and says, "Fifteen minutes."

"Thank you, Michael." Pacing back and forth, Chris begins his pitch. "I call it—working title—'Resurrection.'"

"They just did 'Resurrection.'"

"OK, 'Absolution.'"

"This some kinda Catholic movie?"

"Redemption."

"Of what, Amex points?"

"Revulsion?"

"Which is what I'm beginning to feel, Christopher. Fuck the title, just gimme the bones."

"OK, OK. This good-looking guy, Richard, marries his dumpy high school sweetheart, Sheila. They lead a quiet, Saturday-dinner-and-movies existence for years till, one day in their young life, Richard's best buddy, Mel, opens a bar and their whole life changes. Richard starts drinking more and more at Mel's place, starts cheating on his wife and falls madly in love. Wants a divorce but Sheila won't give him one so, guess what, he kills Sheila, murders her, and—listen up—he gets away with it."

"How?"

"He gets away with it. Don't know yet. So now he marries this new love, Janine. Fast forward fifteen years . . . Mickey? Mick? Your eyes are shut."

"I'm listening, I'm listening."

"So, fast forward fifteen years and Janine, who turned out to be a hopeless alky, drinks herself to death. Or maybe it wasn't the booze that did her in, you get my meaning? I mean, who knows what goes on in Richard's twisted mind, right? Now Richard is once again alone and hungry for love. To escape his 'grief'—whatever—he books a singles cruise to Tahiti and, sure enough, on it he meets this gorgeous woman, Carol. A few hours . . ."

"Chris?" interrupts Mickey, taking an exaggerated look at his oversized Patek Phillipe.

"Stay with me one more second, Mick. A few hours strolling the deck, a few candlelight dinners and now Richard and Carol are curled up in the sack. But it's not just a shipboard romance, Richard's in love again. For real. I mean fucking smitten. He and Carol get . . ."

"Chris?"

". . . married and . . ."

"Chris, for crissake, is this guy a serial killer, a serial wedder . . . what? Where's the arc? Does this 'concept' of yours have an ending?"

"I'm there, Mick. Richard and Carol get married, OK? But it turns out that Carol is the resurrection of Sheila!"

"Who's Sheila?"

"His first wife. C'mon, Michael."

"OK, OK. But it's getting way too woo-woo for me. You got an old love, a new love, a newer love who used to be the old love. I'm confused here. And where's the fare-thee-well, Chris. Get to the goddamn end."

"I will if you let me, Mickey. If I had an ending. But I'm working on it. So whaddaya think, Mick? Good enough to pitch the Tower? Mickey? Mick? Your eyes are closing again."

Another long silence. Mickey's eyes have closed, but he ends the silence with a softly spoken, "I like it."

"You like it?"

"Yeah, sit down. Let's talk about it some more."

"I thought you were having lunch with C.K."

"Yeah, well that's actually tomorrow. Anyhow, your little tale just might work after all."

"You really think so?"

"Yeah, but it needs something."

"Like what something?"

"Like a thread to weave it all together"

"A thread. What thread?"

"Lola."

"Lola? Who's Lola?"

"My wife's dog."

The silence is now initiated by Chris. "What, Michael, does Carmelita's dog have to do with my 'Resurrection?'"

"What does Lola have to do with your movie?"

"Yes, Mick, that's what I just asked you."

"Well, Christopher, I'm going to be honest with you. Carmy loves her little black Scottie more than anything else in the world. Including, maybe, me. Anyhow, she made me promise I'd find a way to honor her little bitch by doing a film—a documentary—about her. But who the fuck will pay to see a doc about a Scottie? Now, I was thinking that maybe we could weave Lola into your little story, you see what I mean?"

"No."

"Carmy would love it and I wouldn't have to pitch the Tower on doing a doc no one wants to see, see? Jeezuz, I hate documentaries!"

"Mickey, Mickey, how am I supposed to 'weave' Carmelita's Lola into what is basically a murder mystery-slash-thriller?"

"Fala."

"Fala? President Roosevelt's Fala? What the fuck does Fala have to do with . . ."

"They're both black Scotties, Chris. Hey, my friend, you're the writer. Find a way. You wanted to write a movie for once, not just pitch another concept? Then write it. You need a writer to work with you? I'll give you one. But, if you want this to be in the package I present upstairs next Friday, then you damn well better have at least 120 pages on my desk by next Thursday. Now get outta here and get busy, buddy." Mickey rises as he's saying this, then adds, with a loving whack on Chris's tush, "Love you, Ham! Ciao! Bye-bye!"

With that, Mickey buzzes Mary Ann to lower the drawbridge for whoever is next on Michael C. Green's extremely busy schedule.

Chris Sinclair now has exactly six days to script, not just conceive, his screenplay. He spends the first two days in a couple bottles of Old Forester, searching for inspiration, the writing kind, not the mere concepting kind. He does not have to remind himself that concepts are as rife in Tinseltown as hookers on Sunset Boulevard.

Not finding what he seeks, Chris panics. In his agitas he goes out and gets good and goddamn drunk. Which he stays till Wednesday morning. Further panicked when he awakens to realize he has just twenty-four hours to write his doggy script, he writes. And writes and writes and writes. And finishes "Lola and Fala" at exactly 9:30 Thursday morning. With no time to edit it, he makes a mad dash to Mickey's office, blows past Mary Ann, slaps down the pages on Mickey's desk, and does not even say hello to the dumbfounded Mickey before rushing out to get good and goddamn drunk again.

Michael C. Green and his co-producing partner, Sterling Fingerman, take their meeting with the upstairs boys in the Tower. Among their offerings is a script about a Scottish Terrier name of Lola, brought aboard President Roosevelt's yacht, the Potomac, to be a companion and possible mate for FDR's world-famous Scottie, Fala. The film is to be narrated—first-person voice-over—by Scarlett Johansson as Lola, with Channing Tatum as Fala. Billy Bob Thornton, Michael insists, would make an excellent President Roosevelt.

In the climactic scene, a horrific storm blows up and sweeps the wheelchair-bound president overboard. But, just as a lifesaver ring is thrown into the roiling waters, Lola and Fala bravely dive in and nose the lifesaver over to the floundering president, saving his life until the sailors can reach him. FDR later presents the pair with the Presidential Medal of Freedom, America's highest civilian award. Fala licks Lola's face, sky cam pulls up and out to a far shot. End of picture.

The Tower loves "Lola and Fala." The film gets made.

At the film's previews, everyone is cheering and bawling throughout the climactic rescue scene in which the action is accompanied by a blaring concert version of Jimi Hendrix' Star Spangled Banner, orchestrated by John Williams. The film is runner-up to the 2014 Cannes Film Festival's Palme d'Or winner, the Turkish film, "Winter Sleep." It grosses an impressive $42 million over its opening weekend and is later nosed out for best picture Oscar by "12 Years a Slave."

On a sad note, Lola, played by Carmelita's real life Lola at the loving suggestion of Mickey, drowned during the filming.

After which, Carmelita filed for divorce.

Venganza

(for Lis Caballero)

As soon as Berto opened the white Caddy's door, he recognized the man in the driver's seat. Rubén "Q" Quintano, never mind he hadn't seen him in fourteen years. You don't forget a face like that. Long, pock-marked, narrow, mean eyes, lantern jaw. The man was tall for a Salvadoran; above six feet. A triangle of three dots graced the web between his right thumb and forefinger, the prison sign of Mi Vida Loca, My Crazy Life. Next to his eye was a small X, the mark of someone who had killed before; a blooded member of Mara Salvatrucha, the dreaded MS-13.

Berto never expected to face the big man again, but here he was not two feet from him, a specter of a past he wished to forget but could not. A shiver coursed through his slim body.

Adalberto "Berto" Estevez, working the 8-to-4 shift at the valet parking desk under the marquee of Las Vegas's Internationale Resort and Casino that day, gathered himself. He did not let on to the don that he knew him. Snapping his fingers, he waved at his bellhop son, Manny, standing nearby, to bring up a cart for Quintano's bags. He wasn't sure Manny would recognize Quintano, but Manny's eyes narrowed the moment he saw him. Berto, behind Q's back, put his finger to his lips to stop his son from saying anything.

Quintano had five bags, not counting the light blue aluminum attaché case he insisted on carrying himself. Berto handed Quintano his parking stub, looking right at him. It was obvious Q did not recognize him. As Berto drove the Caddy away to park it below, he was distinctly aware of the scent of marijuana, a scent that had always defined Quintano. Three days later, Q, never having left the hotel, pressed a hundred-dollar bill into Berto's hand before returning to the airport, then on to his sprawling home in San Salvador's wealthiest community, Santa Elena.

This scene would be repeated every three months for the next year. The high-ranking MS-13 courier, no longer making his rounds in a sweaty undershirt, was now dressed expensively in designer clothes, always with a panama hat tilted low over his shifty eyes. And he would never fail to arrive in a white

rental Caddy with a load of bags including the aluminum attaché he'd always carry straight to his room himself.

Berto knew what the briefcase contained. Stacks of Franklins, probably half a million, maybe more. Had to be. He knew what Q was up to because, after all these years at the Internationale, he knew all about the well-dressed mules from Colombia, Guatemala and Honduras, and from Berto's native El Salvador. They were not mere delivery men. Anyone could do that, women included. The Quintano types bring up suitcases full of drug money to launder at the Internationale and other major casinos in Las Vegas. They'd deposit the cash at the casino cage, be comped for everything including their penthouse suite, gamble maybe a hundred thou over several days and graciously allow the house their fifteen percent. Then they'd cash in and fly back home after pocketing cash for the substantial balance, bleached as white as the resort's finest linens; a win-win for the cartels, for the casinos.

Las Vegas, Nevada, U.S.A. The biggest laundromat in the world.

The moment he saw Quintano at the I, Adalberto Estevez could not get his mind off him. Especially off what he would like to do to him. Venganza—vengeance—was all he could think about. His thoughts drifted back to the day he first faced this *hijo de puta* at the Estevez groceria in San Salvador's Santa Benito district. The shop had been in Adalberto's family for three generations. Until the day "Q" walked in to offer protection from the rival gangs taking over the local turf. But the cure was worse than the bite. No gang was more cruel, more vicious than Quintano's MS-13—the Maras. In the name of protection, the Maras were extorting every shopkeeper in town. Worse, they were selling drugs in the open, threatening, then committing violence upon anyone foolish enough to defy them. Quintano, the local Mara honcho, only occasionally showed his face to a shopkeeper after he'd first faced him. His tattooed thugs would do the collecting. Any resistance was met at first with vandalism. Slashed tires, smashed windows, fire-bombed cars. Then it escalated to mayhem and, often enough, murder. Of course, it did no good to complain to the authorities because they looked the other way, bribed by the gangs to do so.

Adalberto put up with Quintano for two whole years. What else could he do? He paid his dues until he could afford no more, take no more. He had no choice but to place a sign in his window, Se Vende—For Sale. Same for his modest, two-bedroom home. But there were no takers. Who would be crazy enough to live and work in the midst of such Mara domination? Berto feared, too, that the MS-13 would soon conscript his nine-year-old son Manuelo. And how could he allow his "happy accident," his one-year-old Dahlia, to grow up in such a toxic atmosphere where rape was seen by the cholos not as a crime but as a privilege?

The year was 1994. Time to leave.

Time to go to America.

But America was not Adalberto's dream. The wiry little grocer was comfortable in the life he and his Estela had made for themselves in San Salvador. This was their home and they loved it. Or did, until the maldito gangs wrested it from them. Honest Salvadorans were leaving in large numbers, the poorer ones atop La Bestia, the refugee trains headed north to the United States.

No, moving was not a dream for Adalberto. It was a necessity.

With only what would fit in his orange delivery van, with its beautifully hand-painted Tienda de Estevez decorating each side, now painted over so as not to attract the attention of hijackers on the road, Berto, his dear wife, Estela and their Manuelo and Dahlia, made their way north. The shortest route to the States was the road along the Gulf Coast to Matamoros, just across the Rio Grande from Brownsville, Texas, nearly fifteen hundred miles away. It took them three days, staying at cheap motels or camping out under the stars along the way.

Near the end of their journey, in San Fernando, about a hundred miles from Matamoros, the van's radiator sprang a leak. The engine, overheating, seized up. Adalberto could not afford a new one and was still short of the amount he'd need for their passage to Brownsville, so he sold the van for a fraction of its value to the garage man. He found another man—there were several such coyotes tracking this route to El Paso—willing to take them north in his moving truck and smuggle them across for the equivalent of twelve thousand U.S. dollars; all the money Berto had. The deal was made and Berto paid the man, Rafael, in cash. But, less than halfway to Matamoros, the man stopped and ordered the four of them out of his truck. Adalberto, incensed, demanded the return of his money, but Rafael ignored his plea and took off, leaving them standing there, helpless. They had little more with them than six hundred pesos—about forty U.S. dollars—pinned into Estela's dress. This plus a package of tortillas, a few papusas, a container of crema and a less than full half gallon bottle of water as they began their trek, on foot now, and on hostile back roads, to the border. Berto had an old gun tucked away in the food sack but never got a chance to use it. And probably wouldn't have, never having shot a man before.

What he and his family would do when—and if—they got to the border, he did not know.

The family barely survived its two days under the brutal Mexican sun. Near the end of the second day, an old woman, a gringa Texas rancher heading north in a Ford F-350 diesel full of alfalfa, spotted them on the roadside. Hearing no more than a minute of Adalberto's story, she stopped him, tucked the lot of them under the alfalfa and drove straight up through Matamoros, then across the Rio Grande, waving at the border guard like the old friend he'd become, and on to the Valley Baptist Medical Center in Brownsville. Though half their remaining water had been preserved for Dahlia, their precious little niña had come very close to dying from severe heat stroke and dehydration. The kindly woman,

Abigail Johnston, had saved Dahlia's life; probably all their lives.

Miss Abby, as they came to call her, did more. She took them in to her home and took it upon herself to sponsor their efforts to remain in America where, due to Congress recently having passed an immigration reform act, they would soon be granted amnesty. A year later, with Miss Abby's help—her favorite cousin was a minor executive at the Internationale—Adalberto and Estela found work together there, he as a parking valet, she as a housekeeper. Six years later, Manuelo would join them on the I staff as a bellhop. The four—citizenship hopefully in their future—took on "American" names: Bert (the "o" would soon find its way back to his name), Stella, Manny. Dahlia—their little flower—would retain her name. And their new niña would be called Abigail—Abby—for the angel who'd rescued them from the Mexican sun.

Even after all these years, Berto, almost daily, swore venganza against Rubén Quintano. Vengeance for forcing his family to forsake their home country. And especially for the near-death —the near-murder, as he saw it— of Dahlia. He could not let his hatred of the man go. Men like Quintano and the pitiless Rafael deserved to rot in hell. Someday he would meet up with this *puta*, Quintano. A picture formed in his mind of his sticking a knife through the big man's wicked heart. But Berto's violence was only in his mind. He would find another way to make Quintano pay for nearly destroying him and his family.

Vengeance, he knew, belonged to God, but, for Quintano's unforgiveable acts, Berto Estevez was determined to make vengeance his own.

He and Manny, biding their time, carefully observed Quintano's movements during each visit. Quintano was a man of habit. On arrival. Berto would alert his son to attend to him. Manny would then wheel Q's bags alongside him, first to the VIP check-in desk where the attendants would fawn over the high roller, then up to his penthouse suite, Q never letting go of his precious attache case.

On Quintano's second visit, Manny got up nerve to mention the attaché to the big man.

"Señor Quintano, I notice you carry that briefcase by yourself. I'm guessing it contains money. I hope you don't mind my suggesting that, for your safety and its safety, if you mean to gamble with it, you might walk it directly to the Cage when you arrive. Security will accompany you if you'd like."

A bold statement, coming from a mere bellhop. Bellhops weren't supposed to notice, much less mention, guests' attaché cases full of money. But Quintano liked the boldness of this earnest and efficient little bellhop.

"Look at me, Manny," he said. Manny looked at Q. "You're quite the observant little hombre. Fuckin cocky, I'd say. But I guess you got my best interests at heart. You wanna know why I don't walk my money to the Cage?" I don't feel like walking a half fuckin mile to get there, that simple. Look, hombrecito, I bank it when I decide, comprende?"

Quintano's menacing look faded to a grin as he pinched Manny's cheek. Hard. "Now let's get these fuckin bags up to my suite, OK? Anyhow, who needs Security, I got you." Quintano roared at his own little joke.

Once in his rooms, the big man complained about his "miserable fuckin flight" from San Salvador, never mind he flew First Class. He talked endlessly about how hard he'd been working. He always took a long, hot shower or Jacuzzi followed by a half-hour nap. After, he drank half a bottle of tequila with maybe a splash of Tic Tack he brought from home. Finally, he'd leave to have a steak—always a steak, a T-bone—at Clouds, the posh grille atop the Internationale. And only then would he head to the Cage, his hand clamped tightly to the handle of his attaché case except when it sat between his legs as he ate.

Manny wondered what Quintano would do if anyone tried to snatch his money. He thought about it a lot.

After depositing its contents, Q would leave the Cage with a container of black hundred-dollar markers and maybe ten or twenty orange "pumpkins"—thousand-dollar chips he liked to click and shuffle in the side pocket of his jacket while he gambled at the Baccarat tables which he liked because of their quiet atmosphere, their remove from the madness of the main casino. If with a woman, he'd have her stand behind him or send her off to Roulette with a stack or two of blacks.

Manny, doing his best to gain the man's confidence, now seemed to have it. He'd bring him, stat, whatever the well-clad courier from San Salvador desired: a meal, drinks, extra towels, cigars, even women—usually a few each trip—whatever the man desired. Now, after three visits, he'd become Quintano's "main man," especially after Manny told him he was from Q's hometown. A demonstrative man, Quintano now hugged his "Manuelito" on arrival at the I, treating him almost like a friend.

Something Manny most certainly could never be.

Quintano's fourth visit to the Internationale was on August 12th, nine months almost to the day Berto first saw the man pull up in his white Caddy. The visit began like the previous three, Berto saluting Quintano, handing him his parking stub, and waiting behind the wheel while Manny off-loaded Q's bags. Quintano had called the hotel from San Salvador, just to make sure his main man would be available. Which assured that Manny would be at Berto's side when Q arrived. Quintano still didn't recognize Berto except as the guy who parked his car. Had no idea he was Manny's father. He'd dismiss Berto by slipping him a ten then greet Manny with his usual hug, almost like he was his own son.

"C'mon, I'm beat, Manuelito. Let's get this shit upstairs. This Vegas heat, ¡Dios mio! I need a shower, maybe a fuckin siesta."

The routine was always the same. The procession to the VIP check-in, Manny hauling Quintano's baggage, Q at his side, but this time rolling a red aluminum overnighter, like the attaché but with three, maybe four times the capacity.

Julie, the new VIP chargé, guessing at what the overnighter contained, suggested, as Manny once had, that a security man might accompany him to his rooms. Quintano made a joke, something about not trusting nobody, not even Security. His business done at the check-in, he and Manny moved over to the B tower elevator. Manny carded it open. Q rolled his bag in. Manny followed, pressing the UP button.

During the less than two-minute express ride to the 64th Floor, Quintano remained silent, something he rarely was. He appeared worn, his cheeks sagging, same as his large, bloated body. He looked like he truly couldn't wait for his shower and his "fuckin siesta."

The elevator opened to a luxurious central gallery off of which were four penthouse suites, each with eight-foot-high double doors of zebrawood. The gallery was hung with original oil paintings. It had terrazzo floors, marble walls and a vaulted ceiling, and might have been mistaken for a gallery at the Louvre. All the double-door entries were bracketed by six-foot Chinese urns spilling over with fresh flowers changed daily. Quintano, picking his nose and, in passing, wiping the findings on the back of a satin-striped Louis XVI chair, headed straight to his suite, P4, rolling his suitcase full of cash behind him.

But, before he reached the double doors, his trusty Manuelito alongside, he noticed a man casually seated on a gray velvet divan at the opposite end of the gallery. The man, short, a Latino like himself, was reading a newspaper and smoking a cigarillo. He was dressed in off-white trousers and a flowered, powder blue linen shirt unbuttoned halfway down to his navel. Squared on his head was a short-brimmed Trilby straw. He was mustachioed, in his maybe late forties, and his neck supported three gold chains, one bearing a heavy gold cross.

Quintano did not recognize the man but he did recognize trouble in the form of small but crudely tattooed numbers "1" and "8" on his slightly caved-in chest. This fuckin cholo was a Barrio-18! The Barrios had become badder asses than the Maras. But not badder than Q. Quintano would have gone for the Glock that sat atop the cash in his roller bag, but the cholo was suddenly pointing a Smith-Wesson revolver directly at his heart.

The "cholo" aimed his forefinger at the bag. "Let's have it," he said, in a high-pitched voice.

"Fuck you, bitch!" said Quintano, stepping quickly behind the luggage on the cart. "Manny, get us back on the fuckin' elevator now." But the gun went off before Q's sentence was complete. A bullet slammed into the Louis Vuitton two-suiter sitting at Quintano's left side.

"Move and the next bullet will find you," said the Barrio, his Salvi accent probably noticed by Quintano. Manny froze. "OK, now roll that suitcase you are holding over to me nice and easy. And do not make any funny moves."

Manny, in front of the cart, standing just a few feet from the Barrio, remained frozen, his mouth open.

Quintano stood his ground. "I'm not going to do that, puto," he said, in a measured cadence. "I will see you fuckin dead before this day is over." Another bullet tore into Quintano's Vuitton garment bag, undoubtedly ruining the Armani pinstripe it contained.

Quintano, cursing, rolled the overnighter toward the Barrio gunman.

"Now leave it there and back up," barked the gunman.

This time, Q did as he was told, cursing some more. But, as the little man bent to retrieve it, Manny, suddenly coming alive, directed a kung fu kick squarely at his gun hand, knocking the weapon into the air and arcing it toward Manny's reaching hands which grabbed it and held it tightly. He looked at it like he'd never held a gun before because, of course, he hadn't.

The Barrio made a grab for the overnighter but Manny said, "Leave it right there," and fired a bullet into the floor to the left of him.

"Shoot the bastard!" screamed Quintano, as he moved toward the little man. But the cholo was too quick for them. Devoid now of both weapon and overnighter, he ran for the exit door next to the entrance to Penthouse C.

"I'll be back," he hollered over his shoulder, sounding like a Hispanic Terminator. Manny shot at him again just before he disappeared through the door. The bullet went wide, Very wide, shattering one of the Chinese vases and sending its myriad of flowers in every direction.

And the little man was gone.

Back in the room, Quintano locked his overnighter into a closet then pulled a bottle of duty-free Demerara rum from one of his suitcases. Pouring a tumbler-full for himself, he carried the bottle with him to his balcony. He gathered himself, looked down at the Strip, shook his head, returned to the room and sank into a chaise. "Want some, kid?" he said, waggling the glass at Manny.

Manny, looking scared and bewildered, shook his head no.

Quintano took a long gulp, then raised his glass to Manny. His roseate face wore a serious look. "You did a good thing there, Manuelito.

A very brave thing. You saved my life, little buddy." Saying this, he arose and returned to the lock closet, opened it, unlocked the overnighter, removed a packet of bills, walked it back to Manny and flipped it into his lap. "I can't put a price on what you did, *cipote*," he said, "because that's worth more than money. But I'm sure you can use some." Manny's eyes went wide. "Lookit, kid," said Quintano, "I may just have a job for you. Pays a few times more than whatever you're making now. A whole lot more. Interested?"

Manny thought for a few seconds. "What's the job?"

Quintano smiled. The bait was cast. "We can talk about it after I have a Jacuzzi. And catch some sleep. You start putting my things away, we talk later."

"I'll fill the Jacuzzi for you, Sr. Quintano. But aren't you going to tell the police, or at least Security, about this?"

The Security question again. Quintano sighed. Maybe this kid wasn't quite ready to turn. Shaking his head, he replied, "I don't talk to police or Security about such matters, Manny. I take care of them myself. Maybe I could teach you a little something about how to do that," he said, closing the suitcase and rolling it back into its closet. "Meanwhile, you get busy while I get clean, eh?"

Manny filled the Jacuzzi, turned its jets on, then hung up the remains of Quintano's clothes. Quintano, wearing a hotel robe, his gun and lock-closet key in one pocket and the cholo's revolver in the other, hauled himself into the bathroom, the size of a mini spa. He was plugged into his MP3 player as, with an audible sigh, he slid into the Jacuzzi, lit up a Havana, leaned back, shut his eyes and began to soak away the craziness that had just taken place by the elevator. He was thinking how he would search out this goddamn Barrio and disembowel him.

The MP3's music—Jennifer Lopez's "Ain't It Funny"—and the Jacuzzi's full-on water flow blocked out the loud voices, the furniture being thrown, the bodies scuffling in the suite's living room, thirty feet away.

But, minutes later, Quintano had no trouble hearing the two quick gunshots that followed, then a body being thrown or falling against the bathroom door. This whole business couldn't have taken more than two minutes, most of it happening before the gunshots. He jumped from the tub, ripped off the MP3, grabbed his Glock and, wet and gross in his nakedness, pulled the bathroom door open, his weapon ready to unload at the Barrio bastard on the other side. The cojones of the sonofabitch, coming back like that. Quintano would have shot through the closed door if he knew it wasn't Manny he was shooting at.

Sure enough, it was Manny, slumped against the door, a gush of blood running from the right side of his bruised mouth. Q shifted his eyes toward the entry door but whoever had been in the suite with Manny was gone. The boy, dazed, his eyes not quite in focus, looked up at him. "They came back." He looked like he was about to black out.

"Did you get shot?"

"No, they threw me around . . . punched me . . . kept punching me, asking where the money was . . . didn't tell them but they figured it out . . . shot the lock out of the closet . . . grabbed the suitcase . . . I was half out . . . called to you but you couldn't hear me . . . wanted to stop them but you had the guns."

"Them? Who's them?" Like Quintano had to ask.

"The 18 guy. And another cholo."

Then Manny's eyes closed. Quintano lifted him onto the bed. Sitting next to him, now in his hotel robe and with gun in hand, he tried to dope out what in hell had just happened. This little Manuelito almost got himself killed. That was one thing. But Q was more concerned about how his people would take this. He was in deep shit now and he knew it.

Now what? What Barrio pricks pulled this off? Once I find them, thought Quintano, they are good as dead. And if I don't find them, he afterthought, I'm dead.

Berto Estevez sat on the long velvet couch in the center hall of the penthouse floor. It was a strange feeling to be in the midst of such luxury, far greater than any he'd seen down below. In all his years at the Internationale, he'd never been up here before. It also felt strange to be holding the old Smith & Wesson he'd kept when the coyote left him in the Mexican desert. He remembered the shopkeeper who had sold it to him saying, "Be careful, mi amigo, this is a truly lethal weapon." He remembered also thinking, what kind of gun was not?

He had taken an afternoon break. One full hour. It began by his slipping into the Penthouse elevator with a plastic bag from Sears containing his idea of Barrio 18 clothing. He changed into it instantly during the ride up to the 64th floor, stuffing his parking valet uniform into the emptied bag. If his timing was right, Manny and Quintano would arrive in less than five minutes. He had thought of loading the gun with blanks because he, like Manny, had never fired a gun before and didn't trust himself shooting live bullets. But Quintano would know immediately if blanks were being used. It had to be real bullets. Smoking a cigarillo, he was thinking along these lines when the elevator door opposite the velvet couch opened. He stood and started walking toward it.

Manny exited the elevator car with the luggage cart, Quintano right behind him. Berto pointed the gun at the pair. As soon as Quintano saw Berto he shouted, "Manny, get us back into the elevator now!" That's when Berto fired at the suitcase to Quintano's left, telling the big man, "Move and the next bullet will find you." It was a line he'd rehearsed many times. He then ordered

Quintano to roll the metal suitcase, whose handle he was grasping so tightly, over to him.

Which is when Quintano replied, "I am not going to do that, *puto*. I will see you dead before this day is over." Berto's answer was another bullet that hit a garment bag. This time Quintano, hesitating for just a second, shoved the suitcase toward Berto.

It was time for Manny's practiced choreography to kick in. As his father reached for the suitcase, he kicked out at Berto's hand, knocking the gun it held into the air where Manny caught it before it hit the floor. Berto, looking suitably shocked, started to grab the suitcase and run, but Manny said, "Leave it right there!" When Berto grabbed it anyhow, Manny shot a bullet into the floor near him then froze while Berto ran toward the exit door, easily outrunning the enraged Quintano who followed.

Hearing Quintano scream "Shoot the bastard," Berto knew Manny would have to fire another round. Which he dutifully did. Berto had to keep himself from laughing when he heard a vase near the exit door shatter as he disappeared through the door.

Less than fifteen minutes later a call from Manny brought Berto back to Quintano's penthouse door. The other three penthouse suites, held for high rollers only, must have been empty, summer being slow season in Vegas. Thus no one had been around to see or hear anything.

Why hadn't the plan been for Berto to simply take the money and run when Quintano and Manny stepped out of the elevator? Because he was sure Quintano would see it as a set-up by Manny. He still might think it was. But Q had reached the top of his trade by being the meanest and nastiest, not necessarily the brightest, of his Mera Salvatrucha compadres.

As soon as Berto entered he and Manny tossed some furniture around. Then Berto fired two shots into the lock-closet's handle, blowing it off. Grabbing the suitcase, he looked at his son with reluctance. He did not want to carry out the next step.

"You know the plan, papa," said Manny. "Hit me a good one. Berto hesitated, then punched his son square on his chin, drawing blood, most of it from the blood pellet between Manny's teeth. Manny staggered back and fell against the bathroom door. Berto moved toward Manny to help him. Manny hissed, "Vamoose!" Berto, rolling the suitcase behind him, ran out the door seconds before Quintano emerged, armed and naked, from the bathroom.

Stella, with her laundry cart was waiting there for Berto who quickly buried the overnighter under the cart's dirty sheets and towels and, a moment later, the pair were safely inside the service elevator heading down to the basement. During the descent, Berto changed back into his valet uniform. Soon as the doors opened, they moved straight to Berto's Dodge Charger in the employee parking area way in the back where he transferred the overnighter to the Charger's trunk. A few minutes later he was at his station, half-empty cup of coffee in hand, looking like he'd thoroughly enjoyed his brief break. Which, of course, he had. Stella, by now, was back changing the linen in her rooms on the 27th and 28th floors.

Rubén Quintano, to his detriment, did not find his elusive "cholos." He was never again seen at the Internationale. Nor anywhere else in the world.

As for *familia* Estevez. . . *venganza* was theirs.

The BB Tube

Arthur Hollister had never been able to retrieve the hidden-away cardboard B-B tube that contained the love letter he'd written more than 60 years ago. It had been on his mind, sporadically, ever since.

Arthur was eleven at the time he wrote his love letter; a simple note really. Though he was generally good at English, he'd never been much for writing. He'd certainly never written a love letter, the kind that bolder boys occasionally passed to girls in class. That's because Arthur had never, up till that time, been in love.

But there's no question Arthur was in love that summer of 1953. The object of his love—an undying, if unrequited, love—was Irene Shoemaker, a fifth grader like him, and unquestionably the prettiest girl in his class. Irene was two inches taller than him but that hardly mattered. She was slim and had piercing green eyes and long hair so blond it was more white than blond. And she had a red bow of a mouth, so red it seemed as if she wore lipstick, but Arthur was pretty sure it wasn't lipstick because girls weren't allowed to wear lipstick in school. She had a slightly turned up nose and always smelled good like she'd just shampooed her hair. Arthur knew this well since he sat behind her in homeroom and, every chance he had, he'd lean over and, making certain no one was looking, he sniffed her hair.

Arthur wanted desperately to express his longing for Irene but he was shy; so shy that every time he came even close to revealing this longing his face would turn a deep red, his blood running to it the very

163

moment he even thought of saying something. This paralytic condition persisted throughout the year that Arthur fell in love. He was thus incapable of speaking his love thoughts or, for that matter, any other thoughts. Ask her to go with him to a movie? Out of the question. If a pencil fell from his hand and rolled under Irene's desk, he could not make himself ask her to retrieve it, he had to just let it lie there. Did Irene return this love? How could she? Arthur correctly surmised that she didn't even know of it.

But if Arthur Hollister could not speak his love, he was more than capable of writing it. His head spoke to his hand far better than his tongue spoke at all. And so, Arthur poured his heart onto three four-by-six-inch sheets of lined notebook paper. When finished, he re-wrote them. Then wrote them a third and fourth time until they contained the exact words he wished to say. He was, however, not quite ready to present his letter. He wanted to rethink what he'd written and possibly perfect even further the words he had so painstakingly assembled. So he carefully folded the three sheets into fourths, rolled them up and slipped them into a three-inch-long red cardboard tube long emptied of the BBs it had originally contained. Here's what Arthur wrote:

Hi, Irene. I think I like you really a lot and I hope you like me too. I think you are the prettiest girl in our class and your hair is pretty and it smells real good, kind of like you just stepped out of a bathtub, or maybe a shower. There's a darn good movie called Shane playing at the Belmont on Saturday afternoon, it's a cowboy movie but I think there's a girl in it. If you'd like to go with me please let me know, I'll pay for you. I hope you like me as much as I like you, but I sort of said that already. Yours very truly, Arthur Hollister

He would hide this loaded BB tube from his nosy little brother, Marcus, until he was ready to present it. He knew that Marcus, the little twerp, if he found the tube, would immediately reveal its contents to Irene, to the entire school, to the entire whole wide world.

Arthur knew of only one place he was certain Marcus would never think of. Off the attic bedroom was an unlit crawl space where luggage was kept. It could be entered only through a four-foot-high door and an unfinished floor that didn't quite cover all the rafters where the roof slanted down to meet the floor. It was under the insulation that lie between the exposed rafters that he secreted his red BB tube with its precious contents.

You understand, Arthur was not ready to present his love letter to Irene. He felt he could do better yet with the words it contained. Or so he told himself. The fact was that, as much as he wanted Irene to know of his love, he was still too embarrassed to present it to her because what if she hated it and maybe even hated him for writing it? This offputting thought was constantly on Arthur's troubled mind.

And so the red BB tube sat there, tucked away under the insulation in the attic.

Half a semester passed during which Arthur could not bring himself to present his love letter, which of course need updating because Shane had come and passed. He then began to think it was rather childish, and he and Irene would soon be in junior high school and, while Arthur still felt strongly about Irene, she had now succumbed to the blandishments of one Nick Giovanetti, a good-looking Italian boy who'd transferred from a parish school in the inner city.

Now Arthur would not forgive himself for failing to have presented the letter. Had his opportunity passed? He blamed not himself for this failure, but Irene for not somehow recognizing how strongly he felt about her. Never mind, he would try to forget her. What he could not forgot however was the letter itself. He had convinced himself by now that, never mind the required revisions, it contained the best, the most honest thoughts he'd ever felt about anything. He believed that someday it would serve to remind him of what a fine writer he really was.

This thought was on his mind when, one Saturday morning when no one was home, he crawled into the crawl space and reached under the insulation between the rafters where he was certain the red BB tube still lay. But no tube was to be found. He inspected the neighboring set of rafters as far as he could reach under the flooring and found nothing. Panicking, he tore the insulation from between every rafter. By now he was soaked with sweat and itched unbearably from the errant insulation fibers. Where was the red BB tube? Had Marcus found it? No, not possible, the little rat would have broadcast every word of it by now.

Of course, he'd have to rewrite the letter if he were ever to present it but, time and again, out of sheer curiosity, over the next six years of junior and senior high school, Arthur periodically inspected and re-inspected the hiding place that had so successfully hidden the tube from him. But nothing ever turned up. His quest became an exercise in futility. The following year Arthur entered college and his family moved from the home that, he was still convinced, held his sacred declaration of love to Irene Shoemaker who, five years later, became Mrs. Irene Patterson and was already going to fat and whose hair had turned a mousy brown.

Still, the letter's mysterious loss remained on Arthur Hollister's mind. And continued to do so, periodically, for the following fifty years during which Arthur moved to California, married and raised a family of his own.

At age 68, Arthur returned to his hometown for his fiftieth high school reunion. While there he drove through his old neighborhood, as he often did on his rare return visits, just to see how it had changed. It now had a population mixed between blacks and orthodox Jews. Though the brick three-story houses were now about 70 years old, they were still well-maintained.

While there, Arthur stopped in front of his old home. He saw a stocky, middle-aged man in a black skullcap reading a newspaper while sitting on a rocking chair on its front porch.

Arthur, on a whim, rehearsed a few lines of entreaty. Would the man allow him to walk through the house "just for old times' sake?" He approached him, introduced himself, explained that his family had been the first to own the home, then asked his question. The man was cordial but hesitated. "I'll have to ask my wife," he said. The wife had just emerged from the front door, a scowl on her face. Arthur stood there as the man spoke to her in Yiddish. She shook her head. He spoke some more. She looked at Arthur with obvious distaste, threw up her hands and went back inside, followed by the man in the skullcap. The man emerged seconds later. "She says it's OK," said the man. "Come with me, I understand how you feel. Come, I'll show you the house."

Which he did.

A feeling of deep nostalgia rolled over Arthur in waves as he wandered through the rooms of his boyhood. The home seemed much smaller than he remembered, but, though it had been extensively renovated, he recognized every corner of it, floor by floor as they rose to the attic.

And there was the four-foot-high door, beckoning him to look behind it. Arthur stood silently before it.

"You're staring at that door," said the man. "Did you play hide-and-seek in there as a child?"

"No," said Arthur, unable to tear his eyes from the door.

"Would you like to look inside?" said the man.

It took Arthur, blinking all the while, a full fifteen seconds to reply before shrugging.

"No," he said.

Just Another Evening

I'm sitting in my boxy old, cat-scratched reading chair, its oil-stained leather arms embracing me. Just another evening, like most in my solitary, 40-year-old life.

Halfway into my martini I take a deep toke of Sativa before dipping corn tostadas into a perfectly picante salsa from the 99¢ Store. Best moment of a day spent staring at my Mac, surfing, admittedly, more than writing. But now, as evening approaches, I'm at a comfortable remove from that machine that usurps so much of my time.

I know from habit that, fifteen minutes into what may be the best novel I've read this year, I'll be stopped by the guaranteed appearance of my insistent muse who actually believes writing is more important than reading. Which forces me to slam shut what may be the best novel I've read this year.

Barging into my befogged brain, she means to do what she does. Shouldn't complain, though. It's not reading I mean to do, but it's better than staring at a blank screen staring back at me.

I close my eyes, waiting for the creative caress of what I've imbibed and inhaled to kick in. Waiting then for her open sesame to tickle my writing buds. Old—OK, young—reliable, she's always there for me, reluctant though I often am to receive her.

I'm relaxed as I've been all day, but this particular one turns out like no other. Suddenly I hear a tapping, as if someone gently rapping, Edgar-style. Not from some dreamlike distance, this rapping snaps my eyelids open like defective window shades.

My eyes jerk right to rest on a very small creature, a disturbingly attractive foot-high female sitting on my rickety IKEA dresser, her legs dangling as she knocks hard on unfinished pine. If she's seeking my attention, she's got it.

I blink maybe five times then blurt "You're my . . ."

"Writing Muse, right."

"You're real? I mean . . ."

"Always have been, Jonah, not just a figment of your gin-fumed mind."

My dropped jaw reflects my shock. I believe in my muse but never expected to meet her as a person, pick your size. If she's actually here, something must be bothering her big time. "Uh, what's going on?" I finally think to say.

"That story I put into your head yesterday." Her abrupt tone says she's not here just to chat.

"About the archaeologist?"

"Have you started it?"

"This morning. Just about finished it." I still can't get over her actually being here.

"Mind playing it back to me?"

'Sure, but . . ."

"Just a synopsis, please." She's not asking, she's demanding.

"Okay, okay. There's this man. Haven't named him yet. Maybe based on me, don't know. Lives in High Tide, a suburb of Mobile, Alabama, a burb that never existed in a city I've never been. This guy, maybe early 40s, is an archaeologist specializing in the Early Etruscan period. Digging in northern Italy, in Lombardy, he uncovers an almost fully intact ancient urn covered with faded glyphs, thousands of them, writ small, painted in the Etruscan language which he laboriously translates. They somehow tell him more about the person who wrote them more than about the subject of her writing. He's certain that the words, painted in a feminine hand, are those of a woman. Through their lyrical content he slowly falls in love with the woman separated from him by well over two thousand years. This powerful love emanates from him, reaches her metaphysically, causing her to fall in love with him and . . ."

"Stop right there," says my little muse, holding up her hands and shaking her green-haired head. "I knew it!" She massages her forehead. Her lips are pressed together. Covering her mouth as if afraid to speak, she finally does, pointing a finger at me. "There's a problem, Jonah."

I blink again. She inspired this story, it's going to be one of my best. Is she going to quash it?

She crosses her arms. "I don't know how to say this, but you are going to meet this woman. I know, I know, this cannot happen, it's not supposed to happen, it's not allowed to happen. But it is happening." Her dark complexion grows darker. She seems angry at me? Why?

"Did you say I'm going to meet Daphne? Don't you mean my archeologist character is going to meet her."

Daphne? That's what you call her? No, Jonah, it's you who's going to meet her."

I've face-met my muse for the first time and now she's telling me I'm going to meet someone who lives only in my mind? What is she saying? My heart is pounding. I have a million questions, but for once I realize I have to just shut up and listen.

"Something's gone wrong with the whole muse system, Jonah. This thing we have, you and I, it's a fixed process that's worked perfectly for years, come whenever you pour your martini. You sit back, sip, start to read, take a hit, then—I can almost time it, fifteen, sixteen minutes—your mind beckons me like you're pulling a cord for a servant. Faithful me arrives, we kick around some ideas, I dust you with a little inspiration and off you go, running your perfectly sharpened Ticonderoga a mile a minute, spitting out words like bullets from an AK-47, prepping for your computer next am. I've done my job, you're doing yours, I'm gone. That's the process we both love, too bad it interferes with your precious reading. Foolproof. Till now."

I nod my head. She's right. Couldn't have described it better. She sounds a lot like me, but then, she is me. "So what's wrong with me meeting Daphne?" I ask.

"What's wrong is it's forbidden. Never happened before. To me, to any of my sister muses. This could be the end of me. And would definitely be the end of us being together."

"You sound almost jealous."

Her comely face darkens. She evaporates into nothingness.

Emerging now through a black hole in the perfectly white wall next to me is—who else?—my three-dimensional Etruscan Daphne, very much of today, wearing a diaphanous, off-the-shoulder linen gown which she fills out beautifully in each dimension. Tall, slim, a few inches shorter than me, she's the essence of femininity, even while looking as startled as me.

I am dumbfounded by what I see. "Daphne?" is all I can think of to say.

"Who are you?" she replies. She's already learned English.

"Jonah. I . . . I guess I created you."

"Jonah? You created me?"

"Yes."

"Are you God?"

"No, I mean I imagined you." Am I actually talking to a character I imagined? Maybe I am God.

"What just happened?" she asks, looking herself over but not looking at all as though she'd just traveled through a two-thousand year time warp.

I'm too stunned to answer. My staring lowers her eyes in embarrassment. She's beyond the beautiful I imagined her to be. An involuntary shiver goes through me.

I finally speak. "I wrote a story about you and a Greek archaeologist who fall in love with each other across the millennia. What happens to you two is something I haven't finished writing yet. I make it up as I go."

"You made me fall in love with Demetrius," says Daphne.

Demetrius? I never gave him that name or any name. What's going on here?

"I thought I was brought here to meet him. What just happened?" she asks again.

"I don't know." I repeat. "My muse ran off before she could explain.

But even she doesn't seem to know. All she says is this wasn't supposed to happen."

"What, our love? I thought I was coming to be with Demetrius but now I'm here with you. Were you and I supposed to be together? I'm confused. If that's so, there must be a reason for it."

And, wham, I may actually have one.

"I think I can explain at least a part of it, Daphne. I wrote 'Just Another Evening' as a love story. I have this odd tendency—you'd be right to call it a fault—to insert myself into my stories. Yes, I had you and your Demetrius fall in love with each other over the words you so painstakingly painted on your lovely urn. But it wasn't Demetrius who was falling in love with you, it was, uh, me. You see, my characters are sometimes—well, usually—an extension of me. The me I fantasize myself to be. You, of course, weren't real. But the more I wrote about you, the more I wanted to believe you were. And now you are. Or seem to be. If this is really happening. And I think it is." Maybe, I think to myself, I'd better stop talking.

Her expression has been blank throughout my stumbling explanation. "You're Demetrius?"

"No, yes, well, sort of. Demetrius is actually me. Or the other way around. Does it matter. Are you disappointed?"

"I'm not sure. Are you telling me I fell in love with you, not Demetrius? Hard to wrap my mind around that."

"Where'd you learn to talk like that?"

"From you. Remember? Look, Jonah, I'm just a character in your story. Or was. But whatever real feels like, that's how I feel now. And I guess you're right; since Demetrius is you, I must have been falling in love with you all this time. May I be truthful with you? Demetrius is something of a flawed man."

"Well, then I must be flawed too."

"Let me look at you," she says. "I want to make sure you're real."

I do not want this conversation to end. "Look, a story can only go so far," I say. "It needs an ending and this one's hardly begun. But here's how I see it so far. Two of my characters—you and Demetrius—fall in love, Demetrius as a surrogate for me. Then you come to me across the years.

My muse shows up for real at the same time, and now no one knows what's going on."

"So where does that leave us?" says Daphne, sitting on the arm of my chair, making what sound like purring noises. Is she beginning to like me? I don't seem to be giving her much help. Is she accepting this insane outcome that hasn't yet come out? This can't be a dream because I've never had such a perfect dream. I've invented a woman and—I'll say it—I've fallen in love with her. And I'm pretty sure she's falling in love with me.

I rise, pull Daphne into my arms and kiss her. Just like that. "Checking to see if you're real," I whisper into her perfectly formed ear, kissing it as well. Then I kiss her a third time. She kisses me back. We move toward the bed. Or, rather, she pulls me there.

Please let this be really happening.

The damned rapping-tapping starts up again as my Muse pops up on my IKEA dresser. Bad timing.

"Where've you been? You didn't look too happy when you ran off a while back."

"Mount Olympus," she says.

"What Mount Olympus?"

"That Mount Olympus. You ever look at Murray's Manual of Mythology? I was summoned there by my father."

"Father?"

"You don't know his name? Of course not. You don't even know mine."

"You're my muse, what more need I know?"

"I'm not just your muse, you know. I happen to be Thalia, the muse of Comedy and Burlesque. And this would truly be both if it weren't such a tragedy."

"Tragedy? You've put me on Cloud Nine."

"Where you do not belong. This monkey business was never supposed to happen. You and your runaway imagination! You couldn't just keep your Daphne on the printed page, no, you had to fall in love with her. That's why she came alive, don't you understand? You did that, it wasn't my idea. You broke the rules. You know how bad that makes me look? Daphne has to go back."

"But why?"

"Because Pater says so."

"Pater?"

"Stop repeating what I say. Pater is Zeus. Blames me, not you. So, to make things right, according to Mater, Mnemosyne, Goddess of Memory, the memory of your Daphne will be wiped out. Gone. In fact, your whole story will go missing from your irresponsible, hyperactive, fairy tale brainpan. In effect, this never happened."

"You really are jealous, Thalia." Wrong thing to say, but I had to say it.

"That's it. Five minutes," she spits out at me through clamped teeth. "You have just five minutes to say ciao, bye-bye, fare-thee-well to your lover woman. And to Just Another Evening. And, by the way, to me. I'm done with you, you're on your own!" By now steam is shooting out of Thalia's pointy green ears as she once again evanesces, this time in a whorl of black smoke that stains my bedroom ceiling.

Five minutes. Damn! I can almost hear them ticking.

"I can't leave you, Jonah. I won't," Daphne says, wrapping her arms around me.

"I'm not sure you have a choice." As I say this I see the black hole reappear in the wall. It begins to grow. At the same time, I feel her being pulled ever so slightly from me toward the hole.

Three minutes left. Got to think faster. Can write other stories. With other women to fall in love with. But they never came alive before. There's a reason Daphne has. This was meant to be. A literal love for the ages. Who knew!

Two minutes to go. How do you fight Zeus? Daphne and I are clinging to each other, struggling against whatever it is that's drawing her toward the menacing hole. Will I ever see her again? Will I even know she existed, that I held her in my arms like I'm holding her now? Her eyes, filled with fear, filled with tears, lock on mine. She's shaking her head, shaking away the fact of her leaving.

Less than a minute now. Can't hang on to her any longer. A

whirlwind force much stronger than me rips her from my arms.

I watch as Daphne is pulled, screaming, into the gaping hole.

The hole begins to close. I shut my eyes and let out the roar of a wounded bear.

And then I dive in after her.

Living Alone Together

Darryl McDermott cared about people. Just didn't care to spend much time with them. A loner, a hermit you might say, but friendly enough in his abrupt way when you ran into him on the street where he'd doff his hat and mutter what sounded like "'lo." It's just that Darryl was more content to be with his overweight 12-year-old beagle, Buster, than with any human.

What Darryl did was, he made Windsor chairs, those gracefully curved wooden chairs with carved, fan-shaped stretchers. On breaks from his shop he'd do his gardening, and the hunting he so dearly loved, especially his deer season treks through the Appalachian ridges and valleys where he lived. As a trained sniper, he'd killed—sometimes at distances of 500 yards or more—eight of the enemy, confirmed, in his year in France and three months in Germany during World War II.

Darryl came straight back home when he was mustered out in November of 1945, and quickly became known as a master craftsman. He'd picked it up in the most natural way from Micah McDermott, the grandfather who raised him in the backwoods town of Pine Ridge, Kentucky, after Darryl's father, Harland, was killed in a hunting accident three years after Darryl was born.

On his return, Darryl had settled into the family clapboard in Pine Ridge, population 1472, situated about 65 miles east of Lexington on the eastern side of the mountains. Not a year later, Grandpa Micah died, leaving him to live a solitary life. His mother had been long gone, having run off with a traveling person shortly after Darryl was born.

Darryl was a tall man, rail thin despite an appetite folks would remark on. Smiles rarely creased his long, hollow-cheeked face, and the ones he did produce were barely seen through his proudly full beard.Besides the beard, he'd picked up a facial tic in the service after cowering in foxholes too close to shell bursts in Ardennes at the Battle of the Bulge. His handiness with a rifle had earned him a sharpshooter's badge. A shrapnel wound earned him a Purple Heart, and he was awarded a rare Silver Star but didn't care to talk much about how these latter honors came about. Or about much of anything else he'd been through. What he never did receive was a Good Conduct Medal. Not surprising, as he'd always had trouble sucking up to authority.

It didn't take long for Darryl to settle into his sprawling home, though he felt he wasn't near filling it. What filled his time was the establishing of his trade, the handcrafting of his nonpareil Windsor chairs.

Though Darryl had chosen to live alone, he was a lonely man with a hole in his heart. He meant to fill this hole but his firm take was, if he came across the right woman he'd know it and would do something about it. Still, he'd done nothing about it for going onto twenty-seven years now since his mustering out. Which is when May Johnson came along, she being the new fifth grade teacher at Pine Ridge's combined junior high-high school. May considered herself a settled old maid at forty-one, not that she was complaining.

One fall weekend she was chaperoning a junior high dance. At the last minute, Darryl was asked by his flu-ridden neighbor to fill in for him as the male chaperone. Darryl near panicked, especially since he hadn't been near a school since his own high school graduation in 1941. Being a kindhearted man, he reluctantly agreed to take on the chore.

Darryl and May, turns out, were the only adults at the dance, but that was OK because the dance was something of a bust, less than thirty students showing up. Two boys had been hired, at ten dollars for the pair, to spin records at a table in the near-empty cafeteria. On the table were an RCA record player and a loudspeaker. A hand-lettered sign on the table read "Music Fast and Slow by Mark and Joe." May remarked that she especially liked Tammy Wynette's "Help Me Make It Through the Night. Darryl allowed that he liked C&W but preferred classical music, particularly opera which he'd stumbled upon listening to radio while working on his chairs. He claimed opera helped him work with better concentration and better results. His "opera" chairs, finished on Saturdays when the Metropolitan Opera was broadcast live, were his best and were always priced a little higher than the others.

With the dance fading to a close half an hour short of its scheduled end, and with Darryl taking something of a shine to May in spite of her overly sentimental taste in music, he suggested that, it being a very nice evening, he might walk her home, especially since it was a dark night, the moon being nearly new.

May Johnson was tall and bony like Darryl. The two looked enough alike to be mistaken for brother and sister. May wasn't certain what Darryl had in mind with his invitation, but she knew him to be a respectable fellow so, as they strolled along, she asked him outright, "Why did you ask to walk me home tonight, Darryl? Did you really think I wouldn't be safe walking alone in this town?"

By now, they'd reached the doorstep of May's rooming house. Darryl, being who he was, proffered an honest answer. "Well, May, I guess the truth is that I rather enjoyed talking with you tonight. Which is to say that I rather enjoyed your company. Especially talking about the dishes you like to make." This broad hint was one Darryl didn't realize he'd dropped. It was said not without stuttering a bit and while shifting from one foot to the other. It was too dark on the porch to see how red his face had become.

May had a sudden thought to do something she didn't believe she could ever do because she'd never done anything like it before. It was an impulse she obeyed. She put her hands on the reticent Darryl's shoulders, pulled him toward her and kissed the unsuspecting co-chaperone squarely on his unsuspecting mouth. Not a heavy-duty kiss, but a meaningful one.

Darryl stood there a moment, his long arms dangling at his sides. "Thank you," he murmured, his eyes still closed. He was unable to think of a better reply. This was followed by a motion to tip the hat he forgot he wasn't wearing. After a softly stated, "Good night, May," he turned and began to walk off May's porch.

May, saying her goodbye to Darryl's back, remained motionless watching him. But, as if feeling her eyes on him, he stopped at the top of the steps, turned, came back to May, took her into his arms and kissed her proper, and she kissed him back with a fervor that resulted, not a month later, in marriage, the perfect union of May Johnson and Darryl McDermott, conducted properly by Pastor Erick Olsen at the First Baptist Church over in Sandy Hook, a good 50 miles west, just to avoid a crowd of overenthusiastic friends, neighbors, customers and students, crowds not being much to Darryl's liking.

Darryl and May McDermott meant to have a child; God knows they wanted them, never mind it was a tad late for that sort of thing. Failing to bring that blessing off, they filled Darryl's house with three dogs and a pair of cats, which, treasured though they were, hardly took the place of a flesh and blood daughter or son. If they saw this inability to procreate as a failure, it did not fail to make their marriage a fully satisfying one. They had a great deal, they figured; they had each other.

May went on to become her school's principal. Her career had spanned 32 years until her retirement at age 69. Darryl, who'd never considered his chair-making as work, continued to ply his trade and take himself to the woods and fields around him to do his beloved hunting.

The two loved to travel, not to far off lands but to America's far off places—particularly its national parks. They made these meanderings in a well-equipped motor home that spent most of its time on the back roads they preferred before returning them to their home in the hills of Eastern Kentucky.

Darryl worked fewer hours after May's retirement, partly so they could travel, but also just to be with May. He did not wish to be deprived of her company as in the past, due to the long hours she'd spend teaching and running her school.

He was thinking of his own retirement when a blow was struck from which he would no more recover than she. May was diagnosed with ALS; Lou Gehrig's disease which gave her just two more years of life. But they were two torturous years. Two rapidly declining years.

From the day Darryl learned of May's diagnosis, he never left her side. She quickly became confined to a wheel chair and soon after had to be lifted into bed, into the bathtub, onto and off the toilet. This, Darryl did with loving determination. He made May's meals using her best recipes and fed them to her, patiently, spoonful by spoonful. Soon, May could no longer speak except in short bursts of a few words. It didn't matter to Darryl, who'd never been much for talking to begin with. Instead, he'd take out as many as six books at a time from the Pine Ridge library and read them to her for hours, even for a while after he thought she was asleep, because he never could be sure if she was. And all during the reading he would hold her hand because she'd told him she liked that.

It made page-turning difficult, but he managed.

One snowy, blustery March afternoon, as Darryl was reading the last chapters of John Steinbeck's "Of Mice and Men," he felt May's hand go limp.

She wasn't asleep, she was gone, just like that.

Slumping in his chair, the first thing he felt was a consuming relief that she no longer had to suffer. The next thing he felt was his loss, the beginning of his grief.

But hadn't May been lost for a long time, trapped in the insidious cage of her ALS? Near the end, she'd been unable to communicate except with an occasional movement of her hand in his, or with her half-closed gray-green eyes. Darryl, stunned at the reality of her death, would not allow himself to believe his May was gone, lost to him forever.

He did nothing for a while. He simply sat there at her side through the night and well past the breaking of dawn, her hand, now cold, still in his. Next, he did what he had to do. He bathed May, dressed her in a fresh flannel nightgown and covered her with a sheet printed all over with small sprays of the violets she'd always favored. Then he made a call to Perry C. Hodges, Pine Ridge's only mortician. Perry was a hunting companion and one of Darryl's few close friends.

Perry came by and the pair sat for a bit, rocking on the porch, Darryl telling of the good life he'd had with May while the two men sipped a few fingers of Wild Turkey. Within the hour they made arrangements for May's funeral, a simple affair as most people Darryl and May had known had either moved away or were, by now, dead.

After May's casket was lowered, Darryl remained until the two cemetery attendants had fully filled the space above it. Alone finally, he placed the handful of violets he'd brought on the mound and left. A large but simple slab of black granite, rounded gracefully at the top, would later be laid at the head of the mound. It would read Darryl's words: "May Johnson McDermott...1928-1996...Beloved Wife." Below these words were three others, much smaller in size: "Wait for me."

Darryl left the cemetery alongside his friend Perry the mortician. As they parted they shook hands. A wan smile appeared on Perry's face, reflected by the same smile on Darryl's.

Darryl McDermott was 74 at the time of May's passing. He wasn't much seen around Pine Ridge after that, leaving home rarely, then just for groceries. Most of his provisions were supplied from his garden and by a single-shot Remington rifle, still aimed with deadly accuracy.

Being the chosen concern of those who held him as a good neighbor and an upstanding citizen, Darryl often received invitations to share a meal. He accepted few on the excuse that he wouldn't be very good company. Never reciprocating these invitations, he soon stopped receiving them. He had chosen not to invite even the few friends he had left to look in on him. Another choice was, upon May's death, to take up a new pastime, so secret that he revealed it to nary a soul.

A year or so after May's passing Darryl tapered off his Windsor chair making not just because of a creeping arthritis but because he no longer cared to deal with the public. But he still liked to putter about in his garden and, occasionally, his woodworking shop, continuing to bend wood from his own willow trees into the lovely arched backs of his chairs and rockers. These he would display on his front porch, each tagged with an outrageously high price—$800 and up per chair, $975 with arms—almost as if to chase away customers. Nonetheless, he sold a number, especially to the city folks passing through Pine Ridge. Perhaps the price, being so high, reinforced the recognition of his master craftsmanship.

With each sale he forced a smile, and he never failed to say thank you.

As Darryl passed eighty, he quit making chairs altogether. He was comfortably fixed and his own health had held out to the extent that he rarely had need of a doctor. His "medicine" for pain and for sleeping had been reaped from the personal patch of marijuana he'd been husbanding for years but the arthritis no longer allowed him to tend it. And so the damned weed died.

As did Darryl McDermott, at age eighty-seven, on the sixth of August, 2006, during a heat wave not unusual for that time of year in Pine Ridge. It took three days before Darryl's neighbors realized he hadn't appeared on his front porch rocker.

When the call came in, Sheriff Ed Schiller, who'd known Darryl for many years, raced out to the house, not forgetting his bullhorn because, by this time, Darryl had lost most of his hearing. Failing to raise the man either by phone or the horn, Schiller authorized his deputy to break in the front door.

They found him in his bedroom. He was lying next to his beloved May. He and May were holding hands. Each wore a beatific smile, hers having been arranged by him years earlier. They both looked like they'd just passed not a day or two before.

Word of the finding got around town fast. At the funeral, it was said more than once, by the many who attended and who'd come to know him, that Darryl McDermott was, along with being a fine citizen and a more than decent human being, the finest chair-maker in these parts. They, of course, were flabbergasted as to how he brought off hiding, but especially preserving, his cherished May for all these years.

They had no idea, of course, that, by way of preserving his hunting trophies, he'd become, in later years, just as fine a taxidermy man as a Windsor man.

Owen Berwalter

"Who did you say you were?" My hearing isn't so good. I didn't recognize the voice on the phone, but the first name struck a note of familiarity.

"Owen Berwalter, Uncle Richard."

Owen Berwalter? I had to think twice.

"I'm your cousin Norma's grandson. Don't you remember? We met when I was a little kid in St. Louis. At Grandma Norma's 60th birthday party at the Norwood Hills Country Club. You brought your wife—I forgot her name—and your daughter, Carolyn. I was a little kid and Carolyn was a lot older than me but I had lots of fun playing with her."

"Owen! Of course. My God, that was what, twenty-five, thirty years ago? Sorry to say I've fallen out of touch with your grandmother. Didn't mean to but I haven't spoken with her in years. A wonderful woman. Is she all right?"

"She's dead. Died a few months ago." Owen sounded like he was speaking of a pet goldfish.

This news shook me more than a little. Our family is small and I'm now one of the last of my generation alive. "I'm very sorry to hear that, Owen," I said. But his grandmother could not be the reason for his calling. "So what's going on with you?" I added.

"Well, I'm here in Los Angeles," he said. "I just got a job here and I've never been here before and I thought it would be great if we could sort of get together because, you know, we're, like, related."

The image of young Owen was coming back to me. My mind's slipped some at seventy-nine, but my long-term memory is still pretty good. I'd only met Owen that one time, but I recalled that he had some kind of unusual mental condition, not sure what.

"Get together?" I said. "Well, yes, that would be fine." I did want to know about him and his family, and about his mother, Maureen, widowed young, who was every bit as nice as my cousin, Norma. I hate driving in this congested city, so I said, "Look, Owen, why don't you come over to my place and I'll take you out to lunch and show you around a bit?"

"Well, I don't have a car, but I guess I could take some buses to get there."

"Buses? You shouldn't have to do that. OK, I'll pick you up." What else could I tell him?

"Gee, thanks, Uncle Richard." Uncle Richard? I'm not, of course, Owen's uncle, I'm a cousin a few times removed, but if that's what he insists on calling me, so be it.

Did I really want to do this? Why not? This young man is my blood, after all, and what else did I have going the next day? Or any day, for that matter, retired and living alone in a two-bedroom walkup in Venice. So, next day, I found myself heading to the address he gave me in Hollywood, just steps from Vine, a nearly twenty-mile drive east through the kind of traffic I've studiously tried to avoid every day since retirement. Convincing myself that a day spent with him would be worth a three-hour round trip, I was at his doorstep by noon.

I was impressed with Owen's striking good looks as he tucked himself into my baby Prius. He greeted me warmly, reaching over to hug me hello. At a good six feet, he was pencil slim and dark-complected. His eyes were nearly as black as the finger-combed mop of hair falling over them. Stubble—the fashion these days—covered his face. A small circle of gold dangled from his left ear. He wore black leather Nikes, a well-worn New York Yankees tee and black jeans so narrow they looked glued to his legs.

As we drove off, he asked if I'd mind his smoking in the car. My no was emphatic enough for him to hold up his hands and blurt, "No problem, Uncle Richard." I informed him he was welcome to call me just Richard, or even Dickie, as the family has always called me.

Over burgers at Off Vine on Leland Way, I learned that Owen, already twenty-eight, had never been west before. He'd arrived a month earlier and found a job at a phone bank doing customer surveys for twelve dollars an hour plus a small commission for each survey secured. "People hang up on me a lot," he said. What he really wanted to do, he told me, was to get into acting.

Oy.

After lunch, we headed west on Sunset past Beverly Hills to the beaches, then up the Pacific Coast Highway into Malibu. His eyes got wider and shinier with each passing mile. He asked me several times to stop so he could take pictures. I could feel what he was feeling. I'd been this moved—stunned—by these same panoramic sights some fifty years earlier on my first visit here, a business trip. I recall the very moment, stopping on the PCH berm and walking across the beach to the water's edge. Fully business-suited, I swore, while crouching and sifting sand through my fingers, that I'd spend the rest of my life in this perfect place. I returned a month later and never left, never looked back. Owen had that same resolve written on his handsome young face as he filled his phone's memory bank with shots of Malibu's beaches, beach houses and the ragged, boulder-strewn mountains rising behind them.

As we were returning, he couldn't stop raving about his newly-found love for the City of Angels. He would work hard to remain here, he said. He would take acting lessons in the evenings and he would make Los Angeles his home. But in the middle of this spill of feelings he stopped and asked me again to pull off to the side. His face had suddenly gone white and he was breathing short, quick breaths. An anxiety attack?

The traffic on Sunset was thick. At first chance, I turned onto a side street and pulled to the curb. "What's happening to you, Owen?"

"I'm having another heart attack."

Heart attack? *Another* heart attack? Twenty-eight years old? "My God, son, what can I do to help? Should I call 9-1-1?"

"No, no. This happens all the time. They'll just kick me out like they always do." As he spoke, his breathing slowed and his color returned. "I'll be OK, just let me sit here awhile." he said. Staring at him for signs that he really was OK, I offered him a bottle of water, which he pushed away. He looked at me in a pleading way, his mouth turning down at the corners, his eyes welling up with tears.

We sat in silence for several minutes while he tried to collect himself. "Are you really going to be all right, Owen?" I said.

He sucked his lips in and bit down hard enough to turn them white. "No, I am not going to be all right. I am not all right and I have never been all right. I need your help. I think I'm dying, Uncle Richard."

Still "Uncle Richard." What was going on here? "What's wrong, Owen? Talk to me." I said this with concern . . . but with wariness too.

As we sat there, parked on a sycamore-lined street in front of a perfectly manicured Brentwood tree lawn, Owen Berwalter, my cousin's grandson, spewed out his troubles non-stop for the next forty-five minutes.

"The real reason I came to L.A. was that it had the only clinic—the Ottinger Clinic in Orange County—that offered an experimental procedure to correct my very rare heart condition, Kappelstein's Syndrome." He described the syndrome in great detail before continuing. "I was admitted there but they released me—kicked me out—after one day. They lied to me, telling me I had no symptoms of Kappelstein's. I kept having heart attacks and going to ERs throughout the city but they too lied, claiming there was nothing wrong with me. I've missed a lot of work because I have to go to these emergency rooms every week, sometimes twice a week, so I might get fired, and my roommate won't help me because he's a hopeless alcoholic and drug user and is very mean to me. He's beaten me up more than once. Uncle Richard, I don't know what to do or where to go. Someone's got to believe me. Someone's got to help me."

At this point in Owen's poignant narrative I stopped him. His father had passed many years earlier. "What about your mother?" I asked. "Can't she help you?"

"My mother won't talk to me. She can barely help herself. She says there's nothing wrong with me, then she hangs up on me. She hates me.

Everybody thinks there's nothing wrong with me. But now you, Uncle Richard, you know what's wrong with me, you just saw it. I keep having these heart attacks! And sometimes I can't even get out of bed in the morning because I think I have some broken bones in my back and I know that I am dying!"

I didn't know what to reply. What to believe either. "Look, Owen, I'll take you to a hospital if you'd like. If you don't want to go because you don't think they'll do anything for you, I'll take you back to your apartment so you can rest for a bit. Give me the information about your condition, that Kappelstein's thing you mentioned, and the name once again of that hospital in Orange County, and I'll call them to see what I can see. I'll do a little research on the Internet and I'll get back to you."

"You don't believe me, do you, Uncle Richard?"

"I didn't say that, Owen. I've offered to help. I'll do what I said I'd do. Please don't judge me and I won't judge you, how's that?"

We hardly spoke during the rest of the slog back to his apartment. I left him with, "Hang in there, Owen. Try to relax. I will get back to you." Did he really have such a miserable roommate? He left me with, "Please help me, Uncle Richard." He was crying again as I pulled away.

Next day, working off information Owen had emailed me, I called the OC hospital. Yes, they worked with Kappelstein's. And, yes, they'd received and examined an Owen Berwalter but were not allowed to release their findings. At my insistence, the woman I was speaking to finally said that they could find nothing wrong with Owen.

I dug up the number for Owen's mother, Maureen. A long conversation revealed that she loved her son dearly but was quite ill herself with shingles and could not deal with what she suspected was Owen's galloping—that's the word she used, galloping—hypochondria. "There's something wrong with my son, but it's more about his head than his heart or his back. He's been this way all his life. I tell myself that I cannot deal with it any longer, but I do deal with it because he is my son. I told him that, if California doesn't work out, he can come back home to St. Louis. But he doesn't seem to want anything to do with me anymore because he claims I think he's lying. The fact is, most of the time I believe he is lying and doesn't realize it himself. So maybe I do sometimes hang up on him. I just can't listen to him anymore. I cry for him, Richard, but I'm alone, I'm ailing myself. I can't do anything more than provide a bed under my roof for him. If you want the truth, I'm not sure I can live with him. Richard, I think my son is, to a degree, deranged. But try to forget I said that. If you talk to him again, please tell him I love him, will you tell him that?"

That . . . was hard to listen to. But I'm certain it was an honest assessment of a son by a loving mother. If my heart bleeds a little, it's more for Maureen than for Owen. Anyhow, what was I getting into here? And just as I asked myself that question, the phone rang. Owen Berwalter was the name on its screen. It rang six times before I allowed myself to answer it.

"Yes, Owen, I was just about to call you." Before he could say anything, I told him what they said at the OC hospital, and I said I'd spoken with his mother and, without revealing all she told me, I told him she'd welcome him home anytime and she loved him. I didn't forget to tell him she loved him.

Owen listened without interrupting me. When I finished, he said, "She's lying. She hates me. I'm never going back to St. Louis. That's not why I'm calling. Uncle Richard. Can I come to live with you?"

That one took me totally by surprise. How to reply. "Uh, I don't know what to say to that, Owen. I, uh, I don't think that would be a very good idea."

Owen took this calmly. Calmly, at least, for Owen. "OK, but will you think about it?" This was said with a cracking of his voice.

"Sure I will, Owen. Just give me a few days."

I struggled with the idea, doing my best to picture what life with Owen might be like. It wasn't a hard picture to paint, even giving every scenario the benefit of the doubt. Everything inside me kept saying no, I'd be a fool to give in. The answer had to be no. My own sanity depended upon it.

Before I could get back to Owen, he called me. "Did you think about it, Uncle Richard? Is it OK if I come?"

"Owen, I'm sorry to have to say no to you, but that is what I've decided."

A long silence. Then: "Why, Uncle Richard?"

"Well, first off, Owen, I'm not allowed to have anyone live here but me, my lease doesn't allow it." This wasn't entirely true, but I knew I'd need a strong excuse to stop Owen's pleading. It was a lie, I wasn't proud of it, but what was I going to tell him, that I didn't want him here?

It was as though he hadn't heard me. "Listen, I could do things for you. I could clean your house and do your chores, maybe do some shopping for you, keep you company."

"Hold it, Owen. You're coming at me a little too fast. There are other reasons too. You said you're about to be fired or maybe already have been fired. Well, frankly, I can't afford to feed you, son. I'm living mostly on Social Security and can barely afford to feed myself." Another white lie. I did have a little extra coming in from my dwindling investments.

"Uncle Richard, that job I had, I did lose it, and I'm about to be evicted. That roommate I told you about, he punched me in the ribs and I'm pretty sure he broke a few. And maybe punctured my liver. I'm thinking of suing him. I know he has a gun and wants to kill me. Please you have got to let me live there."

The more Owen talked, the wilder his claims, the firmer became my resolve. "I have to say no again, Owen. I'm sorry, but I've got a pot of water boiling for tea, I've got to go." And I hung up before he could reply.

I knew this was not the last of it.

It wasn't. Owen called two hours later. I didn't pick up. He called again each succeeding day for three more days. I kept letting it ring through but knew I couldn't avoid him forever. On the next call, I picked up on the first ring. "Yes, Owen?"

"I was just thrown out of my apartment. They actually hauled my stuff to the sidewalk. And now they're about to cut off my cell service. A guy I used to work with is letting me stay with him tonight, but only tonight, and I'm having these terrible migraine headaches which I never told you about. You can't imagine the pain I am feeling. Please, please, please, Uncle Richard, let me come stay with you."

"I can't, Owen," I said, as calmly as I could. I almost said I won't. "You have got to think about going back to your mom's in St. Louis. If you can't afford a bus ticket, I'll take you to the station and I'll buy it for you, but you can't live here. You cannot live with me. You want to really know why? I'm too old to be dealing with you, Owen. You have got to understand that. I'm terribly sorry, but that's the way it is."

And I hung up on him once again.

He called the next day. I picked up. He repeated his plea. I replied, firmly and, I'm afraid, not too pleasantly, "No, Owen, you absolutely, positively cannot live with me. That is my decision, it is final and it is irrevocable. Do . . . you . . .understand me?"

No answer. A brief silence. Then a hang-up from his end.

Half a year has gone by. I haven't heard from Owen. Not once. Maybe he no longer has a phone. Or maybe I've seen him emerging from a tent under a bridge or pushing a rusty shopping cart on some distant corner of this traffic-infested city, and I just didn't recognize him.

Or maybe my cousin's grandson, Owen Berwalter, is dead. If so, I'd like to mourn for him.

Can I?

Punc Rock Operetta

LIGHTS UP:

INT. AUDITORIUM, LIBRARY OF CONGRESS - TODAY - CONTINUOUS.

A stage has been set and brightly lit for a panel discussion. Seated on the panel at stage-center are COMMA, COLON, SEMI-COLON, QUESTION MARK, EXCLAMATION POINT, PERIOD. The moderator, at stage-left, is WIKIPEDIA.

WIKIPEDIA

Hello, and welcome to the Library of Congress. I am Wikipedia, your moderator for this panel discussion featuring some of the English language's best known and best-loved punctuation marks. The subject of tonight's discussion shall be "Who Amongst You Best Serves the English Language?" Panelists this evening require no introduction. You all see them daily and have come to know them intimately. Please hold your applause until I finish introducing them: From the left, the Comma... the Colon... the Semi-colon... the Question Mark... the Period... and last, the Exclamation Point, or as over-users prefer to say, the Exclam. I also wish to acknowledge other important puncs in the audience. In the first row are the Apostrophe, the Parentheses and their first cousins, the Brackets, and, at each end of the row, the Quotation Marks. In the second row we have the Hyphen, the Dash, the Slash or Virgule, the Ellipsis, Ampersand, and—ah, I didn't see you down there—the Underline. Not to be forgotten, we have with us that reclusive, rarely used, but highly useful Twentieth Century invention, the Interrobang, child of tonight's panelists, the Question Mark and the Exclamation Point. Finally, in the rear, the Interpunct or Middle Dot, and the Guillemet, reintroduced to modern usage as the At Sign by Twitter. Also let's put our hands together for the Tilde, Caret, Back and Forward Slash, a.k.a. Whack, the Pipe, or Vertical Bar, and the interruptive but informative Asterisk. Far back in the balcony are the way-too-popular Emoticon and the disgusting and even more popular newcomer, the Emoji.

We'll open our discussion with the Period.

PERIOD

If you don't mind, I'd like to come at the end.

WIKIPEDIA

OK, who wants to kick it off?

You each have five minutes to state your case.

Question Mark, go ahead.

QUESTION MARK

Most of you on this panel aren't that certain of where you belong. Ask yourself if the world could get along without you. But a question is a question. I go at the end of a question. I know exactly where I belong. Commas? You can live without 'em. Most people sprinkle 'em like manure, all over a sentence. Not sure of what to use? Throw in a Comma. Throw 'em out, I say. They're like Legos spread over a nursery floor. Something to trip over.

COMMA

I damn well resent that, sir. Without Commas, sentences would run on like your mouth.

WIKIPEDIA
Dignity, gentlemen, please.

(Question Mark and Comma stare each other down.)

QUESTION MARK
Did you ever look at a Comma? Reminds me of the tail in that Pin the Tail game. And we all know where that usually winds up. And the Exclamation Point? Generally speaking, if you have something important to say, you don't have to shout to say it. And you certainly don't have to repeat it three times.

EXCLAMATION POINT
I resent that, sir!!!

QUESTION MARK
You and Mr. Comma can do your resenting in your five minutes. These are mine. Take the Colon. . . please. If you want to give me an example of, say, half a dozen things, give 'em to me. I'm not an idiot. I don't need two self-important dots to warn me they're coming. And you, Semi-colon, do you have any idea where you belong? Don't give me that Question Mark; there never was a Semi-Colon that couldn't be replaced by a Period. Period, am I right?

PERIOD
(Stoically)
I said I'd come in at the end. I guess this is it.

WIKIPEDIA
Coming in December: those brotherly rivals, Diacritical Marks versus Editing Marks in the first-ever Library of Congress Marks Brothers Speech Slam. This panel is adjourned. Over. Finished. Period.

The Bookkeeper

Bookkeeper. That was the title of my new civilian job after mustering out. Never mind that I'd been a highly competent accountant in the army, a three-striper and a quartermaster, no less.

In my first week home, October of 1945, I snagged this job at Hoffman & Moreland, an independent insurance agency that's been around Trenton for three generations.

I felt good wearing my brand new Hart, Schaffner & Marx three-piece suit. but working there was more than a little like still being at war, that's how demanding the job was. Until I got the hang of it.

Not a vestige of my army accounting smarts seemed to remain at first, including whatever it took to screw the army out of half the supplies delivered to our base in Hamburg; something I could do with just a few keystrokes. Back then, if three trucks were needed for transporting supplies to the bridge our engineers were building over the Elbe, I'd manage to "mistakenly" order four, liberating one and shipping it to a private freight yard, thereby pocketing a serious amount of change, some of which I necessarily spread around to the guys in on the scam with me. Made a lot of friends that way. You might say I was a thief but you'd also have to say I was a fiduciary whiz. You needed something in this man's army, you came to Wisnewski. Staff Sergeant Arnold S. Wisnewski. Me. Now I'm just plain old Arnie Wisnewski.

But that was there and now I'm here. And, screwing-wise, I've come to find that the army was easy, selling insurance is not.

Until an idea came to me with something of a brilliant flash.

If I could get a few of my old army buddies to buy a Hoffman & Moreland auto policy and a few others to buy maybe a homeowners policy, and they somehow should have a certain kind of auto accident or trip over a badly laid rug in their home, a few bucks just might possibly be made. What's more, I knew that one of my GI pals was already a budding personal injury lawyer and would likely come aboard for lawsuits that'd provide some extra moo-lah-lah.

They all agreed that my scheme was perfect. Foolproof, even. I was their good old quartermaster sarge once again. And who would ever dream of giving a hard time to a bunch of brave heroes just back from risking their very lives in the European Theater of Operations?

Over the next few months, the policies were bought and the scheme was launched. Our policyholders had the right to select their own repair shops should they, God forbid, get into an accident. And, wouldn't you know it, one of my other guys actually set up some phony repair shops just for the ability to float estimates substantially higher than the norm.

Of those who bought home policies, two soon reported thefts of "valuable" jewelry for which yet another army pal, working in a jewelry shop, had provided bloated estimates. Another "slipped" in his tub and sued the insurance company, through our lawyer pal, because my agency didn't offer a high enough settlement. Within half a year our pockets were stuffed.

In time, Mr. Hoffman started to question me when they somehow learned that I personally knew several of these fellows whose claims far outmatched the profit from their premiums. I quickly admitted that, of course, I did know them and had recommended the agency to them precisely because they were friends and we'd be helping each other out as well as bringing in business for the agency. Hoffman seemed to understand, but I knew it was time to move on before they really got wise.

So move on I did. To another agency. With my pals in tow. And the merry-ground continued to spin, with pals of pals added. Did it ever stop? You'd think that schemes like mine couldn't go on forever, but I covered my tracks well—something the army taught me well—moving on to the point where, within a year, I was able to establish my own insurance agency, this time finding ways to extract cash, not from my agency, of course, but from the insurance companies I represented. Meanwhile, I was providing work for old war buddies, two of whom worked in my agency.

I'm pleased to report that this went on for nearly twenty prosperous years. To avoid suspicion, I'd frequently switch insurers. The Wisnewski Agency was now the second largest in Trenton. I had sixteen people working for me. At 43 years old, I was on my way to becoming a true millionaire.

Until I tripped over a rock. In spite of my conservative ways, claims losses were gradually surpassing policy revenue. And, though sales were up substantially, income somehow wasn't keeping up with outgo. A spate of auto accidents and home theft and damage claims was threatening to lose me our key insurance companies. I inspected every one of the claims myself and gathered all the data possible that might lend a clue as to where the trouble lay. I could not figure it out. Or was someone cooking the books. But it couldn't be an inside job because I knew all the inside tricks. I was truly baffled.

I called my chief accountant into the office, along with his staff which included a man recently hired, a man I'd met but hadn't yet got to know. His background seemed impeccable. He loved his work and was very good at it, finding several cracks through which some of our income was falling.

He was attending night school to become a CPA and had indicated that he'd like to go on for a law degree. Anyhow, our meeting ended with no clues to help solve the mystery of our losses.

A week later I invited our new man—Ed Ross by name—to lunch. Over filet mignon at my intown club I questioned him about his background. Turns out he'd served a three-year gig in the army including two in 'Nam. Casually, I asked what he did over there, thinking his type might well have been in combat. In fact, I asked specifically if he was.

"No, Mr. Wisnewski," he replied, with his eager smile. "I lucked out. No combat for me. I was a quartermaster."

Walking Out

Never mind why I'm in solitary at Quentin, I'm there. It wasn't for anything nice. OK, the state claimed that I, Alvin Czerny, committed a little bit of murder; a matter of beating a man to death for the act of rape committed against my girlfriend, Bettina Lopez. The bastard deserved it but most who know of my case said I never should have received a death sentence, even though they claimed I'd stalked the rapist and carefully planned the murder, very much in the first degree. With inadequate representation in court, next thing I knew, the jury convicted and the judge decided that I must die by lethal injection to be administered at San Quentin Penitentiary where I'd have to spend the rest of my shortened life.

San Quentin—the "Arena" to its inmates—sits on Point San Quentin, twenty acres of the most beautiful outcrop in Marin County, overlooking San Francisco Bay, and with the kind of view, even of the Golden Gate Bridge, you pay for by the square foot. If it were a resort, which some day, if they ever razed the place as has been urged, my cell, as a single, would probably go for half a thou per night.

Instead, the Arena is the last resort and I am nothing more than one number—267446—among its current 76, the largest population of Death Row inmates in America. Not the land of the free for us.

Everyone knows what's on my mind. Escape. It's all I ever talk about when I feel like talking at all. Oh, it's been done before. Last time was in '86. I guess it's obvious that all men in my hopeless position think of escape, but that's not quite so. Take it from me, most of us lifers have learned just to live with it.

I'm seen as a loner who talks to himself a lot. I guess that's right because, besides getting out of here, I do talk a lot about my Bettina, the only one in my whole life who ever gave a rat's ass about me. She's waiting out there still, but for what, a loser like me? I'm a lifer at best if they don't choose to inject me. And I'm WP. Without Parole. But still she waits. And loves me and says so in ways I don't care to reveal. Her every letter makes me believe every word she's written. And they are some sweet kind of words. All I want is to put my arms around her once, just once, instead of us having to kiss each other through two inches of reinforced glass while these goddamn prison goons leer at us. And it'll have to be in an open place, a woods or a field or something; someplace with sky above us. And without walls. But, if there's no end date to my being here, just how can I make it to my woods, to my field with the sky above us?

I'm working on it.

There are five inmate units at Quentin. I'm in the smallest, CU2; Condemned Unit #2. Solitaries represent only four percent of our population. I occupy one of a dozen cells in our detached North Seg, so called not for the direction in which it lies but because it's on the sixth, the top or "north" floor. You get up there by "dropping the bucket," a cage elevator that stops only at 1 and 6. Above its entrance on the first floor is a sign that reads "Condemned Row." It's there because the warden says we prisoners sometimes need reminding of where we are. We Rowers are considered so dangerous, so violent that North Seg guards must, by the rules, wear riot gear all the time.

As a condemned man a prisoner is not seen as a man at all in the eyes of some guards. Few guards stay around long. But then, a lot of citizens don't see us as human either. Me, I've tried to be a decent man, even if I made the most serious mistake a man could make. I'm always polite and respectful and I don't complain, not out loud, because it's smart not to, and because my attitude is that I'm the one who got me here, I'll deal with it my own way. By blaming only myself, I manage to dredge up a little respect. From the inmates, even from some of the guards.

The way I see it, I'm in lockup for life. Or until they take my life. Or until I take off.

I sit here and think as I gaze out of my one-square-foot barred window at the sometimes snow-capped Mt. Tamalpais to the near west. It's a slightly more beautiful sight than North Block that houses the execution chamber next door. Man, I'd love to be atop Mt. Tam now, touching the sky.

I've come up with every escape scenario. I can't tunnel my way out of a six-story tower. Or get through a tiny, barred window and lower myself on torn bedding like in the movies. I can't work in the laundry and hide myself in a cartful of outgoing dirty linen because solitaries can't work anywhere here. And I can't jump a fence they never let you get anywhere near. There's a lot more I can't do so what I have to do is concentrate on what I can do. Problem is, I've got nobody to help me but Bettina.

And then, to my surprise, along comes Billy Hislop. No, seriously, I really am thrilled he's here. But don't get me wrong, Hislop's no friend of mine.

Sgt. Clarence William "Billy" Hislop, an ex-paratrooper, is new to Unit #2 but hardly new to the Arena, having been a Quentin correctional officer for the past nine years. I'd heard a lot of scuttlebutt about him long before he was assigned to #2. Definitely not the sweetest cherry on the tree, Hislop loves to piss us inmates off every minute of his shift, like repeating, in the middle of the night, the repulsive rat-a-tat of his steel baton on our bars just to wake us up. Calls it "rattling the cage." Laughs his ass off every time.

But not all the guards are pricks like him. His streak of sadism stands out like a bad goiter. If it weren't for his union, he'd have lost his job twice over beatings he gave inmates for small infractions on the yard, like whispering or not lining up fast enough. His attitude—always in your face—is "If you ain't white, you ain't right." Look very carefully at the back of his left hand, between his thumb and his forefinger, and you can spot a swastika de-tatted before he applied for his job. Another thing that gets me off is how he's always chewing bubble gum like he's a little kid or something, always smugly grinning after he blows a big bubble, like he's expecting a standing O.

What I liked about Hislop, soon as I laid eyes on him, was that the man looks a lot like me, especially in the face. He's about six feet, I'm 5-11, and we're built alike, built well, he by lifting in the gym, me by doing up to five hundred pushups, sit-ups and leg lifts every day in my cell. What else I got to do? I could almost pass as his double. All of which got me to thinking, if I can't get out of here as me, maybe I can as . . . Sergeant Clarence William "Billy" Hislop.

But if this is to be a workable plan, I can't be kind of like Hislop, I have to *be* him! So I get to work. The hair. I can get the prison barber to give me a buzz cut like Hislop's tomorrow, no problem. But how do I make my face even more like his in a way that holds up long enough to get me out of here as him and in his gear. How do I turn me into him?

I need what they call a prosthesis. A mask of Hislop. I'd have to, of course, get him to cooperate with the loan of his uniform and his face. So I'd have to catch him unawares and knock him out. Or kill him. Hell, they can't kill me twice. But is killing the only way?

Jeezuz, I have got to think this through.

Prosthesis. I love that word. Discovered it reading The Master of Disguise, about a CIA operative. If I could get my hands on a pile of those latex gloves the kitchen crew uses and maybe melt them down over Hislop's face—maybe his dead face—and . . . but who am I kidding? That's complicated. I've got to do it the KISS way. Keep It Simple, Stupid. When I get the chance to act, it's got to be quick. Take only seconds. Bang, bang and I'm gone. But how? How do I get Hislop into my cell when he's only supposed to stand outside of it? I'm starting to think this can't happen. But I can't think that way. It has to happen. I have to make it happen or I will go insane. Maybe I already am. I'm halfway there just for thinking what I'm thinking.

This yin-yang kept me up half of last night. Fell asleep about 3 am then was awakened about 4 because a blackbird was sitting on my windowsill. A Raven? Aren't they supposed to be asleep at that hour? It kept singing the same two notes, one low, one higher, before it took off.

Came off as Free-DOM! . . . Free-DOM! . . . Free-DOM! Was it really there? Was I dreaming? Didn't matter. I saw it as a messenger and I was ready for its message. It was telling me I could do this thing. And then, in minutes, the whole plan unfolded itself like an accordion taking in air.

I now know what to do.

I need to start a riot. I will start a riot. The match I light will be chaos. And the best way to create chaos in North Seg? Back to the simple. Attack a guard. Hislop, of course. My man. The me I am to be. But what did I have going for me, going against a tough thug like Hislop? I'll tell you what. Something he has that I don't. Like the blackbird said, FreeDOM! Its sorry lack, its desperate need, that's what will give me the strength I need to get out of this rotten hellhole. Even if just for one day alone with Bettina. Or maybe a whole life alone with her. I would give my life for that. I may have to.

I am ready.

Another day passes. It's Saturday. My hour on the yard passes. But I haven't filled in the important details, the moment to strike. I don't have a timetable. Things just have to feel right. Will I know when they are? Can't wait for another blackbird to speak to me. So it's got to be tomorrow. The fourth Sunday. Before the start of our daily hour on the yard. 4 PM. Only once a month, every fourth Sunday, we can trade our hour for a visit from what they like to call a "loved one." Most of us don't have a "loved one." Some of us never did. If anything is going to happen, it has got to be on a visiting Sunday. At 4 PM.

It will happen. I will make it happen. In my cell.

My cell. I'll describe it to you. It'll let you know what I'm up against for resources. It's five by eight and seven feet high, more or less. It has a two-and-a-half-foot wide bunk made of a concrete slab fixed to the wall on one side and supported by two concrete legs, each about three inches square and eighteen inches high. The bed is mounted with a six-inch foam mattress. The only other furnishings are a two-by-four-foot wood table with a small drawer, a heavy wood chair, a three-foot built-in shelf above the table for my few books and framed photos of Bettina, and a sink and toilet in the far corner. The only metal in the cell is the faucet tap and the wire cage that covers the ceiling light, never turned off. Even the toilet tank is locked so we can't use the hardware inside. The plumbing's all plastic. Nobody trusts us, nobody should. In my day I've seen the wire arm of a toilet tank ball shoved through a man's heart, then blithely put back into place for the next flush.

I've been working on one of the bed's concrete legs, giving backward kicks to it for the past two weeks until it developed a small crack where it joins the concrete slab. It now appears ready to break off. I'm guessing, with its heart of iron rebar, it weighs about twelve pounds. Enough to do some serious damage to a man's head.

Same night, I rehearse my plan in my own addled head. Its simplicity gives me confidence. Quietly, I practice Hislop's voice, using its cadences I now know as well as my own. Having daily observed every gadget on his uniform, I know what each is and how it operates. Ballistic helmet, vest, shield. cuffs, OC spray pouch, tear gas cylinders, gas mask, baton, shield, Taser. Everything but a gun. A gun is too much for a guard to answer for, so they're not allowed to carry. Only the tower guards are armed. To kill, not wound.

Edgy as I am, I sleep better than I have all week. Because, repeat, I am ready. I am ready for tomorrow. And the tomorrows after that. With Bettina. Tonight, throughout the night, I dream only of her. With me. On the other side of the wall.

Next day, Sunday, I pace like I'm sleepwalking, not aware of moving though I never stop moving, until the approach of 4 PM. At which time I'm in my bunk, under the covers, reading. The concrete leg from the rear of the bunk rests in my concealed left hand. I grip the leg at the opposite end of where three inches of rebar sticks out. I take slow, even breaths to keep myself calm; the way I must before the storm.

At exactly 3:55 the bucketful of riot-geared guards begins rising to North Seg to escort us out for our hour on the yard. A minute or so later the nettling sound of Hislop's baton, playing its maddening tune on his way to my cell, reverberates in my brain. And I hear the pop of his stupid bubble gum. It's the last I mean to hear of both. He now stands, legs spread, at my door, slapping the baton on his left palm. And smirking his sidewise smirk through the raised mask of his helmet.

"Are you ready for your ex-er-cize, Mister Czerny?" A smarmy tone like that can get a guy killed. But, yes, I am ready. If not for exercise, I'm very ready for you, Billy Hislop.

On the snapped P.A. order, "Open," from the captain, the cell doors unlock themselves and slide aside. Hislop steps into the doorway, as far as he's allowed to go. At this particular moment, no one outside can see what's happening in the cell except the unblinking 24/7 roto-camera mounted above the door.

"What's wrong, Mr. Czerny, not feeling well this lovely afternoon? Perhaps you'd like me to bring you a nice cup of hot tea."

"Right, Hislop. But, you know something, I really don't feel well. I'm going to skip the yard today." I know he's not going to buy this. I'm counting on it. And sure enough, he bites. He looks over one shoulder then the other to see if anyone's watching, then comes at me.

"Up and out, you lazy Polack sonofabitch," he snarls. "Yard time is yard time." Saying this, he gives me a nasty poke in the ribs. And repeats it, raising it to whack me. He knows where to do this so it doesn't show. He's very good at this. Reminds me of my old man, the bastard.

"OK, OK," I say, holding up my right hand in surrender, "I'm getting up." I roll to a sitting position, more like a crouch, then instantly explode upward, and with me, from under the blanket, comes the concrete leg, blindingly fast, arced up in a two-handed uppercut square to his jaw, with a force I never knew I could generate. The rebar rips through the soft flesh below his chin and sinks in until the concrete squares with his jawbone. This meeting of concrete with bone sounds like a coconut dropped from a rooftop. He never sees the blow coming, never expects it. He's actually lifted off his feet by its force, half his teeth flying from his bloody mouth. He drops like dirty laundry. He's likely dead before he hits the floor.

I whip off his blood-spattered pants and blouse and roll him onto the bed under the covers, face up, before the camera comes around. The camera doesn't see all that well. And the man watching it sees what he expects to see: a subdued inmate. Me. Or a damn good copy of me. I stare at him for a second. "It's not personal, Billy, it's business," I say, paraphrasing Michael Corleone's remark to his brother, Sonny, before he does murder in the first Godfather movie. Hislop stands between me and the outside. Stood between me and the outside. He doesn't anymore.

Wearing his bloodied gear now, I pull on the gas mask, let go of a few tear gas cylinders, an excuse to keep my mask on, then tap my mic alive and spit out my best imitation of Sgt. Billy: "Hislop here. Code 212. Trouble with Czerny. Using tear gas. Lock down now!"

Code 212 is a red alert. I've just triggered a riot alarm. I've just created chaos. The riot horns start whooping. The bucket is half way down. It squeals to a stop, rises again and its inmates are shoved out onto a tear-gas filled walkway and frog-stepped back to their cells by guards all now wearing gas masks.

A guard, rushing past, stops to glance into my cell. "You OK, Hislop?"

"It's all good, Jankowski. I put the sonofabitch down." Jankowski leaves. It's working. The cell doors are now all locked and the guards, including me, head for the bucket.

"What happened, Billy?" Jankowski asks, through his mask.

I practice my Hislop through mine. "Czerny grabbed a can off my belt and let it loose. Don't know what got into him. Got a dose before I could kick it away. Can't talk no more."

"The captain meets us when we land on 1. "I want you all to report to the infirmary now for observation, then we'll meet in the squad room at 1700."

The six of us head for the infirmary. I peel off when we're ten yards from it. "Where you goin', Billy?" shouts Jankowski.

"Left my cell in the car, Chuck. Wanna call my wife to let her know I'm OK. Be right there."

I walk, I do not run, to the gate and, to avoid suspicion, drop my mask half off. The gate guard stares as me in my splotched riot gear. He's fairly new and doesn't know the other guards too well yet. I'm hoping he'll catch Hislop's name on my blouse. "Hold on, I want to talk to you," he says. I stop, my heart about to pop out of my chest. But he too sees what he expects to see. "Word's out, Hislop. What was it like?"

"Tell you later, man. Headin' home for the day."

"Sorry I stopped you," says the guard. "Just wanted to say good job up there, guy."

He's right. It was a good job up there. And suddenly I'm walking out. Walking out of San Quentin.

Outside the gate I stroll over to Bettina's car, now tagged with fresh, untraceable plates, waiting for me in the visitor's lot. I take a minute to drink her in. She's wearing some kind of little off-the-shoulder baby blue dress and her blond hair is in what I think they call a Swedish braid. I want to take her right there but I open the trunk, jump in, she closes it and takes off. Slowly. A mile away, she stops, lets me out of the trunk, I ditch Hislop's outfit and gear, put on the Adidas jump suit waiting for me and we take off again.

We hardly exhale, don't even say hello till we're out of Marin County heading north on 101, then onto the back roads to who the hell knows where. It is 1993. Alvin Czerny is outside the bars. He means to stay there for the rest of his days.

A knock is heard on the door of a three-room farmhouse near a town called Albertville in northern Saskatchewan. The year is 2017. There is no bell to be rung. The man standing at the door knocks again. With no answer, he steps to a front window and peers in. He can see no one. There is smoke rising from the chimney so the man knocks once more. A minute later a viewing slot in the door is pushed aside. A grizzled voice comes through it. "What is it you want?"

"Are you Harold Manford?"

There is a five-second hesitation before the voice replies, "Yes. Who are you?"

"Rex Huddleston. I'm a reporter with the Saskatoon Express. It's a weekly."

"What do you want from me?"

"I'd like to talk to you."

"About?"

"Well, I'm researching a story about stateside convicts who escaped up to the north. A lot of them do. And a lot wind up in northern Canada. Maybe one or two in Saskatoon, just like the Yank draft dodgers back in the '70s, you know?"

"No, I don't know. I don't know anything about escaped convicts or draft dodgers. I'm busy. I can't help you, Huddleston, I'll have to ask you to leave."

"Wait a minute, Mr. Manford. Have you ever heard of a Lester Cobb?"

"No."

"A J. R. Malinowski?"

"No, no, go away." The slot begins to close.

"Arvid Jackson?"

"No, dammit!"

"Alvin Czerny?"

Manford stops and straightens up. His chin muscles and fingers began to work. He reopens the slot and stares through it at the man anchored before it. The man is tall and lanky and has a wispy blond mustache. He is very young—earliest twenties, likely a green neophyte. But the intense focus of his pale blue eyes is not that of a green neophyte. It takes Manford a full ten seconds before he slips back the bolt and opens the door.

"Come in, Huddleston," he says in a voice so soft that Huddleston asks him to repeat what he said.

The reporter wipes his feet carefully on the sisal mat that fronts the door. Entering, he grabs the farmer's hand with both of his own and shakes it almost violently. "Thank you, Mr. Manford, I really appreciate your inviting me in. You're the first person willing to talk to me about this."

"Not surprised," says the farmer. "Sit down, I'll have the missus bring us something to drink. Betty!" he calls, "come and meet this gentleman. And bring us some Pepsi-Colas if you will." Which Betty does. In well-iced glasses with a slice of lemon in each. They sit in front of the fireplace, still dormant in early September. Betty, in her late forties, is a handsome woman, slender, blond, but gaining on white.

"So anyhow, Mr. Huddleston, how did you happen to come upon me?"

"Well, it was kind of a stab in the dark. I mentioned that a lot of stateside cons head north. Far north. You don't get much farther than this without running out of towns to live in. These cons seem to think no one's ever heard of northern Canada. Anyhow, I did some digging and put two and two together and . . ."

"Young man, if you're going to be a reporter you'd better learn to use fewer clichés."

"I'm not sure what you mean, Mr. Manford."

"Never mind. So you came up with all those names, all who headed north when they escaped. Seems you're playing a rather dangerous game doing this all on your own. Might have thought you'd want to bring a posse with you."

"Are you kidding, sir? I haven't even told my editor. If I let it out what I'm up to, some Regina reporter would get wind of it, fly up and grab my story right out from under me."

"OK. What's next for you?"

"Soon as I can confirm a few more facts, I'll write my story. I mean, if I find what I'm looking for, what would some old man do to me?"

"Old man?"

"I'm sorry, sir, I was referring to those men I just mentioned, I wasn't referring to you. But do you mind if I ask your age? It's my job to ask questions."

"Sixty-two. Old enough but not ancient."

"Sixty-two. So, if you were one of the men I've been looking for, what could they do to you if you admitted it? I'll bet they'd look the other way. Or maybe there'd be a statute of . . ."

"There's no statute of limitations on escaped murderers, Huddleston."

"Murderers? I wasn't talking about murderers, Mr. Manford, just escapees, but, well, one of them actually was a murderer. Anyhow, you called your wife 'Betty.' Alvin Czerny was the murderer I mentioned. He was on death row when he escaped. His wife—or maybe she was just his girlfriend—was called Bettina. I've done some research. A coincidence?"

Manford laughs. "A coincidence? Wouldn't know about that. Look, I wish I could help you but I'm afraid I don't know any of these old 'cons' you've mentioned."

"You're sure you're not one of them, Mr. Manford?"

Huddleston says this with a smile but Manford does not smile in return. "That's a pretty cheeky statement, young man, but I'll let it pass." And then he adds the non sequitur, "We don't usually get what we deserve, do we? Usually less, sometimes more. What do you deserve, Mr. Huddleston?"

Huddleston doesn't know how to answer Manford. Nor what to make of the older man's offhand remark. Was there a touch of menace to it? Then Manford breaks out laughing, much to the reporter's relief.

"Look, son, while you're here wouldn't you like to see a bit of my farm? Nice background for your story. I mean, if you weren't kidding me, if you were right, then I can see your headline: 'Convict escapes, reforms, turns farmer, lives happily ever after until young reporter comes along and . . .'"

Huddleston's grin expresses his further relief. He likes what he's hearing enough to interrupt, "Sure, I'd love to see your place."

"God Himself lives up here, Rex, just judging by the sheer beauty of what surrounds us. Lakes, firs and white birch, mountains, snow and rich, black earth. You could spit on soil like this and up would come nothing but rich feed crops for my hogs, and corn so sweet you could eat it right off the stalk."

As the two walk out the door, looking like old friends who are about to lock arms, Betty stares at their backs, smiling benignly. She calls after them, "Make it a quick tour, boys, I'm fixing you some nice bacon, lettuce and tomato sandwiches for lunch."

Betty's man stops the reporter. "Hold on, son, let me just grab my pitchfork first. Have to feed the pigs. Got over half a hundred, last count. A pig's almost like a goat. A pig'll eat just about anything."

Huddleston, jotting background notes, falls in behind Manford as they head to the deep mud of the sties. So deep it resembles quicksand. Deep enough, when it's watered enough, to swallow a careless piglet.

Or a careless man.